Someone
Like You

A **SOMEONE TO LOVE** BOOK

Someone Like You

ADDISON MOORE

SKYSCAPE

SKYSCAPE

This is a work of fiction. Names, characters, organizations, places, events, and incidents are either products of the author's imagination or are used fictitiously.

Published by Skyscape, New York

www.apub.com

Amazon, the Amazon logo, and Skyscape are trademarks of Amazon.com, Inc., or its affiliates.

ISBN-13: 9781477847114
ISBN-10: 1477847111

Printed in the United States of America

Books by Addison Moore

Someone to Love (*Someone to Love* 1)
Someone Like You (*Someone to Love* 2)
3:AM Kisses (*3:AM Kisses* 1)
The Solitude of Passion

Ethereal (*Celestra Series* Book 1)
Tremble (*Celestra Series* Book 2)
Burn (*Celestra Series* Book 3)
Wicked (*Celestra Series* Book 4)
Vex (*Celestra Series* Book 5)
Expel (*Celestra Series* Book 6)
Toxic Part 1 (*Celestra Series* Book 7)
Toxic Part 2 (*Celestra Series* Book 7.5)
Elysian (*Celestra Series* Book 8)

Ephemeral (*The Countenance Trilogy* 1)
Evanescent (*The Countenance Trilogy* 2)
Entropy (*The Countenance Trilogy* 3)

Ethereal Knights (*Celestra Knights*)

To Dutch. God, I really do miss you.
Never again will there be someone like you.

1

THE HOOKUP

Ally

My mother believed in happily ever after. She said it often found you in the last place you'd think to look, but I'm pretty sure a strip club deposited at the edge of a college town isn't one of those fabled places.

I peer from behind the velvet curtain and watch Kit, a girl I know from Garrison University, move her body in ways meant to hypnotize entire herds of inebriated men. The long metal pole creates a shadow over the platform, bisecting it in two like a broken heart.

The Pretty Girls Gentlemen's Club is filled to the brim with patrons who can be described as anything but gentlemen, mostly stoned-out boozers with their tongues and other body parts wagging. Their fisted dollar bills are few and far between.

An ebony-haired god sits off to the side with a gaggle of bare-chested girls slithering over him. He seems unmoved, perhaps even allergic to the mass of silicone as he continues to watch the show. Something about his glossy black hair, those bottomless-pit dimples in his cheeks, reminds me of why this was a piss-poor idea to begin with. He glances in my direction and our eyes lock. My breath gets caught in my throat as I'm transfixed by those pale-blue eyes. A lewd grin plays on his lips, and I duck backstage, clutching my chest like I've just averted a head-on collision—more like hard-on collision, although I'm pretty sure I shouldn't be entertaining sex with the patrons quite so soon in my budding dancing career.

"Shit, shit, shit," I hiss.

Tess, my older, far-from-protective sister, struts over in her ultra-high heels, her long shiny hair pale as milk.

"Tessy!" I haven't called her that since I was three, but suddenly my chest feels like it's about to explode and I can't catch my breath. "I think I'm having a coronary malfunction."

"A heart attack?" She averts her eyes while adjusting the strap on my glittering bra. "And it's not Tessy—it's *Fan*-tessy." She raises her brows seductively. "By the way, you need a name." Her lips twitch because, God knows, she's having a rare moment of contemplation. "How about something scholastic like the Luscious Librarian? Or School Spirit?"

A slew of protests try to gag their way out of my throat.

"How about something *sane*"—I say—"like Look at Her Leaving, or Oh Shit, She Just Puked All Over the Stage."

"Ha, ha. Very funny." She gives a wry smile. "No puking—you got that?" She tugs down my panties so they sit just below my hips. Her bright green eyes shine like cut jade as she expands her toothy grin. "If you knew how many strings I had to pull to land you this job, you wouldn't be whining. You'd be kissing the bottom of my stilettos for letting you anywhere near this stage. These are practically sacred grounds, Ally."

"What?" I'm not sure I want to get into a debate on the sacredness of this gloried pussycat salon. Typical Tess. Always making my problems seem impossibly small to coerce me into yet bigger problems with possible legal ramifications. "I do not whine. You're the one genetically cursed to sound like a three-year-old brat. I used to go to bed each night thanking God I didn't sound like a chipmunk on fire."

"Really, Ally?" She pulls her lips into a thin line. "Well, maybe I'd rather sound like a brat than an uptight sorority girl who spends her Friday nights blue-balling with the best of them."

I consider this a moment. She's not too far off base, but I'm not ready to be bested by not-so-sweet, dear old Tess. Oh, what the hell. "Touché." She got me.

"And please, save the three-dollar words for your professors."

The crowd erupts in aggressive hoots and decidedly dirty hollers on the other side of the carnal curtain.

"You still need a name," Tess reminds me.

"I'll take the Bitter Bitch for five hundred," I tease. "Better yet, the Ballistic Blue Baller."

"I think you're on to something with that one." She cuts a look out at the crowd. "And I'm still not laughing." She pivots on her heels, examining me for a moment. "I think Midnight Angel suits you. You've got that girl-next-door vibe going on— all wide-eyed and quivering with innocence."

"That's called *fear*."

"Relax, would you?" She dusts her fingers over my bare shoulders. "It's all about subtlety. And would you stop with the panic attacks?" She reaches back and thrusts a bottle of champagne at me. "Hold this, I'll get some glasses."

"*Oh*—trust me, I don't need a glass." I take a nice long swig and give it back before sneaking another peek into the den of depravity. The ebony-haired god is still glued to his seat. He's looking around as if he expects something to happen, not paying attention at all to the show on stage or the one playing out around him.

God, he's gorgeous—hair as dark as pitch—T-shirt that shows off everything that bulges and ripples on top. That boy's got muscles for miles. Tattoos in muted shades of blue and green run up both arms, giving him that bad-boy appeal. He holds a beer bottle on his knee, and ironically he looks perfectly bored while panning the stage. He glances in this direction and our eyes meet again.

"Oh shit," I whisper as my stomach implodes with heat. I yank the curtain around me so hard and fast, I think it's going to fall and smother me. It would serve me right to die one of those humiliating freak accident deaths. I can see the school paper headline now: "*Garrison Sophomore Ally Monroe Dies in Fabric Avalanche While Topless Onlookers Helplessly Sip Champagne.*"

"What's the matter?" Tess struts back with her boobs one bounce away from escaping the rhinestone-studded carnage she's trying to play off as a bra.

"Front row, left side—tall, dark, and way-too-freaking handsome."

She brazenly pulls back the curtain and gawks at his hotness.

"Now we're talking." She lays it out there, low and guttural. "He's a cute one." Tess bounces in her five-inch heels as if she were on springs. "If things move in the right direction this could be your lucky night."

"Lucky indeed," I say, releasing myself from the ridiculous stuffed snake, coiled around my belly. "He has definitely moved things in the right direction because I can't go out there now."

"*What?*" Her features pinch as if I've decided to quit school and become a stripper, and ironically there is nothing Tess would love more than for exactly that to happen. And now it sort of has, with the exception of the quitting school part. If I had a dollar for every time she referred to my scholastic endeavors as a "distraction from the real world," I wouldn't be stuffing myself into snakeskin-print panties and wondering if I should have opted for a Brazilian rather than the blunted business end of my razor.

"He's your *get*." Tess shoves me back toward the open mouth of the stage. "That's where you'll make the big bucks. Make him feel—special—*important*. If you make it a personal experience he could become your regular." Her eyes widen at the psychotic prospect.

"Geez, Tess." I loosen her grip on my elbow. "Thanks for making me sound like a hooker in training. I can't go out there and dance for him. It's like going to the gynecologist and finding out you have a cute doctor. It changes your perspective, and your knees go into lockdown. The cuter they are, the less they get to see. It's genetic discrimination employed by women the world over."

"*Geez*, Ally"—she mocks—"would you stop acting like Ms. Goody Two-Shoes? You're here to foster hard-ons, not relationships. You have a goal, remember? You're helping Dell out with his girl shortage in exchange for help with your *cash* shortage. As soon as you get enough for your own place, you can run back to your little job at Starbucks for all I care. Just appreciate the favor, would you? There were at least thirty different girls on their knees for this spot, and I made sure he gave it to my little sis."

On their knees? I'm almost afraid to ask if she's being literal. Although knowing her sleazebag boyfriend who owns this place, I have a feeling that very position is a staple of the interview process.

"You're right. And thank you, because I am grateful," I whisper. Ever since my Starbucks supervisor, Gretchen, cut my hours to almost nil I've been having a tough time making ends meet. I swear that woman hates me. Besides, it's my last night at the dorm before I officially turn in the keys and land on the couch of Derek's RV. Not that I mind my brother, but a bathroom the size of a closet is involved, not to mention the tiny detail of no actual closet. I'm hoping a few nights at Pretty Girls will help me earn far more than I could at Starbucks in a month.

"Can I see that again?" I pluck the long, green bottle from her and take a few more swigs of the carbonated vinegar before handing it back to her. It's becoming increasingly clear the only way out of this mess is to pass out or vomit.

The room sways for a moment, and I remember exactly why it is I don't drink. Puking and passing out are never high on the priority list.

I peer out and watch as Kit jumps up on the pole and falls backward into the splits. My entire body tenses up at the sight.

"Crap. It's like she's trying to make me look bad on purpose. She's an impossible act to follow." I turn to face my sister. "I haven't done the splits since the fourth grade—that just proves I'm totally underqualified to be here."

"You'll do fine." Tess scoots me closer to the stage where the stench of beer and cigarettes clots the air. "Pretend you're someone else—someone who actually enjoys what she's doing." She wrinkles her nose as she looks out at the crowd. Tess's features harden. "You better loosen up, Ally. They're like dogs. They can totally smell fear. Take this"—she thrusts the champagne back in my direction—"bottoms up."

I take the cool bottle in my hands and force the rest down until my insides feel as though they're disintegrating in a vat of acid. The room pulsates like a heartbeat, and I hold on to her shoulders to keep from toppling.

"This stuff goes straight to my head," I whisper, as the echo reverberates in my brain like a boomerang.

"That's what all you sorority girls say." She gives an approving wink. Her red lipstick shines like glass, and for a moment I want to lose myself staring into it.

"I'm not a sorority girl." I glance back out at the crowd, and then at Kit, who I know for a fact belongs to Tri Delta. "And if I was, I wouldn't be in this mess to begin with."

"What mess?" She rolls her eyes. "You go to Garrison and hang out with snobs all day. Fix my handcuffs, would you?" Tess holds out her wrists. She's opted to costume herself as law enforcement, which, in and of itself, is slightly hypocritical since Tess has walked in the shadow of all things legal since the tender age of twelve when she was caught giving herself a five-finger discount on a pack of cigarettes.

"Since when do cops arrest themselves?" I ask, securing her cuffs.

"Since they had to deal with uptight little sisters like you. Hey . . ." She gets that fiendish look in her eye that's usually followed up with something just this side of a legal violation. "I know a great way to help you loosen up. You should have a one-night stand."

Tess percolates with glee as she dispenses her not-so-sage sisterly advice. If I haven't learned by now to run like hell from Tess and the brain aneurisms she tries to pass off as good ideas, I never will.

"I should *not* have a one-night stand." I glance back out at the ebony-haired god whom I'll be mortifying myself in front of shortly.

"Oh, come on." She peers at him from over my shoulder. "Look at him. Walk on the wild side for once, would you?"

"I tried walking on the wild side, remember? It turned into a felony and almost landed me in prison. By the way, the jackass who was marching next to me is still being housed in a federal institution, trying not to pick up the soap. And besides the unlawful offense, I ended up with a baby—who by the way I had to give away." To say it ended badly would be an understatement.

I shake my head, trying to push Ruby out of my mind. I've sunk so low. My heart breaks in half just thinking about her. I miss her, but thank God I had the wherewithal not to raise her. One of the most difficult things about the whole situation is that if I had a million dollars, she'd probably still be with me. It's money I hate most. It's the one thing that's always managed to hold me under water a little too long, struggling to breathe, making me do things like inaugurate myself as a Pretty Girl.

"Yeah, well"—her lips twitch like she might cry—"you're lucky you still get to have her in your life. Tell her Auntie Tess can't wait to see her on her birthday."

Kit twirls her way backstage out of breath. Her bright pink tassels rotate over her nipples with glee and, in all honesty, it's embarrassing to watch. Kit is gorgeous and wealthy, both of which are usually prerequisites if you plan on attending Garrison University. Of course, I'm far from gorgeous, more like the vanilla girl next door—and for damn sure I'm not wealthy, nor is "stripping" on my bucket list. The only reason Kit's doing this is because she's an adrenaline junkie. Unlike Kit, I prefer my adrenaline to mimic my bank account and run on empty. Oddly, she somehow sees stripping as a move that will advance her social status. I'm sure it will have the reverse effect on me if anyone finds out, resulting in complete and brutal social rejection at the hands of my peers.

"That was fantastic!" Kit's dark hair is slicked into a neat bun. Her sharp features look like they belong in a magazine. "It's just like the time I zip-lined across the Serengeti!"

"And"—I hold back the urge to mock her—"much like the wildlife at Serengeti, the animals native to this watering hole have prehensile tongues and are unable to repress the urge to mate at random."

"Oh, Ally"—she rolls her eyes—"you're gonna love it." A wad of bills fringes her jewel-encrusted bikini. "I'll see you on the floor." She rushes back out to a mosh pit of dollar-wielding patrons.

A single dollar bill remains in her wake, and I glare at it for a moment.

I take a breath, bracing myself at the sight. That's exactly why I'm doing this—money. It's just for a few weeks. I'll get a place, pay off my credit cards, and have enough to buy Ruby something nice for her fourth birthday.

"Go on." Tess pushes me gently until I reach the lip of the stage.

My heart picks up pace. My skin breaks out in a cold sweat, and my breathing grows erratic.

"Shit," I pant.

The speakers crackle overhead as a deep voice booms, "Let's give it up for our next Pretty Girl, Midnight Angel!"

The bright lights blind me momentarily, and I shield my eyes as I try to get my bearings. The crowd ignites in a choir of catcalls as I try to focus all my energy on the long, metal post at the other end of the stage. The faces, the hungry hands clawing out for my attention, all turn into a dizzying blur.

"I'm going to kill Tess," I whisper. "I'm going to *kill* Tess." I chant my newfound mantra while I muster the courage to glance out at the crowd melting in a cigarette haze.

The full effects of my guzzling efforts come into play as I take a few uneasy steps onto the glass-bottom stage. The lights beneath my feet go off in a dizzying pattern of purples and blues as I attempt to inch my way to the pole. One twirl. That's all Tess said it takes to get the "clientele" to open their wallets. Then I can collect cash like candy at Halloween and run like hell all the way back to Garrison.

The music switches up to one of my favorite songs, or as it will be referred to from this moment forward, *that stupid song!* Way to bookmark this catastrophe in the making. I'm sure I'll recall every loathsome moment whenever I have the misfortune of hearing it again.

"Here I go," I whisper.

I make a mad dash to the pole as if the room were on fire, and my foot slips out from underneath me, sending my limbs flailing in all sorts of unflattering gyrations.

The crowd breaks out in a fit of laughter, followed by whoops and howls, as if I've accidentally managed to do something right. It's not until I grab onto the glorified metal staff that I note my left boob has made an Alcatraz-worthy escape from my studded brassiere.

"Crap," I whimper, quick to correct the clothing malfunction. "Bastards," I hiss as the laughter and sneers pick up some serious steam. I manage a quick twirl, which apparently is mandatory per management, and the room spins out of control. "Oh God, oh God, oh God . . ." The words gurgle out of me as I attempt to stagger my way back to Tess so I can carry out the felony I've been destined to commit right from the beginning and wrap my hands around her irresponsible throat.

"Let's see it, baby!" A voice bellows from the rear as I continue to stomp my way toward the red velvet curtains with my arms spread wide, and suddenly I feel like Godzilla ready to trample an unsuspecting Tokyo.

"Come to Papa!" A greasy-looking character with long straggly hair tries to climb onto the stage, and Dell, the owner-slash-bouncer, plucks him back. Oh wait, that's Dell. The fact I'm seeing double is not a good fucking sign.

The lights in the platform go off in a spasm, right along with the music, and it feels as though the floor just opened up and swallowed me whole. I take a few unsteady steps to my left and the crowd gives a collective gasp. I try to catch my bearings in my five-inch killer heels but end up running to my right—so dizzy, so damn tired.

My ankle turns as I do a rather inglorious swan dive right off the stage.

Oh God, don't let this hurt.

I fall like a stone right into a pair of strong, heavily inked arms. I look up very much expecting to see Dell, or some I'm-Going-to-Hack-You-to-Pieces-Later-With-a-Butcher-Knife sleaze, but I don't. Instead, it's Mr. Tall, Dark, and Handsome with his unholy grin and alarmingly deep dimples.

"Whoa, you okay?"

"Mostly not." Unless you count the fact I've reduced our metric distance within my first five minutes as a Pretty Girl. Then I'm totally okay.

"How about you and me take this party someplace else?" He broadens his sexier-than-hell smile and my stomach pinches tight. Why do I get the feeling I've just stepped into some frat boy's triple-X fantasy? Although judging by those bulging biceps, and the carefully choreographed tattoos that swirl up his arms, this is no ordinary frat boy.

I bounce out of his grasp. Clearly I've sent him the wrong message.

"I'll pass. The last thing I'm doing tonight is aiding in my own abduction." The truth is, I'm just about willing to help him tie me up. The thought of what a boy like that could do to me has me halfway to that ever-elusive orgasm I've yet to master. I peer up at him from under my lashes. I bet his fingers know how to work more than a little magic, his gorgeous full lips too. God knows my fingers are useless. I jolt out of my sexual stupor and shake the thought away.

I dust myself off for no apparent reason and oddly my skin feels numb, most likely from the lethal levels of alcohol I've ingested under my sister's twisted supervision.

"I'm not an abductor, so it's not a problem." His grin widens and my insides squeeze tight. I take in his lean, mean body while the tat on his left arm explodes to life as a fire-breathing dragon. "In fact, I'll let *you* take *me* someplace. Hell, I'll even let you bring a weapon." He smiles widely and his dimple winks at me.

"A weapons-grade date, huh?" I lean in, amused, only the leaning doesn't stop until my face ingloriously smacks into his granite-like chest.

"My eyes are up here," his voice rumbles through my skull, deep and baritone. There's a boyish quality about him, and I'm finding it alarmingly attractive. "And if you're interested, I've got a baseball bat in the car I can give you."

I straighten at the thought.

Gah! He's a freak!

"What the hell kind of pervert keeps a baseball bat in the trunk of his car? I bet it's sitting right there next to the duct tape and garbage bags." Crap. Did I just say that out loud?

He picks up his beer, and I proceed to swipe it from him and take a nice long swig.

Tess strides up and snatches the bottle from my hand.

"*Ally*," she snipes. "Do not take beverages away from customers. And for God's sake, try not to get ripped on your very first night." Tess gives a little bow as she returns the bottle to Mr. Tall, Dark, and I've-Got-a-Baseball-Fetish.

I wave her off and snatch the bottle back. Since when did Tess become a roadblock for liberal inebriation? The occasions might be few and far between for me, but tonight the portal to my sanity is definitely ethanol based.

She lets out an incredulous breath before scuttling over to her moronic boyfriend. She's convinced Dell is going to make an honest woman out of her even though she's clearly aware that he shares the same relationship status with at least six other girls at the club. Dell is the biggest douche she's ever dated and the scariest as well. He has a reputation for making people disappear: piss him off and your soul becomes eligible for the dimensional relocation program. But those are just rumors, and Tess doesn't believe a single one of them.

"So it's your first night, huh?" The dark-haired god raises his brows as if this new information took the sheen off my metallic panties.

"Everyone has a first day." I glance down at my right ankle, and wonder when I wrapped a red bandana around it, only to snap out of my drunken stupor long enough to realize I've already managed to rack up a work-related injury. "God, it's swollen."

"Are you okay?" He leans in, and his warm spiced cologne intoxicates me twice as much as the champagne.

"Actually, I'm Ally," I say, glancing down at my foot. "It's just tweaked—I'll live."

"Let me see." He gets down on one knee like some sort of baseball-bat-wielding Prince Charming and gingerly plucks off my high heel. I'm just one foot rub away from adding "feet" to his growing list of fetishes. Something in me sizzles at his touch, and I'm pretty resigned to the fact I'm about to let him have his way with more than just my foot. "You should probably ice it," he says, carefully caressing the back of my calf, and a fire rips through me all the way up to my belly. Every inch of my body begs to have his hand ride up a little higher.

"Ally!" Kit runs over with her curls escaping her bun like little black snakes. She gives me a discreet smile at the quasi-medical attention I'm receiving at the hands of the man with the dragon tattoo. Although judging by those tats, that bad-boy smile, something tells me the medicine he practices is anything but traditional. "Okay. I see you're in good hands." She licks her lips after she says it. "Dell said you can take Amy's spot in ten but if you're hurt I'll totally do it."

"It's all you," I say, plucking off my other heel. "I'll be sitting out the rest of the night." And most likely every other night that follows, but I leave that part out.

She squeezes my hand with excitement before hopping her way back toward the entry. I'm pretty sure Kit just added a heavily inked wannabe med student to her You Only Live Once wish list.

"Wait," I shout after her as she dances farther away. "Bring my purse. The doctor says I need to get home and ice this!"

Her mouth opens wide as she takes in the dark-haired suitor who manned up and caught me like a pop fly. She gives an approving wink before disappearing in a sea of bodies.

"Ice, right?" I glance up at the good doctor. "Among the other alternative treatments I'm sure you have in mind."

"Alternative treatments?" He smolders into me, and my panties try to slide down my thighs on their own volition.

"Let me guess, you've got a thermometer in your Levi's and you'd really like to take my temperature."

His chest vibrates with a silent laugh. "Everyone knows an internal temp is the only way to go." His voice rumbles, deep and secretive. "The name is Morgan. And I'm no doctor. But tonight I can be anything you want."

My insides explode with a rush of pleasure at the blatant innuendo Morgan just employed.

"Consider it an honorary title I'm bestowing upon you." I glance around for signs of Tess. I'm pretty sure she's going to drag me away from Dr. Dragon at any moment. But do I really *want* her to?

"Bestowing upon me?" His brows rise, amused.

I'm guessing the word isn't in his lexicon. But his dimples deepen as he bursts into another heart-stopping grin, and at the moment I don't really care if he understands a damn thing about the King's English.

Crap.

I try to hobble the hell away from him and his medical equipment in the event my alternate champagne-guzzling personality decides to pull him under a table for that one-night stand Tess prescribed. She's no doctor either, but since I'm playing fast and loose with medical degrees there's no telling where things might lead.

The ground sways as I struggle to gain my bearings.

I glance back and catch a brassy blonde wrapping her arms around him while assaulting his neck with her overblown lips. He tilts his head as if he wants it, and his eyes close for a moment, getting lost in the nirvana before he gently peels her off.

"I'm good," he says sweetly but curtly, and she cuts me a death look as if I'm personally responsible for the rejection.

Kit reappears with my bag, and I'm quick to thank her.

"You can have my spot for the rest of the week." My voice reverberates in my head like a tuning fork. "I'm taking off."

I glance down at my barely there accoutrements: my ridiculously high heels that are better classified as stilts, the glorified nipple shields, the G-string I might be moved to fashion into a noose. I'm not exactly sure where it is I'm taking off to. Tess pulled a disappearing act with my street clothes hours ago.

"Hey, you need a ride?" Dr. Dimples offers, and a part of me desperately wants to say yes.

"I'd better not." I press my lips together because everything in me is ready to jump into a moving vehicle with him and beg him to show me his baseball bat.

It's obvious I'm in no condition to drive. The only way I'll get home is either to call Lauren, or Kendall—or hang out at a bus stop dressed like a human anaconda. God knows things will get interesting fast if I choose door number three.

"But thank you," I say, latching onto his steel-colored eyes as my body begs to surrender to any offer he's willing to make. "And thanks for catching me."

A moment sweeps by and the room—the world—stills as his gaze lingers over mine. I'd like to think this would all play out differently if this were some party back at school, but as it stands the only place I'm dressed for success is the Gentleman's

Club. That's probably all he sees in me, a "Pretty Girl" desperate for dollars.

I take a step back, and my knees buckle.

"Whoa," he says, picking my arm up and wrapping it over his shoulder. "Let me help you get wherever it is you're going."

My insides clench because I know what's coming. I've walked into plenty of my sister's misgivings. I've taken her advice and deep-sixed myself in a landmine of crap a time or two.

I swallow hard.

"I'm headed to the back," I say, securing my fingers over his, our eyes never losing contact.

I can feel a one-night stand coming on like a cold.

"You do house calls?" I ask as we hobble into the cold night air. "I'm impressed."

We make our way toward the back of the Pretty Girls Gentlemen's Club, where Tess and Dell have their love nest conveniently located. It grosses me out just to think of the rampant debauchery that takes place behind those doors, not that it stopped me from asking if I could crash on their couch for a few weeks. Of course, Dell said no.

"Fan-*tessy* is my sister. This is her place," I say. Tess keeps a spare key behind the pot with a cactus in it. I lean over to grab it, and stab myself in the process. I don't care what the hell Dell says, I'm way too toasted to drive.

"*Ouch.*" I draw my hand back like pulling it out of a fire.

"Looks like I might need to stick around and inspect you for further injuries." His dark brows pitch, giving him a devil-like quality that I'm finding hard to resist. My heart picks up pace as I steady myself against his thick, treelike arm.

"Why do I get the feeling you're interested in inflicting a few injuries yourself?"

"I promise not to inflict an ounce of pain—unless, of course, you say please." Something in him softens, and he presses out a dull smile. "You got a friend you can call to help you out tonight?"

"I thought that's what you were for?" I say it so low I'm not sure he heard. His eyes hood over, and he's bedroom-eyeing me—reducing me to moronic substandards I swore I would never call my own. He's luring me toward the nearest mattress without even trying. I'm one breath away from surrendering my sanity—*hell*, my body——right here at the corner of easy and hussy. "I don't know where you get off looking so damn hot."

Did I just say that out loud? I close my eyes a moment and the world does a cartwheel.

He lets out a low gurgle of a laugh as he comes in close. His heated breath sears over my cheek, and I can't help but think I'm getting a little too close to the fire.

His lips touch down just shy of my temple, and I close my eyes and moan. Maybe walking on the wild side just one night wouldn't be such a bad idea.

The scent of his spiced cologne makes me heady as our lips find one another—soft and hot, the slight taste of mint and beer lingers over his tongue.

Dr. Morgan detonates like a firecracker in my mouth, only a lot less painful and far more delicious. I pull him backward into the house and shut the door with my elbow. A series of soft moans escape from my throat as I dip into his Levi's.

He rides his hot hands over the bare flesh of my back before pulling away and examining me with those "I'm going to make you come hither" bedroom eyes.

"I think I'd better go." He reaches for the door, and I pluck him back. I place his hand back over my waist, where every drunken fiber of my being believes it belongs. He presses out a sad smile and his dimples ignite just for me. "Once I get going I'm not going to want to stop."

"Who says you're allowed to stop? And for damn sure I don't want you to go anywhere." I pull him backward, and my ankle explodes in a ball of fire. "Ouch," I whisper, righting myself. "Besides, I have a bedroom." I mean bed. "And protection." I'm thinking condom but a forty-five wouldn't be a bad idea in the event things go south. I glance around and note I'm not in Russell Hall while a vague memory of the Gentlemen's Club wafts through my mind. I'm weak, and dizzy, and far too hormonal for anything good to come of this night.

He plucks a metallic square from his back pocket and waves it in the air.

"I don't leave home without it." He gives a crooked grin that has the potential to commit ten different felonies all on its own. And I'm hoping to God he will. "You sure you want to do this?"

My ears pulsate with a heartbeat, and my body gyrates with slight panic. In theory, one-night stands were something my dorm sisters did, often and without regret—hell, I even cheered a few of them on. But as for me, and my girl parts, we've deferred to the traditional dating pool for all our penile endeavors.

"Yes, I want to do this," I hear myself say. It's like I'm in a cage locked away in the farthest reaches of my mind. All of that champagne ushered any good sense I might have held onto and strapped it to the bedpost, much like I'm hoping he'll do to the rest of me in less than five minutes. "The bedroom is this way." I try not to slur as I lead him further into the tiny living room.

"Oh, sweetie." He gives a dark laugh. "We're not gonna make it to the bed."

Morgan pulls me in. His hot, viral tongue lashes over mine, and a series of moans get caught in my throat.

The tugging and pulling of clothes ensues along with the clatter and banging of shoes being missiled across the room. My bra flies off, and I jump out of my panties a little too eagerly when they hit the floor.

My back lands hard against the tiny kitchen table, and the room does a silent spin.

Dr. Feel Good rises above me and takes his shirt off, revealing well-chiseled abs, and another tattoo that covers his shoulder, rounded blades that look like a series of sharpened knives.

He fiddles with the metallic square and the sound of paper tearing and crumbling fills the air but I refuse to look and ruin the magic.

His body lands hard over mine, and a fire erupts as our skin fuses together. His dark hair lands just below my chin as he peppers me with kisses that trail from the hollow in my neck, straight to my lips.

"Last chance to get off the train," he whispers sweetly into my ear, and a line of excitement tracks all the way down my spine.

"Shh," I say a little too loud. I reach down and guide him in.

Morgan thrusts into me with powerful force, and I let out a cry that rips the most innocent part of me into pieces.

Morgan

A mean streak of sunshine bears down over me and my lids crack open to find a beautiful blonde snuggled up beside me.

I seize for a minute.

Shit.

I close my eyes again, hoping for a different outcome, but she's still here, or, more accurately, I am.

A dry laugh rattles from my chest. I swore I wasn't going to revisit old habits—the first one being rounding out my nights at strip clubs. Then again, I never could resist a "Pretty Girl." But in my defense I had only planned on hanging out long enough to hand in an application for the bouncer position advertised out front. It wasn't my fault I fell into another "booby" trap. Once I spotted Ally I knew I wasn't going anywhere.

I untangle our limbs as carefully as if I were defusing a bomb, and sneak off the bed. We made it to the bedroom after all—hell, we made it to *every* room, and even to the edge of the kitchen sink.

For a minute I think about staying—about letting her wake up in my arms. But with my luck, the booze that was talking would have long worn off, and the last thing she'll be asking for is seconds.

I'm pretty sure bailing me out of jail on assault charges isn't what Mom was talking about when she mentioned she wanted to get "all this wedding crap" off her mind for a while.

I fumble into the tiny living room and snatch my jeans off the floor, flinging my wallet clear across the room in the process.

Shit.

I hustle around in the dimly lit room looking for my left shoe and my phone as I get dressed—like a burglar anxious to leave the scene of the crime.

My wallet sits on the coffee table, and I pick it up only to have it slip from my fingers, rattling the thin glass square as it drops.

I snatch it up and run the hell out of Midnight Angel's private abode.

A small grin edges on my lips as I head for my truck.

Ally was a lot of things last night, but she was no angel.

That's for damn sure.

———

WELCOME TO CARRINGTON. An oversized sign greets me as I pull off the highway and drive onto the rural country road. Tall evergreens line either side of the highway as if they're hiding the residents, and I kind of like it this way. Quiet, unassuming. I like the idea of leaving all my troubles behind, clear across country, and disappearing for a while.

A soft bell goes off letting me know I'm flat on empty, and a service station magically pops up on my right. If I didn't know better I'd think fate was twisting all the green arrows in my direction for once. First Ally, then having insane sex with Ally, and now a miracle of the petrol variety. I could get used to this.

Carrington should consider a new motto: *Welcome to Carrington, where all your wet dreams come true.*

I pluck my wallet out only to be greeted with the dark hole of poverty. I stare at it for a second. I know for a fact I had sixteen dollars left because it was my last sixteen dollars and it happened to have breakfast written all over it.

What the hell?

Could Ally have taken it? Nope. She was too busy taking things I was willing to give her, like myself. A loose smile plays on my lips because, hot damn, my balls and I appreciated the attention to detail that girl put in.

I don't give it another thought, just gas up with a credit card and hit the road before heading for the Elton House Bed and Breakfast.

A lone stretch of highway expands in front of me like a silver asphalt tongue. And just as my thoughts meander back to Ally, a body jumps out onto the road.

"Holy shit!" I hit the brakes so fast the car skids off to the shoulder.

A pair of long creamy legs crop up on the horizon along with a gorgeous sandy-haired girl to go right along with them. She's got her hip hiked out and her thumb jabbed in the air. I crawl to a stop, and she runs over to the passenger's side window, laughing. She's hot—not in the turn-your-boxers-into-a-tent kind of way, but with a wide-eyed innocent nature. Although something tells me she's nowhere near innocent.

I crack the window an inch, half-afraid she might jump in the truck if I give her any leeway.

"You sure hitchhiking is a good idea?" I lean over to get a better look at her. Shit. She's barely street legal. She's nothing but a kid.

ADDISON MOORE

"I wouldn't be doing it if it wasn't a good idea. *Besides*, nothing ever happens in Carrington."

That's doubtful. If I had to guess I'd say she was designing an incident of the sexual variety as we speak.

"I haven't seen you around here before." She peers in through the glass and inspects me with those childlike eyes.

"How far do you need to go?" I bark it out, annoyed. It was one thing to help Ally out. A part of me needed to know she got home safe and sound. Her sister's got a screw loose letting her get tanked wearing next to nothing around a group of hopped-up assholes.

"Less than a mile to the bed-and-breakfast down the road." She bites down on a dirty grin as if she is hungry for breakfast and she wants her meal to begin with me.

"Elton House Bed and Breakfast?"

"Yes!" She jumps and her chest ripples from beneath her low-cut top.

"Just wow," I say, lackluster. "What are the odds? Hop on in, sweetie." I let out a disparaging breath as I unlock the door.

"Oh my God! Like, thank you so much!" She buckles up and shuts the door before I can change my mind. "You would think it would be against the law the way people around here pretend they don't see me."

"Probably is," I say, heading back on the road.

Her hand glides over my thigh, and I place it back in her lap.

Knew this was a bad idea.

And exactly what the hell is happening? Did I hit my head when I crossed the state line? Who gets bombarded with gorgeous women left and right after I all but made a vow of celibacy once I left the West Coast? It turns out the people in

Massachusetts are a lot more *friendly* than they are in Oregon—hell, or every other part of the country, for that matter.

"So does your mom know you're out doing whatever it is you're doing?"

"What?" A choking sound emits from her throat. "I'm *eighteen*. It's none of my mom's business where I am or what or *who* I'm doing." She gives a sideways glance as if I might be the "who" she's referring to.

A weak groan escapes me. "First, you don't look a day over twelve, and yes, it's your mom's business. That's why she's called your mom."

"I turned eighteen last April. And no, my *mother* doesn't know I'm out. She thinks I'm tucked in my fluffy pink bed like a good little girl." She looks out the window when she says it. "I'm Molly, by the way. What's your name?"

"Morgan." I press my lips together as a small sign reading ELTON HOUSE BED AND BREAKFAST comes up on the left.

"Anyway," she continues, "most people think I look much older than I am, like say, twenty-one. That would explain why the bartenders here never card me." She pulls at one of her blonde curls as if to entice me. "They give me free drinks and everything."

"I'm sure they'd like you to pay them in other ways." I pull in just shy of an undersized hotel painted an offensive sunny yellow. And why the hell does Molly here want me to drop her off at a place like this anyway? Crap, I bet she's underage and I'm about to get busted in one of those sting operations the networks put on to boost sagging ratings.

A white picket fence runs the periphery of the property, and a heavily chipped archway stands about twenty feet from the establishment. The place looks run-down if you ask me. The plants under the windowsill look as if they committed suicide.

I park and we get out.

"Molly and Morgan," she says, a little too loudly for so early in the morning. "I think we sound really cute together." Her voice dips low and her hips swivel like a hula dancer. Molly here could give any one of those girls at the titty bar last night a run for their money.

Swear to God, if I didn't just leave another girl's bed I might have seriously considered the offer. Plus, Ally wasn't just another girl. There was something genuine about her, I could tell. I'm glad she had to take off after her inglorious jackknife off the stage. I didn't want to see her get mixed up in something sinister. Sure hope she forgets the directions to the strip club.

"Honey?" Mom's voice streams from a set of oversized doors. "Oh my God! It's really you!" Her shock of dark hair is still rumpled from sleep. She's wearing a robe and slippers and accompanied by an equally disheveled man in matching robe and slippers, and oh, holy hell. Just looking at the two of them in their matching disheveled states makes my skin crawl. "You've met Molly!" She wraps her arms around me and gives a big rocking hug. "Isn't she a sweetheart?" She pulls back and makes a face as she takes me in. "Is that lipstick by your ear?" She hisses it out low, suddenly fearing for Molly's not-so-sweet heart.

"Maybe, but I assure you it's from no one you know," I whisper to keep prying ears from garnering any carnal knowledge.

"*Morgan*"—Mom chastises playfully—"there's someone I'd like you to meet." She pulls in her accomplice in early-morning fashion crime. "This is Andrew." She sweeps her eyes over him as if he were a prize. She *should* think so since she's about to marry the guy. Truth is, I've lost track of how many jaunts she's taken down the aisle, but I'll support her if this is what she wants to do. One thing's for sure, when I hit that petal-riddled aisle, the plan is one and done. I'd never put my kids through half the crap she did by hosting a revolving door to her bedroom. Not that I'm angry. Well, maybe I'm a little angry, but despite that I still care about her—she's my mom. And the thought of her getting her heart broken time and time again pisses me off.

"Nice to meet you." He gives a broad grin, exposing a row of perfectly veneered teeth. He's got that silver fox look going on up top, and he seems nice enough. He's not too big, so I could take him if things go south between the two of them.

"Nice to meet you too." I offer a firm shake that says both *welcome to the family* and *I'm not afraid to break your dick.*

"I'll get Kendall," Mom squawks with excitement like I just came back from the dead. "She's been so thrilled that you're coming out." Mom busies herself texting spastically.

"Oh, duh!" Molly jumps in her flip-flops and her boobs say hello again. "You're Kendall's brother. No wonder, you look just like her—but you're all *boy*." She leans in close and nestles up to my bicep, inspiring me to take a conservative step back.

"Morgy!" Kendall screams into the virginal morning as she barrels from a tiny cabin behind the property. Her hair looks like a bat just flew through it, and she's wearing nothing but a white T-shirt that's not quite long enough. I'm guessing it belongs to the dude trekking up behind her who also looks freshly laid.

"Morgy, Morgy!" she sings.

"Don't call me that," I tease, as she flings herself at me. I miss Kendall. I miss having someone to hang out with. I miss seeing her smiling face every single day. We didn't have a lot growing up, but we had each other.

She buries my face in her neck before pulling back. And I try not to comment on the fact she smells ripe, like she hasn't showered in days, and so does the goof just that sprung up beside her.

"This is Molly." Kendall makes a face as she introduces me to the mistress in training. "And *this*"—she bounces with excitement—"is her brother, *Cruise*." Kendall bows when she says his name. "Cruise, this is my brother, the *famous* baseball player. He's going pro right after graduation, right, Morg?"

"I don't know about that." I shake my head. Kendall has a knack for building me up for greatness. "I'm okay. If I'm lucky the coach throws me in." I may have downplayed my abilities, but I'm all for balancing out the modesty when meeting prospective new family members. Kendall mentioned they, too, were engaged.

"Kenny showed me some online footage." Cruise offers up a knuckle bump and I accept. "You're a terror out there, man. We'll have to toss the ball around. Get a game together. My buddy owns the local gym. He's got some batting cages on the property. So you don't need to worry about getting rusty while you're out here."

I'm still stuck on "Kenny."

"Cool." I nod, trying to overlook the fact he just made my sister sound like a dude. "I'll be here all summer. I plan on getting a part-time job."

Mom wraps her arms around my waist and pulls "Kenny" in on the other side.

"Both my children are here," she coos. "Carrington is finally starting to feel like home again. I still have so much planning to do before the wedding; a job sounds just like the thing to keep you out of trouble." She gives my ribs a squeeze.

Molly steps in and licks her lips like a promise. That's trouble in a tank top right there. And for damn sure I want no part of it, especially now that I know she's Cruise's little sister.

I glance around at Mom, Kendall, and their respective disheveled bedfellows. Seems like Carrington is the place to be if you want to get lucky. I should know, I already did.

Sure wouldn't mind seeing Ally again.

I can't help but wonder if I made a mistake by leaving this morning without so much as a good-bye.

The entire state is smaller than a hiccup. I'm betting I'll see her again.

And a part of me hopes she won't remember a damn thing.

2

DINNER AND A MOVE OUT

Ally

I dream of white sandy beaches. I'm holding hands with a handsome dark-haired man as we run down the slippery shore. He wears his tattoos like battle scars. They race up his arms—a kaleidoscope of color on one, a ferocious dragon on the other. The warm summer sand thumps beneath our feet. The ocean is as blue as his eyes. He presses himself into the pages of my heart like a dark exotic flower. He takes me in his arms and sears his skin over my chest and my bare belly before covering me with a kiss. His hips grind against mine and it all comes back to me as I wake with a start.

My hand slaps down over the empty space next to me. It takes everything in me to peel my eyes open, gritty as sandpaper.

"No." I moan as a bolt of pain ricochets through me.

We hadn't made it to the mattress, had we? It must have been a dream—a deliciously dark and twisted dream. Nevertheless, something that wicked could only be produced from the bottom of a champagne bottle. I take a breath and lean up on my elbows. Gone is the Pottery Barn comforter I purchased at Goodwill for eleven dollars, my Garrison

University pendant has been snatched from the wall, and my entire Disney snow globe collection is suspiciously missing.

What the . . .

A mild panic ripples through me as I note all of my things have up and vanished.

He ripped me off! Son of a bitch. He took my bedding and my pendant and who knows what the hell else he pilfered while I was passed out cold. And what kind of asshole steals snow globes? God, I bet he's got some twisted décor-based fetish too.

Next to me, there's a foreign-looking nightstand and an annoying blinking alarm clock—wait . . . I don't have an alarm clock. Do I? My head bursts as a racking pain spears though me.

"Oh shit." I fall back on the bed as it all comes back to me. That's right. Pretty Girls equals champagne, equals one-night stand in Tess's Fan-tessy suite. "Why am I so stupid?"

Wait, did that really happen? I glance around the room for evidence of said gorgeous boy toy but nary a tennis shoe is left in his wake. I probably landed here all by my lonesome. I bet Tess and Dell had to carry me—*drag* me. Figures. Not only did I get severely tanked, I had a grand delusion of the sex-god variety. But damn was it good—*he* was good.

What was his name again? Miller? Maximus? Minimus?

I sweep my legs over the side of the bed and my insides feel as if they've regurgitated themselves all night long. I toss on an oversized sweatshirt and go into the living room. That slight raw, burning feeling between my legs confirms that indeed Dr. Dragon Tattoo had done a thorough internal examination before he so rudely up and left. God, he probably looked nothing like I remember. My knees shake as I bring my legs together, and my insides alert me to the fact that what happened last night was very much indeed real, and perhaps worthy of a visit to the ER.

It was most likely that greasy-haired douche from the back who kept yelping at me to take it off. I'll be dead of some exotic strain of venereal disease in approximately nine months once I give birth to a litter of greasy-haired puppies. This is precisely why I never drink. Everyone knows beer goggles are a proven scientific fact, and champagne goggles are twice as likely to make the common household douche transform into a Times Square underwear model. Just fuck.

The toilet flushes, and the door to the bathroom swings open.

My heart seizes as footsteps head in my direction.

"Morning, sunshine!" Tess smiles, her teeth glittering like a row of tiny mirrors, and everything in me sighs with relief.

"Thank God it's just you. Why was I in your bedroom? Where did you sleep?" Panic shrills through me like an alarm.

"One—you were wasted. And two—you *needed* the bed." She gives a little wink. "Dell and I slept in the spare." A smile twitches on her lips. "You want eggs?" She moves the party into the kitchen, and I follow.

"No thanks. Is there anyone else here?"

"You mean someone around six foot three, black hair, laser-blue eyes?"

My stomach jumps. He *so* did look like that.

"Um, there wasn't any greasy hair involved, was there?" I'm almost afraid to ask.

"No." Her eyes widen just before she dives into the fridge and plucks out the eggs. "And, no he's not here. It's just you and me." She gives a quick wink before yanking a pan out and firing up the stove.

I blindly take a seat at the table.

"He was cute and sweet and helped me home, sort of. He even offered me an out before he impaled me with his impossibly perfect body, but then he just up and left."

"That's why they're called one-night stands," Tess shouts over the sizzle in the pan. "Don't get all weepy-eyed because he didn't write you a poem and leave you a roadmap to his apartment. He was simply following the rules."

"Rules?" This is the very reason I should never have listened to Tess in the first place. Deep down I knew I wanted something more from him. I'm stupid that way and apparently hardwired to believe in sappy, happy endings. I guess it turns out saviors in blue jeans aren't my destiny. Nope, for the rest of the summer I'm going to be living with Derek and his pot-smoking girlfriend in their not-so-comfy RV while I save for a place. *That's* my destiny.

Okay, don't panic. It's only until September and then I'll go around and beg all the sororities to take me in. It's not like I'll be homeless. Plus the savings will help me buy a killer gift for Ruby. Last year I thought I'd buy her something nice to wear from the Gap and scored two sundresses from the clearance rack, but Ruby didn't even glance at them. She was too busy trying to ride the Sit 'n Spin she had just unwrapped from someone else. I got the message loud and clear: toys rule, clothes drool.

I migrate over to the couch and catch a glimpse of a few crumpled bills lying on the coffee table, my panties and bra just beneath them.

Holy shit.

"What's this?" I lean over and inspect the sixteen dollars like I've never seen US currency before.

"Looks like he left you a tip." Tess leans over the counter and bites down a smile.

He didn't.

He couldn't.

I mean, that would make me a . . .

A strangled scream erupts from my throat.

Good God. I think I just turned my first trick.

———

Resentful and angry are not two good ways to drive.

I nearly mow down an entire herd of Pretty Girls as I careen out of the parking lot on my way to Starbucks. I need to ask to get off before three to clear my crap from Russell Hall, and it always works better if I'm not late while begging to be let off early. I'm more than bummed I'm not at Russell now to experience all the fun. It's officially moving day, and everyone is excited to get summer under way. All week the dorm has been buzzing with talks of summer vacays to Europe, the Hamptons, private islands with five-star chefs held captive for my dorm sisters' nutritional benefits. And what do I have to look forward to? At the rate I'm going, an entire array of STDs. Oh, and that tiny detail of having no actual home in which to enjoy said STDs. Ironic since Russell Hall will be empty as a haunted house. Nevertheless, I'll be joining the ranks at the U-Haul rental station later this afternoon.

I sent a 911 text to Lauren and Kendall before I left Tess. Who better to man-bash with than two women who've been stung by cupid's crooked arrow? Oh, who am I kidding? The only one getting screwed sideways by that demonic cherub is me. Both Lauren and Kendall are engaged. It's just me who wants to commit mass penile decapitation. And there's no coincidence about the fact I'd love for my hacking spree to begin with every man misfortunate enough to have the name Morgan. It's probably not even his real name. Sleazeballs like him are forever changing their aliases, making women believe they're astronauts and brain surgeons, only to have their license to lie revoked once the FBI takes them down in a sting operation. Of course, by the time the Feds get involved there are already an entire bevy of dumbasses like me left in his wake.

I take up two parking spaces and breeze inside like I'm going to hold up the place.

Penelope waves at me from behind the counter. She's a sophomore who sounds like a squirrel and perhaps the only natural blonde on the planet I know. In my haste to spew my disdain for all things testosterone I breeze past her. I'll make it up to her later. She's forever asking to swap hours and days, and no matter how hard management tries to shuffle her around, she's never content with the schedule. And if they hadn't cut my hours to nil I would never be in this psychotic mood to begin with. I completely blame last night's fiasco on my supervisor. That entire default to one-night-stand mode was nothing short of her doing for forcing me to seek employment elsewhere.

"Get over here, girl!" Lauren springs to her feet, and her hair bobs around her ears. She's been my roommate for the past year and like a sister since I've been at Garrison—*better* than my actual sister because she's never landed me as the not-so-star attraction of a peep show. Although unlike Tess, she doesn't know every little bit about me. Not that I'm deliberately keeping anything from her, it's just that I find some things unnecessary to bring up, like the truth about Ruby's father, and my recent stint at Pretty Girls. *God*, if Lauren knew I bared my assets in front of dozens of inebriated sausage slingers, and that they all but saluted me with their swords of flesh—she'd fashion a noose out of her copy of *The Feminine Mystique* and kick out the chair herself. Nevertheless, I miss her as a roommate—especially since she's taking her designer closet with her. Of course, Garrison offered to find me a replacement roommate come fall, but the truth is Lauren paid for the dorm in its entirety, so there's that.

I offer her a brief hug and do the same with Kendall. Kendall is far too gorgeous to comprehend with her dark hair and bionic-blue eyes—sort of like the douche I had the misfortune of sleeping with last night.

"What happened?" Lauren coaxes me into the seat between them. "Is this about a boy?" She's already ordered a drink for me, an iced hazelnut macchiato, soy, easy ice, no whipped cream. Only a true friend can order your drink just right.

"Oh, I don't think he qualifies." I slump into my seat. "Tess gave me some advice," I start heroically, and then think twice before revealing any more about my poor judgment last night. It's not like I'm going to mention anything about Pretty Girls, or the fact that US currency changed hands at the end of a long disastrous night during which my questionable services were employed.

"Tess gave you advice?" Lauren looks as if someone just swiped her Prada bag. "And you took it?"

"She's my sister." Not that I'm proud at the moment. "It's not my fault she's prone to dicey advice." Among other things.

Lauren cuts me with a look that could slice steel cables. "Her stripper name is Fan-tessy and she runs a quasi-escort service." She wastes no time filling Kendall in on all the fun little deets. Sure, they're all true, but they sound so much worse coming from a pair of perfectly glossed Stila lips.

Kendall's mouth falls open and appropriately so because for one, she's sane.

"Anyway"—I clear my throat—"I met this guy . . . um, while visiting my sister." I lower my lashes and my cheeks burn with heat. "It was stupid. He was far too gorgeous, which should have been my first red flag. But I didn't stand a chance. I brought him back, and we did it. He left before I got up this morning. End of story." It all sounds so vanilla now that I've pushed it through my vocal cords.

"Oh, *hon*, is that what's got you so upset?" Lauren wraps an arm around my shoulder. "That was just your run-of-the-mill one-night stand. It's your first—"

I cut her off. "And my last. Believe me, there was nothing run-of-the-mill about this guy." Then again that bottle of champagne could have played a part in my exaltation of him and his baseball bat. "It's not happening again." But if those dimples go off I might just be tempted to melt into one. "He's an ass of the highest order." A perfectly rock-hard ass, but still, he's nothing but a double negative. "Jerks like him eat decent people like me for breakfast." Or, as evidenced by his sudden urge to partake of the first meal of the day elsewhere, maybe not. "I swear I'll knife his balls off if we ever meet again."

Kendall and Lauren gape at me as if I've already committed the lewd felony.

"Don't just sit there," I say, incredulous at their sudden urge to plead the fifth. "Raise your coffee and say something encouraging." I grip my cup so tightly my fingers turn white.

"You'll find someone else." Lauren touches her hand to mine with her dime-store consolation. "Someone special." She nods with an equally false sense of assurance.

ADDISON MOORE

"And he'll be Mr. Right," Lauren adds. If I didn't know better I'd swear she was mocking me.

"Easy for you to say. You've got Cal"—I look to Kendall—"and you've got Cruise. And I've got nobody, per usual." I sink in my seat, and my vagina lights up with the remnants of last night's grand slam that held all the magical ingredients of a happily ever after, minus the love and genuine affection, and the general knowledge of his surname. "*And,* I've got to *move* today." It comes out pissy as if this, too, were somehow his fault. "There's nothing like moving to magnify the fact you don't have a strong pair of arms to call your own."

"I'm so sorry, Ally." Kendall combs out her long, black bangs with her fingers. "Not all guys are assholes. I swear to you there are a ton of great ones out there." Her shoulders droop before she springs back to life. "Look, my brother just came into town and he's dying to check this place out. Why don't we help you move and if you like, you can show him around? I'd really appreciate it, and I know he would too. I'd show him around myself, but I can tell he's already itching to get away from me and Cruise."

"I don't know." I shake my head at the idea. "I'm sort of allergic to blind dates in general."

"It's not a date." Lauren smacks me in the arm. "He's going to help you move, and you can take him to dinner as a thank-you."

Kendall nods a little too eagerly.

"Okay. But I have to warn you I have a long-standing track record of not falling for my friends' brothers. No offense. I'm sure he's great and all, but I'm gun shy when it comes to next of kin." It's a certified fact there is no quicker way to kill a friendship.

"I promise—you're going to *love* him!" Kendall beams at the thought of playing matchmaker. "He's totally fabulous."

38

Odd how she's undeterred by the fact I've got a seed of vengeance blooming in my heart for anyone slinging a procreation device between his legs. And, unless he rids himself of his miniature tail, he'll be a guest on my "shit list" for the interim or at least until my anger for an entire gender subsides—and judging by the knot in my stomach, that would be never.

———

After a brief stint at the Bux, I return to Russell Hall and endure hours of playing throw everything you own into garbage bags, plus sixteen boxes. Where the hell did all this crap come from anyway?

My phone buzzes. It's a text from Kendall.

Downstairs!

Perfect. That means her brother is here. My stomach pinches at the thought of meeting up with another card-carrying member of the Trouser-Snake Society. I've been in a pissy mood ever since Dr. Morgan-Douche decided to check me for a fever with his own personal dipstick, then made a run for the border like some kind of carnal convict.

I take the elevator down to meet with Cruise, Kendall, and her oh-so-fab big brother. I spent the majority of the afternoon hauling all the little boxes down and playing a real-life version of Tetris in the trunk of my Honda, but Kendall made me promise to leave all the heavier boxes for Cruise and her big bro. The dorm came furnished so there's that.

It's already warm for June, which is a nice change of pace since I don't usually feel like putting on anything summery until well after the Fourth. But in honor of my newly declared male fast I decide to torment the opposite sex by looking as cute as humanly possible. I hope to drive entire droves of sexed-up frat boys insane with my barely there Daisy Dukes, my add-a-size Bombshell bra paired with the designer wifebeater left by Lauren. When she moved out, half my closet moved out with her—the better half.

Anyway, I called Derek and warned him of my impending arrival. He said dinner involved a big greasy bucket from the Colonel, and me delivering it, so I guess that means I'm buying. We really didn't discuss rent, so I'm assuming endless trips to any and every fast-food locale within driving distance will be my major contribution—that and cleaning. Derek and his girlfriend Raya aren't too keen on that whole hygiene thing. You'd think their humble RV was a getaway resort for the local rodent population the way they gathered around the vicinity in herds. And Raya doesn't help the situation by setting out a five-star buffet for them in her bevy of birdfeeders. I keep telling them the last thing those rat cafes see are winged creatures, but they're the first to call bullshit on just about anything that flies from my mouth ever since "I've done got myself an *edjamacation.*" Everything in me sighs at the thought of what a long, drawn-out summer this is going to be.

The elevator doors open, and I hurry outside. The air is thick and muggy, already perfumed with the familiar scents of summer: suntan lotion mixing with the evergreens.

Kendall stands next to a large white pickup, waving like she hasn't seen me in months, so I wave back and freeze with my hand in the air like I'm about to swat someone and honest to God I just might.

"Holy shit," I hiss under my breath. It's the dark knight from last night's romp and stomp. He's sporting a goofy grin that melts off his face faster than a glacier in hell, and that's exactly where I'm about to send him.

Crap. He's going to ruin everything. Here Kendall was nice enough to show up with her better half and her brother . . .

Oh, no. Oh, God.

Everything in me freezes.

Shit, shit, *shit*.

"Ally!" Kendall bounds over and drags me to the ebony-haired Adonis. His lips twitch a devilish grin and his dimples press in deep.

Just fuck.

"Ally, this is my brother, Morgan." My stomach clenches when she says his name. "And Morgan, this is my good friend, Ally."

Here it is. That awkward moment when you want to gouge out your best friend's brother's eyes, and perhaps a few other unnecessary appendages.

Our eyes lock. Kendall, Cruise, and all of Garrison disappear for a moment, and I'm left contemplating a homicide with nothing more than the nail file I stuck in my pocket an hour ago.

"Hello, *Morgan*." I draw my weapon first. It comes from me a little more aggressively than necessary but I figure I should set the tone for this, the next leg of our nonexistent relationship. "Who I have *never* met before." I shake his hand like a threat. So help me God if he spews the inglorious details of our little carnal cash exchange right here in the parking lot in front of his blood relation, and the meandering ears of my dorm sisters, I might be moved to perform a spontaneous castration with my teeth.

I cringe a little at the idea because I distinctly remember something of that nature occurring before I blacked out.

"Nice to meet you, Ally." He leans in with his seductive gaze, a smile playing on his lips but he's too cocky to give it. "Who I have *never* met before." He drips the words with sarcasm, and it makes both Kendall and Cruise sit up at attention. I glare over at the two of them and they're quick to duck into the safety of Russell Hall.

"It's *you!*" It rips from me like the expletive it is.

His brows rise. His chest vibrates with a silent laugh as if he's indignant at how unimpressed I am with his tightwad ass.

"Sixteen dollars?" I hiss, just this side of tears.

"Sixteen dollars?" He moves in close. "You have my sixteen bucks?"

My eyes widen. What the hell? Does he honest to God think I've got a pimp in the mix? I bet he gave it to Dell. It's obvious he's done this before and is up to date on the protocol.

He holds out his hand like he's expecting something.

"I want my sixteen dollars back." His lips pull into a line and my mouth drops open because swear to God if he's not shitting me there's going to be a knifing.

A group of girls from Alpha Chi stroll by in their matching luau wear and rainbow-colored leis. Two of the girls crane their necks to get a better look at my *john.*

"Oh. My. God." It takes every ounce of self-control not to snatch a neighboring lei and strangle this dipshit—the symbolism alone would be worth the prison sentence. "Are you asking for a refund?" It comes from me smooth, and surprisingly restrained.

"A refund?" He pushes in with those storm-colored eyes. "You thought I paid for sex?"

"Shh!" I dance around in a fit of delirium. "I refuse to discuss last night's brain malfunction out in the open.

Prostitution is *illegal,* by the way. And, yes"—I give a wild-eyed stare—"you left sixteen lousy bucks! What's the matter? All out of pocket change?"

"I'm confused." He holds out his hands in surrender, and his chest expands to the size of a refrigerator. "I'm a guy. I'm not the brightest. I don't attend Garrison." He says *Garrison* with insulting air quotes that only douchebags use to mock institutions of higher learning. "Are you saying I shouldn't have left the money? Or that I didn't leave enough?"

A choking sound emits from my throat because, damn it all to hell, he's guilty of *both* charges. My entire body goes rigid. There are so many insults storming my vocal cords I'm literally gagging.

"Ally?" Kendall pops up from behind lugging a giant box. "I'll just put this in the back of his truck since your car is full." She gives a little wink.

"This is it." Cruise drops off a stack of boxes he muscled down all on his own. Figures. Morgan here is proving himself useless already. Typical male—love 'em and leave 'em, then let someone else do all the heavy lifting. "You guys want to meet us down at Pete's Fish and Chips tonight? My treat."

Kendall leans in and whispers something in his ear.

"Okay"—Cruise looks uneasy—"how about the Della Argento restaurant, instead?"

Kendall nudges him in the ribs. I can tell she's gunning for this to be special for her big bro and me.

"My treat," he grits. Cruise gets that faraway look in his eyes as if he's trying to mentally rework the mortgage on the B and B just to pay for our impending nosh-fest. Cruise wipes the sweat from his brow with his shoulder. Cruise is gorgeous *and* courteous, unlike Morgan here who only has the first half down;

and seeing that genetics played a huge part in that, I'm back to finding him useless.

"Sounds good to me." Morgan pushes out a grin with the hint of a dare.

"Sounds good to me too." I bite the air with my response.

Morgan ticks his head back with that cockier-than-hell smile spreading slow across his face. "Why don't we get those boxes out of your car and we can ride to your new place together?" he offers, tipping his head back with those hooded eyes set to seduce as if he's trolling for more of that bargain-basement affection.

"That's perfect." Kendall is quick to motivate Cruise to evacuate the boxes from my Honda as if it were about to combust. "That way you can get to know one another right away."

I ride a quick glance up and down his body and the memory of him writhing over me reduces me to cinders.

I wonder what Kendall would think if I told her that we got to "know" each other rather proficiently last night.

I give a depleted smile as Kendall and Cruise take off.

"Looks like it's just me and you." His dimples implode and so does my stomach.

"Nice to see your deductive reasoning skills are intact. You're a sharp one."

He huffs a quiet laugh. "And you've got a sharp tongue." He steps into me with his lip curling on the side. "But I already knew that."

My body lights up like a flare. Morgan Jordan already knows far too much about my body. I wish I had never had slept with him.

The only one deficient in reasoning skills around here is me.

Morgan

swear to you, I never meant to leave that money. It must have fallen out of my wallet," I say for the third time as we drive down the long stretch of highway.

It's gorgeous out here but Ally outshines anything Mother Nature is trying to impress us with. Every now and again you can see a touch of the ocean through the pines, and if I weren't hauling a psychotic to her brother's trailer park I'd offer to take her to the beach for a while.

"Sure. Whatever." She spits it out like a death threat. "It's not like you're going to admit it now that you know Kendall and I are friends. By the way, I'll be a bridesmaid in her wedding come December. We'll probably be forced to dance together. In case you're wondering, my favorite bills are Benjamins."

I pump a smile in her direction.

Smart ass.

Her lips quiver as if the thought of throwing some moves on the dance floor with me makes her want to cry.

She gives a hard sniff and the potential for waterworks has just been upgraded to DEFCON 1.

"Look, I'm really sorry," I start out slow. "If I knew you were that close to Kendall I would have never even caught you.

I would have let you fall right there on the floor and watched your skull crack open to see if butterflies flew out."

She gives a little laugh.

"Okay"—she flattens her hands in the air—"so you're less of an ass for catching me, but could you please do me a huge favor? Don't tell her about Pretty Girls, or all that stuff that happened after. I'd die if she found out."

All that "stuff" that happened after? And really? Dying of mortification? I could have sworn those moans she gave last night meant pleasure, not pain.

I run my hand over the wheel before gripping it. I also happened to think that *stuff* was pretty damn spectacular, but then again, I was the only sober party present.

"You got it," I say as we pass a deer on the side of the road. It's not like I was about to babble to Kendall anyway. "It's nice out here." I change the subject on the off chance tears are still a work in progress.

Ally is pretty and, from what I can tell, sweet to anyone who's not me. The last thing I'm in the business of doing is making a *pretty girl* cry.

After an arduous drive that's anything but close to campus, I pull off in the Shady Oak RV Park complete with enough children running wild to outfit an elementary school.

"So why aren't you living with your sister?" I'm guessing Fan-tessy pulls in quite a haul at the end of the month, not to mention she's probably not camping out in the boondocks with the miniature punk posse running afoot.

"Her boyfriend, Dell, is a freak." She makes a face. "He's the owner of Pretty Girls, and thinks that entitles him to every girl on the planet." She shrugs. "Anyway, Tess didn't exactly offer and Derek did." She inspects the dismal rows of metallic structures and her pink polished nails glow off her tan skin. Ally looks sexy as hell without even trying. "So, I hear the bed-and-breakfast is full and you're stuck with Kendall and Cruise."

"It's *Kenny*," I tease. "Actually, I'm pretty sure that nickname's off limits to me."

She lets out a little laugh and her features soften. "We should have sickening nicknames for each other. You could be Midnight Morgan and I can be Angel Ally."

I laugh dryly. "How about I can be Mega Man and you can be *Amazing* Ally?"

"Mega, huh?" She lowers her gaze to my crotch and when she looks up again, she's got a dirty curve on her lips. "Amazing Ally sounds perfectly boring but I accept."

"No, it's true. You were amazing and anything but boring. I've got the replay going off in my mind to prove it."

"You're a perv." She rolls her eyes.

"I'm a realist."

My eyes stray to her long honeyed legs. The memory of tracking my tongue along the inside of her thighs perks my hard-on to life in my jeans.

Shit. I'm pretty sure working myself up as we park in front of her brother's place is *not* a great idea.

I wonder if Ally would be interested in me? She was pretty tanked last night. I'm sure half the guys at the club could have scored the same home run. But damn, I'm glad I was there to knock it out of the park. Sure had fun running those bases.

I press out a gentle smile and tap her on the knee.

"Let's do this," I say, looking at the beat-up RV on cinder blocks. The back window is cracked, with aluminum foil added as a decorative touch. A row of dead plants hangs off a makeshift sill.

We get out and she shouts hello through the murky screen.

"Ally?" A female voice rises a few destructive octaves as she opens the door, revealing herself—a tall, disheveled woman with greying hair, her face as worn as shoe leather. Her arms are thin as rails with track marks etched from her wrist to her elbows. She's sporting some serious raspberry welts, and I'm guessing that's where the needle penetrated a few times too many. "This your boyfriend?" She smiles, exposing two rows of perfectly rotting teeth.

"She wishes." I wrap an arm around Ally's shoulder and give a squeeze.

"*He* wishes," Ally says. "This is Morgan. Morgan, this is Raya."

"I cleared out three compartments for you." She points to a series of small cubbyholes that line the bottom of the RV. "Derek's asleep but you two can come in and have the place to yourself. I'll be in the back." She whispers that last half before disappearing.

"Shit," I say under my breath as I take it all in. I can't seem to look away from the wreckage. No offense, but I can spot a junkie a mile away and Raya here certainly meets the criteria. I'm betting good old Derek isn't sleeping as much as he is passed out, or dead. "You sure you want to do this?" I squint at her. Something in me wants to pick her up and run her back to the truck.

"Do I look like I have a choice?" Her gorgeous sea glass eyes widen, and suddenly I wish I had enough cash to give her an entire list of choices. "I'll be fine," she says, making her way back to the truck and retrieving a small box before heading inside. I follow her in, mostly to see what infestations they might be fostering. There's no way in hell I'm going to off-load her stuff and leave her here like rat bait.

It's dark inside, smells like piss and beer, with something else much more lethal layered underneath. A threadbare carpet meets up with a square of laminate flooring in the kitchen and an odd assortment of beakers and bongs clutters up the tiny counter space.

I nod over to the mess. "I'm guessing this doubles as a science lab."

Ally gives an easy smile and pulls a large square book out of the box while patting a seat beside her on the couch.

"What does your brother do for a living?" I ask, falling into the seat next to her. The cushion depresses straight to plywood.

And she'll be sleeping on this? A casket would be more comfortable, and judging by the atmosphere, it might be an option if she's not careful.

"He . . ." She bites down on her finger and pulls it out of her mouth slowly, as if she were teasing me. Ally leans in tight and her cleavage moves in just under my face. Her sweet perfume grabs me by the balls and gives a gentle squeeze. Damn, she smells good—vanilla and strawberries, my favorite combo. "They rob liquor stores for a living."

"Very good." I straighten. Ally just affirmed the fact there's no way in hell I'm letting her stay. "So they spend a lot of time running—from the law. That would explain the fatigue."

"You think you're funny, don't you?" She rubs her hand over the book she's cradling as if it were a pet.

"I think you're funny for wanting to stay."

She bites down over her cherry-stained lip and lets it out nice and slow by way of her teeth. Her entire person sags as she crosses her butter-smooth legs, and my dick feels the sudden urge to stretch to life.

"What's with the book?" I ask before my hormones start rooting for another home run.

"It's a scrapbook." Her eyes glitter with tears as she blinks them away. "It's of my daughter."

My stomach drops like a stone.

Ally has a daughter. I don't know why this makes her look different, feel different to be around, but it does. It makes me want to protect her twice as much from Derek's pharmaceutical felony in the making.

"Look," I say, shaking my head, "if you've got a little girl, I can't let you stay here. You said this guy is knocking down liquor stores? That means he's got firearms and bullets and all kinds of safety hazards kids shouldn't be around." Honestly, I have to tell her this?

"I don't have her." Ally's voice stills to nothing. "I gave her up when I was seventeen. It's an open adoption." She nods as if she couldn't push out another word. "The Christies are real nice people. Ruby is their middle girl." She wipes a tear from the side of her face, and my heart breaks for her. "Anyway, I get to see her once a month. Ruby knows who I am, and she's fine with everything. In fact, her fourth birthday is coming up this summer, and I'm saving up to get her something special like a bike. I've already cleared it with Janice, her mother." She swallows the word *mother* down as if it hurts to say it.

I brush the hair from her cheek and hook it behind her ear. My chest pounds like I just ran a marathon. Life usually isn't fair, but it doesn't have to be this hard either.

She opens the book and a cherub-faced infant stares back at me. My stomach clenches. It makes me think of Paige back in Oregon, who might be carrying my child. Case in point why I'd sworn off one-night stands, or week-long flings as was the case with Paige. She was taking a break from her then-boyfriend, and I was just letting the general and two colonels I keep tucked in my boxers have a little fun. Of course Clint, her fiancé, wants her to have nothing to do with me—said he'd pay me to stay the fuck out of their lives. But I won't. If those paternity tests point in the direction of a Jordan then I'm stepping up to the plate. There's no way in hell I'll do to my kid what my dad did to me.

I offer up a quiet smile.

I'd tell her all that, but I think one deep, dark confession is enough for now. Besides, I don't want to turn this into something about me. This is about Ally and the little book she's holding as if it were her baby.

"And this is her now." She brushes her thumb over an eight-by-ten photo of a beautiful little girl, blonde curls, big green eyes—she's Ally's doppelgänger in every way.

Something in me galvanizes when I see Ruby's picture, and suddenly I want to protect both her and Ally.

"She's gorgeous, just like her mom." The words come out low, barely audible.

"Thank you." Her eyes lock over mine. Ally holds me hostage with her gaze, and I want to wrap my arms around her, tell her everything will work out.

A quiet moment passes between us. Every cell in my body wants to lean in and kiss her, but it seems like the scrapbook has grown two sizes, and a part of me wonders if she's using its girth as a barrier.

What the hell.

I lean in and she reciprocates. Her hot breath sweeps over my lips like an erotic sensation meant to torment rather than please. I open my mouth and dive in only to fall into the void she created by moving away.

"I can't kiss you," she whispers.

"Why not?" She didn't seem to have a problem doing a whole lot more than kissing last night, but I don't remind her.

"You're *you*." She shrugs as if that alone is enough to qualify a rejection. "You know . . . you've got tattoos and probably a piercing I can't see. You have one-night stands with *dancers*." She says that last part as if it is the invisible line in the sand.

My mouth falls open at the verbal massacre of my character with nothing more than a shallow assessment—not to mention the fact she was the dancer. And she knows damn well I don't have a piercing.

"You always so quick to judge?"

"Don't get testy," she snips. "I waited twenty-four hours to judge you."

"To my face." I give a wry smile. "But then again you were too loaded to argue about my tattoos last night. By the way, you gave your oral approval of the one on my chest for a half hour straight."

Her fingers fly to her mouth.

"Okay." She closes her eyes and tries to compose herself. "First, I'm not trying to insult you. I simply mean that you and I are both from the wrong side of the tracks, and two wrongs don't usually make a right."

"Are you shitting me? What kind of math are they teaching at Garrison anyway?"

"I just think we shouldn't get involved any more than we did. You should find a nice girl, and I should find a nice guy. We need someone who'll refine us. You know, show us there's more to life than gentlemen's clubs and an RV filled with rifles and hypodermic needles."

"Are you saying I'd drag you down?" I really didn't need the clarification, but I want her to zero in on the insult.

She averts her eyes while settling her hips from side to side, driving me wild in my Levi's. Little does she know she's ten times more enticing now that she's put down my social standing as a means of playing impossible to get.

"I'm saying it would be easier for someone else to raise us up. Face it, Morgan, we'd just hold each other to the bottom." She brings her scrapbook to her lips and presses in a kiss. "And believe me, nothing good ever happens down there."

I think I see what's stung Ally so badly that she's given up on finding love in her own backyard. Something tells me she's been to the bottom and has no plans on diving back. Little does she know assholes come in all shapes and wallet sizes.

Ally just needs the right person to show her a relationship can work on both sides of the tracks.

I'm betting all Ally Monroe needs is someone like me.

———

The sun sets in bands of pink and gold as Ally and I make our way to the Della Argento restaurant where Cruise and Kendall wait to meet us. I made it a point not to unload a single box, but Ally put in the elbow grease and had the back of my pickup empty faster than her brother could manage a ten-dollar heist.

"You look nice," I say as we make our way inside. Ally did a quick change into a short black dress. Her long blonde hair sweeps down her back, her legs rise to the sky, and my boner is in the midst of a revival just looking at her. Hate to break it to my dick but I have a feeling Ally's girl parts don't want to be *held down* by it tonight or any other night for that matter.

Wrong side of the tracks. I shake my head as we hit the entrance. Who the hell says that?

I open the door and let her in first. It's nice inside, low lighting, enough candles to burn down an RV park and I'm wishing they would. A bouncy blonde takes us over to Kendall who's waving like a lunatic. She's wearing a tight dress like Ally's that shows way too much of my baby sister to the world, and I don't like it one bit. It's one thing for Ally to wear it—she looks downright hotter than hell—but I want to throw a tablecloth over my sister. Cruise pops up next to her, looking like Mr. GQ with his hair slicked back, his matching suit and tie.

"Oh my gosh!" Kendall jumps up and pulls Ally into a hug. "You guys are the cutest couple!" She jets her lower lip out like she used to do when we were kids and she wanted to get her way.

"I think so too." I give a quick wink to Ally. Nothing like getting under her skin a little to start the night off in the right direction.

"How'd the move go?" Cruise offers up a knuckle bump, so I reciprocate.

"He didn't help." Ally is quick to rat me out. "He stood around and watched as I lugged out box after box all by my lonesome." She cuts a private smile in my direction.

"Morgan!" Kendall is mortified by my lack of box-moving bravado.

"Relax. I didn't want her to go. You haven't seen this place. It's a crime scene in the making."

"Excuse my brother." Kendall's jaw goes slack in the wake of my shorthand analysis. "He's usually not this rude." She glares over at me a second. "Or is this something new?"

"He speaks the truth," Cruise confirms. "No offense, but I've met Ally's brother."

"Oh, that's right"—Ally holds back a laugh—"he wanted to rent the land behind the bed-and-breakfast for his organic farming endeavor."

"Let me guess"—I venture out on a limb—"medical marijuana?"

"How'd you know?" Her eyes brighten as she lets out a laugh.

"I had an inkling." I grew up with a half dozen fools who are barreling down Derek's regrettable road in life. I guess Ally is right in that respect: some people never get off the ground. They get their feet stuck in the mud and only sink deeper.

I wonder what she would say if I told her I'm prelaw, that I have no intention of farming hemp in an effort to make myself and others feel better ten years down the road.

Kendall excuses herself, then a few moments later Cruise does the same.

I glance over at Ally, her long hair—that smoking hot dress—and can't help but feel like I want a do-over of last night's carnal festivities.

"So"—her shoulders bounce to her ears—"there's a huge party in a couple days at one of the fraternities. Sort of a kickoff to summer, if you want to go." She pinches her lips to the side, and a little dimple appears in the corner.

Not quite the invitation I was hoping for, but it's a start.

"Sounds like a date," I tease. Let's see how fast she cuts off her right arm at the thought of pairing herself with a lowlife like me.

"Actually, I will be on a date. There's this guy, Rutger—"

"Rutger?" I cut her off. "Let me guess. *Rutger* is from the *right* side of the tracks."

"Exactly." She nods at her own idiocy. "And trust me, there will be a sea of nice girls just dying for you to corrupt them, so it'll be a win for both of us." She wiggles her shoulders and a visual of her riding me, with her hair lashing over my face, pops up and ticks my cock to life.

"So what's up with the dancing career? You hanging up your tassels or you going to give it one more go at the pole?"

She frowns at me a second. "*Shh.*" She glances around for signs of life in this mausoleum. "It's part-time. Don't judge."

"I don't judge. That's your department."

Her eyes narrow in on mine. "Anyway, I suck at it. I didn't make any money the first night."

"You made sixteen dollars," I correct. Which she's been slow to return, but I'm calling it a loss at this point.

"I did *not* make sixteen dollars." Ally squirms in her seat and her cleavage springs to life.

We make small talk and stare out at the scenery for what feels like a small eternity. It's clear I have the ability to tick her off spectacularly with the simple act of opening my mouth. Ally's a little spitfire, and I like that.

Kendall and Cruise come back looking like they just mopped the floor with one another's heads, and my body tenses up in one giant knot at what their disheveled state of being might mean.

Kendall and Ally engage in their own private conversation while Cruise peruses the menu because I'm pretty damn sure he just worked up an appetite.

"*Dude,*" I whisper, disgusted at what I'm about to ask. "Did you just fuck my sister?" I might have to kill him if he says yes. I have a feeling I'm going to have to kill both him and his boner, anyway.

Cruise glances over at Kendall and Ally still locked in their heated debate over whether or not people still wear capris, before darting a look back at me like it was none of my damn business.

Shit.

I slide down in my seat and gloss over the menu. The prices are conveniently over the top. I pull the menu down and give a quick smile to Cruise I'll-do-your-sister-wherever-the-fuck-I-please. He mentioned earlier dinner was on him.

I'll be sure my meal comes stock with a lot of heavy-handed digits.

"Kobe beef," I muse without breaking his hostile stare. His eyes enlarge as if I just threatened to crush his balls with a sledgehammer.

That's right, Cruise.

Screw you and your little credit card too.

"So, Ally"—Kendall picks up her napkin and tosses it into her lap—"if things don't work out with your brother and his RV, you can move in with us." She wrinkles her nose at her brilliant epiphany.

"That's a great idea," I chime. Not sure why I didn't think of it.

"And you can sleep on the couch." Kendall nods over to me as if it's a given.

I tweaked my back twice last season. There's no way in hell I'm sleeping on the couch. It'll end my baseball career before it ever begins. I'll be forced to leave the field of dreams and change my name to *Rutger*, thereby scoring girls like Ally who want to use me for my social standing.

I don't say a word, just offer a brief smile to the blonde bombshell seated by my side.

"I'll be fine at my brother's." She's quick to wave the idea away as if it were a fly on a shit sandwich. "Unless of course something unexpected happens. I guess you never know." She gives a sideways glance in my direction.

Oh, I definitely know. In fact, I predict something unexpected of the legal variety will happen to a Mr. Derek Monroe as soon as I can alert the Carrington sheriff's department of a hostage situation brewing in the Shady Oak RV Park. I'm guessing the hypodermic needles will give the authorities a whole other reason to hang around once they realize it was all a hoax. In fact, I'm betting Derek has experimented in a little farming on the side that might interest the fine folks over at the DEA.

I'll be keeping a spot warm on the bed tonight for Ally. I'm pretty sure she'll need a mattress to land on.

I reach into my pocket and pluck out my cell.

"Excuse me." I head off down the long, dark corridor in the direction of the restroom.

I Google Carrington sheriff's department and hit CALL.

Sorry, Ally—just want to be sure you're safe.

Funny, I don't think I've ever wanted to protect anyone like I do Ally.

Too bad Derek has to lawyer up for me to do it.

3

LIGHT MY FIRE

Ally

Morgan Jordan is a cocky ass. I ruminate over this well-established fact as I drive what feels like a million bleak miles in my hatchback on the way to shack up with Derek and his unfortunate girlfriend. An oily darkness leads the way past acres of nothing but brush and evergreens. If living off the grid was my brother's goal in life it's safe to say he achieved it. It's going to take me forever to get to work from here.

Morgan and those heather-blue eyes of his come crashing back to the forefront of my mind. It's like he's haunting me, mentally stalking me with his ironic smile, those rippling abs my fingers seem to remember so well.

Mega Morgan had the nerve to continually grill me, all the way to my car, on my stance on dating people who share my socioeconomic disadvantage to which I cited, case in point, dumbass and ass hat, aka Raya and Derek. Met in high school, spontaneously dropped out to "spend more time together," and are now a moment away from living out their days in his-and-hers prison garb.

A glow of red-and-blue lights marks the sky as I near the RV park, and a horrible feeling comes over me.

"Crap." I'm in full panic mode as I take the final turn to Derek's place.

A stream of bright-yellow caution tape encircles Derek's tiny RV, and a bevy of men in navy jackets with the word Feds emblazoned on their backs swarms the area.

"The Feds?" I hit the brakes fast, inspiring a half dozen of them to look at me. I give an overeager wave and start in on a sixteen-point turn. From the rearview mirror I can see at least three of them hunched in the lower compartments where I stowed away my boxes while another one hoists all my stuff into the back of a windowless van.

Shit.

I hit the gas and hightail it away from Derek and the ill-timed narcotics seizure that happened to take down all of my worldly belongings in the process.

For a second I think of sending him a text to see if he's okay, but I'm guessing this is a bad time. Clearly he is not okay, so I text Lauren and Kendall instead.

Drug bust. Need a place to crash.

Lauren texts back. **Good God! Your family is shit!**

Lauren is always the first to comfort and support. Another text comes in, this time from Kendall.

So sorry! I have a bed for you. I'll wait up.

I stare at it a very long time. I'm pretty sure she's not the only one who'll be waiting up. In fact, I bet Kendall's tattoo-bearing brother is already warming the sheets.

The moon washes over the landscape and the fireflies spread their magic under a nearby willow. It looks heavenly—like a sign. If I were a sane person, I'd think it meant things were about to turn around for me—that rainbows and unicorns were in my future—but I know the truth. Fireflies are magic for other people. For me they're just something else to splat across my windshield. Their fiery asses are probably just trying to warn me that the rest of my world is getting ready to burn down to cinders.

Morgan Jordan.

I shake my head at the thought of him as I get back on the highway. He's going to be the next catastrophe to cross my path. I can feel it.

One thing is for sure, I refuse to get burned.

———

The tiny cottage that Kendall and Cruise call home is lit up like a pumpkin on Halloween night with the curtains pulled tight.

Mega Man's oversized dirt bomb is parked obnoxiously outside, all cockeyed and crooked, and for a moment I'm convinced he's parked this way just to piss me off.

I pluck my purse off the passenger's seat and make my way up the porch. It's cold out, and I don't even have a sweater to call my own. Crap. I'm going to wring Derek's neck. Leave it to the Monroe family to get all of our earthly possessions seized in an FBI sting operation. The door opens before I have an opportunity to knock. I half expect Morgan to be standing on the other side, wielding a *mega*-sized condom and his killer grin, but it's just Kendall.

"What the hell happened?" She pulls me in and offers a quick embrace. Thank God for Kendall. She's so much more caring and supportive than Lauren. At least with Kendall I have a shoulder to lean on. She'll probably make me a cup of hot tea, and run a bath for me, then we'll sit at the kitchen table and talk into the wee hours of the night about what imbeciles we have for brothers.

"There were cops," I say, "and caution tape, and all my stuff was floating in the sewer . . ." Okay, slight exaggeration.

Kendall cuts me off. "Horrible." She stretches her hands over her head. "Well, I'd better get to bed. Morgan said he'd help you get settled." She gives a quick wink. She grins deviously, as if she's the last person who'll stand in her brother's way while he pins me to his mattress. Correction, *my* mattress. "Don't do anything I wouldn't do. Night!" She skips all the way to her bedroom and bolts the door shut behind her.

What the hell?

A gorgeous bare-chested male enters from the hall with his dark hair slicked back from the shower. His body looks as if it's hewn straight from marble, with tattoos running up and down his arms and stamped across his chest like a cityscape I suddenly have the urge to explore.

Great. I've just been seduced without him having to utter a single word. And as soon as those dimple bombs go off, I'm going to spontaneously drop to my knees in an act of carnal worship.

"Heard what happened." He struts over with water still beading over his chest. He slings his towel over his shoulder. He has on a pair of navy sweats but my eyes ride up to the labor-intensive pictures he's permanently impressed upon himself.

The scene from Derek's flashes through my mind, and I freeze for a moment.

"Ruby's pictures." I bury my face in my hands. "It's all too much to process right now. I'm sure Janice will help me replace them, but I'm not looking forward to sharing how I lost them to begin with."

"They took the pictures?" His arms circle my waist, and I let him pull me in. The light scent of musk and soap mingle,

SOMEONE LIKE YOU

creating an intoxicating combination that causes my underwear to disintegrate in the process.

"They took everything. I'm homeless, and the only thing I own in the world is this little black dress."

The beginnings of a lewd grin twitch on his lips, then in an instant he grows serious as death and leans in just enough. I push in just a little and his lips descend closer to mine. He stops short of a kiss and circles over my mouth with his oven-hot breath, forcing me to make the first move, and God, I want to make the first move.

"Whoa." I push him away. "Thanks but no thanks. I'm not in the mood for some sexual healing." And even if I were, I would totally deny it.

He pulls his cheek to the side, no smile. "I'll make a fire." Morgan busies himself by tossing a few logs into the mouth of the fireplace before squirting enough kerosene to burn down the entire western hemisphere. He lights a match and a ball of flames shoots out a good three feet.

"I knew you were dangerous." I slip out of my heels and fall beside him on the sheepskin rug. I stretch my legs and sigh. "My feet just said thank you in ten different languages. Be glad you're not expected to wear high heels."

"I am glad I'm not expected to wear high heels," he says, landing beside me. "But I do it just for the fun of it." He knocks his shoulder into mine playfully, and my body electrifies just being near him.

"Look"—I sigh—"I'm not easy." Mostly. I put it out there in the event he thinks he's getting a free ride on the Ally express because we happened to have crossed that bridge already.

"Never said you were." He cocks his head to the side. "Not that you were difficult, but I'm definitely not holding it against you."

"You're a pig." I close my eyes and roll my head over my shoulders. "Never mind. You make pigs look bad. You're worse than a pig."

"Why am I a pig?" He lowers his lids, giving me those bedroom eyes, and my stomach squeezes so tight I can't breathe for a minute. "More importantly, why do you have the incessant need to be mean to me?"

"Sorry. You seem nice enough." And oddly he does. "It's mostly because I have a weakness for bad boys, and we've both already determined you are one."

"You have a weakness for me?" He gravels it out slow and seductive as if this were the crack in the armor he was hoping for. He gives the hint of a sly grin, ready and willing to explode at his command.

"Not *you*. Boys like you in general. You know, trouble with a capital *T* and that rhymes with *P* and that stands for pregnancy."

"Oh." He mouths the word, and I fight the urge to trace his mouth out with my finger. "The Music Man, I get that part. The pregnancy part I'm betting has to do with Ruby's dad."

"Biological father," I correct. "It was as if dirt and scum had married and he was the product of that unfortunate union. Thankfully Ruby escaped his criminally insane genetics. She's all me." I blink a quick smile.

"Lucky girl." His brows twitch and my stomach spikes with heat. Morgan has a way of melting me without even trying. "Look, I'm really sorry about what happened." His features soften as if he actually means this. "Can you get more pictures?"

"I think so. I'm afraid to ask. I guess I can just take a bunch when I see her next." I try to shake all thoughts of Ruby's scrapbook out of my head. It's sort of a miracle I've shared so much with him to begin with. But a part of me wanted to. There's something about him that makes me want to spill all of my deepest secrets.

"I'll help you." He pushes his shoulder into mine. "You know, buy the book, get the pictures in it just right. If you want." He dips his chin and holds on to me with those sky-colored eyes.

I examine him for a moment and wonder what kind of sexual favors he'll expect in return and whether or not I'll deny him. People always seem to want something in exchange for "random" acts of kindness—especially boys who look like Morgan. Usually fantasies and other women are involved.

"Thank you," I say, feebly. "I'm sorry I called you a pig." I lean into his chest and lay my head on his shoulder. I can feel the hard contours of his abdomen tighten under my skin. Morgan Jordan is a work of art in more ways than one. "Let's see the ink," I say, pulling back so I can properly assess the crafts-manship, or lack thereof, but at one glance I can tell a skilled artist left his mark over Morgan's flesh.

"This one hurt the most." He tips his head down toward the one over his heart of an eagle-looking creature with the body of a serpent. "So you might want to kiss it first." His dimples wink in and out as if they were flirting with me in turn.

"I'm not kissing any of them," I correct. "And this one?" I run my fingers over his left bicep and trace out the long tail of a dragon. Its head roars over Morgan's shoulder and its fire breathes toward his neck. "Does it mean anything?"

"They all mean something." He bites his lower lip until it goes white. "The dragon is to remind me to stay strong—to never be like my dad. I wanted it to remind me of the hell he put me and my sister through." He shrugs. "Things like *sticking around* are important to me. I don't want to become some mythological creature in other people's lives."

Everything in me loosens as he gives his thoughtful explanation. Morgan Jordan is nothing but a softie—and one who plans on being responsible, at that.

"Plus, it kills the chicks at the bar." He gives a quick wink. And there it is.

"Thought so," I say. "That dragon is nothing but a means to an end. Way to go. Always have a visual to wow them when you're no longer cognizant of what you're saying. I bet you've got your pockets lined with condoms too."

He lowers his head and grows mysteriously quiet, and a little part of me is disappointed. I was sort of looking forward to a half-witted remark that I could come back at, slashing his masculinity to pieces and forcing him to bow to the master of underhanded comebacks. But he doesn't say a word.

"What's the matter?" I nudge him playfully. "Dragon got your tongue? Is your resident dildo depressed as hell he can't come out and play?"

He ticks his head back, somewhat annoyed at my potshots at his nonvital organ.

"Let me guess," I tease. "You want me to kiss it and make it better?" God, I can't even remember if I kissed it and made it better last night, and my cheeks burn with a fire all their own.

"You got me." He rises to his feet. "I'm all out of ammo. You win the first round, but I won't be so kind tomorrow," he says, heading into the hall.

"Where are you going?" I'm quick to sprint in front of him and claim the room by hopping onto the mattress.

It smells clean inside, no sign of an exploding suitcase with the aftermath splayed out in the four corners of the room. In fact, everything is laid out neatly and folded on top of the dresser.

I lie back on the bed and prop myself on my elbows. A glint of silver catches my eye from the edge of the bed.

Holy shit. There are bona fide *chains* hooked onto the bedpost.

"I see you've unpacked the hardware." I rattle it with my foot.

"Not my equipment, baby." It comes from him almost morose. "But if you feel the need to be bound and gagged, just say the word." He bounces on the bed and groans as he throws his arm up over his eyes to block the light. "I'll be happy to comply."

"Excuse me? I believe it's me who's sleeping here tonight."

"Good night, sweetie, try not to snore this time."

I open my mouth to protest and a brisk knocking sound emits from Kendall and Cruise's bedroom—repetitive, endless knocking.

Morgan pulls his arm back and looks over at me with wild disbelief as if to confirm his headboard-banging theory.

A series of hearty moans comes from the next room and my mouth drops open.

"Awkward," I whisper.

His face bleaches white.

Kendall reaches a crescendo, screaming her satisfaction into the night as if she were shouting her endless chorus of *yes, yes, yes* right into our ears.

"No, no, no," Morgan groans, pulling a pillow down over his face.

On second thought, maybe the worst form of torment Morgan can receive is sleeping right here next to Kendall and Cruise.

I snatch the afghan from the foot of the bed and head out to the couch for the night.

All night long I dream of Morgan helping me piece together that scrapbook.

Morgan

A few days float by with Ally working a series of steady shifts down at Starbucks, where I'm guessing she doesn't hop on the counter and dance for customers under an assumed name.

She's been pretty good about steering clear of me and my hard-on at all hours of the day and night. She's even slept on the couch voluntarily, but I don't fight her on it. In fact, I might have to take her to dinner one night to thank her for preserving my back and therefore furthering my baseball career.

Cruise offers to take me down to the gym and get me a temporary membership so "I don't get rusty on the field." As if. But I take the bastard up on it anyway.

The Carrington Fitness Center meets all the criteria necessary for a workout facility—spacious, well stocked with the latest and greatest in fitness technology, and most importantly, it's co-ed. Since Ally has firmly made up her mind not to entertain me or my balls under any circumstances, my dick has made the executive decision to move on. As much as I'd like to hang on for her, the head of my committee has vetoed my decision.

"So how did you and Kendall meet?" I ask as we head into the weight room. Cruise looks lean and mean, as if he lives at the gym, but in reality all I've seen him do these past few days is disappear to the bed-and-breakfast, the questionable business venture he's nailed himself to.

"Frat party." He gives a smile that disappears as quickly as it came. "She didn't have a place to crash so I let her hang out at my house. Glad she did. Kenny's the best thing that's ever happened to me." He says it like it's no big deal.

"Nice," I say, unimpressed by the fact *Kenny* up and moved in with a guy she met at a frat party. "So you're ready to tie the knot, huh?" I make my way over to the equipment, while he sets up a weight bench for himself. "Let me guess. The proposal came on night two?" I'm only half kidding. It looks like Kenny and Cruise give new meaning to *speed* dating.

He shoots me a disgruntled look. "Yup. Wedding's set for December. I would have done it sooner but she wanted to mark our one-year anniversary. Plus since your mom is getting hitched this summer, Kenny didn't want to rain on her parade."

Weird how Mom and Kenny are marrying father and son. I guess his sister would be the next illogical piece to the quasi-incestuous puzzle, but I'm not into her. For one, she's not Ally, and for two, I'm pretty convinced she's jailbait.

An all-too-familiar beauty wearing a skintight leotard struts in, and when she sees me her eyes expand as if I've just morphed into her favorite dessert. I shake my head as Cruise's sister heads our way. Speaking of the horny devil.

"You go here?" Molly speeds over, snapping a huge pink bubble as wide as her face. "I totally work here." She bounces into me and chest bumps me by accident, inadvertently cluing me in on the fact they're real.

Cruise sits up from the weight bench, takes note of the titty-tap, and glares at me as if I had somehow initiated it.

"So, like"—Molly tips her head toward the exit—"you wanna see a movie later or something?"

I glance down at Cruise Elton with his balls in a knot over the idea I might be even remotely interested in his baby sister, emphasis on the baby, and I consider this. Pissing Cruise off seems like a pretty fair trade for boning my sister in a rather loud and obnoxious fashion, night after inglorious night. I've had about enough of his ape-like grunting, and to be honest wouldn't mind an hour or two away from the freeze zone Ally put me under.

"Yeah, okay." I nod toward her like I'm interested. "We can grab a bite then figure the rest out later. Pick you up around six?"

"*Six!*" She dips her knees, shouting it out like it's her new favorite number. "I can't wait!" She jets out of the room as if she's off to get ready for our outing right this fucking minute.

"What the hell are you doing?" Cruise says it bored, as if he's on to the fact this little stunt was designed to solely piss him off.

"Dinner and a movie, dude. Plain and simple." I slip down on the weight bench next to him, more than pleased that I managed to make him uncomfortable. It's about time I return the favor. "Nothing wrong with it."

"Yes. It's very fucking wrong. Stay the hell away from my sister. She's off limits."

"So is mine." I say it just under my breath.

A blonde trots over in our direction, skinny as hell but decent in the looks department.

"Well, well"—her mouth falls open as she gives me the head-to-toe inspection—"who on God's green earth is this?" She twists her hips as if showing off the goods. On a scale of one to bed I'd say she was three beers and a maybe, but then again she's no Ally.

It's just dawned on me that I've got a permanent hard-on for Ally Monroe with no cure in sight.

"*This*"—Cruise points to me—"is none of your business." He secures his weights, and she leans in low as if she's about to slip under the bar and join him. Something is definitely up with the bimbo ready to limbo.

And what's with the diss? Now that Kenny is safely chained to his bedpost, he's free to show off his curt and rude demeanor to the rest of society? I bet if Kendall saw how rude he was to this poor girl, she'd sock him in the nuts.

The blonde struts over and extends her hand, unmoved by Cruise's douchebag behavior.

"Blair Lancaster."

I cut a quick glance to Cruise, who has ceased all weight-training operations to witness the exchange.

"Nice to meet you, Blair Lancaster." I give her bony fingers a firm shake. "Morgan Jordan."

Her mouth drops like a stone. "*Jordan*? As in *Kendall* Jordan?" Her eyes widen as if she were mesmerized by this bit of information.

"That's right. I'm her brother. I'm here for the summer for my mother's wedding."

"Oh my God," she whispers. "You are amazingly gorgeous." She bites her lower lip as she appraises me in this new light. "Don't you think so, Cruise? He's like the male version of Kenny." She says *Kenny* in a mocking tone. "You know—I do believe you need someone to show you around." She brushes her fingers down my arm as if petting the dragon and cuts a quick look to Cruise to see if he's watching the show. "I'd be more than honored to be that person. *Hey.* There's a big frat party tonight. You should go. It's a year-end thing. Trust me, you won't want to miss out."

I nod. I think I remember Ally mentioning something about a frat party.

"Yeah, I'll be there." I cut a quick glance at Cruise. Sure enough, he's frowning ten times harder than he was with Molly, although something tells me he doesn't get the big-bro warm fuzzies over my new friend Blair.

"Good." She gives an aggressive nod. "I'll be sure to find you." She licks the circumference of her lips before strutting out of the room.

"*Dude.*" Cruise leans up with a crazed look in his eye. "You can't go to the party tonight. You just set up a date with my sister."

"You said to stay the hell away from your sister. I'm just obeying orders."

"I didn't say to rip her heart out."

"Relax. I'll take her to the party. She'll probably meet some nice kid and make out in the corner, and I'll get to know my local tour guide better. It's win-win."

He shakes his head. "Trust me, you don't want any part of that twisted tour guide."

I stifle a laugh. Watching Cruise squirm is more than a pleasure. "What to do, what to do . . . date Molly or Blair? Let's see . . ." I pretend to mull it over while Cruise does his best impression of a raspberry. I press out a satisfied smile. "Oh, hell, I'll just have 'em both."

Molly and Blair. I shake my head.

Still not Ally.

———

I pick up Molly at the B and B, and we ditch the movie for the frat party. Molly was more than onboard with the idea of rubbing elbows with the upper echelon of the future beer pong champions of America. Plus, the dildo debutants cluttering up the vicinity seem to be impressing the hell out of her.

The music rails through a set of pristine Harman Kardon speakers, rattling the windows as we mill around inside. An entire army of well-dressed bodies moves through the dimly lit room of the supersized frat house. I didn't catch the name out front but for all practical purposes it could be called Alpha Sigma Dollar, or more appropriately, Alpha Sigma Living-Off-Daddy's-Dollar. But I'm not here to focus on frat boys. I'm strictly here for the ladies. Well, one lady, but that seems to be beside the point.

The nice thing about the Greek system is that the girls don't give a shit about the lettering as much as they do getting laid by a letterman. I've donned my team practice shirt for the night. It's a magnet for the jersey chasers and usually doubles as an icebreaker. Molly and I make our way deeper in to the supersized frat house, which just so happens to be fully equipped with a keg in each of the four corners of its universe.

"Can I get something to drink?" Her eyes enlarge at the sight of the beverage bar.

"Sure. Knock yourself out." I'll have to monitor her in the event she blacks out in some frat boy's arms. Just because I'm not planning on taking advantage of Cruise's sister doesn't mean I want others to.

A hot blonde in the corner winks at me and ticks her head as if inviting me over.

I pretend not to see as I pan the crowd for signs of the only hot blonde I'm interested in—Ally. Not sure why my dick has its compass set on Ms. High and Mighty. Maybe the fact she has a kid has something to do with it. Plus, she's nice. She's just misguided when it comes to guys who can't wipe their ass with legal tender. If money were all it took to keep a relationship afloat, the wealthy would never divorce. Maybe I should clue Ally in on that well-known fact, but, then again, she seems hell-bent on exploring that theory for herself.

A pair of long, soft arms slip around my waist from behind and my mystery girl grinds her hips against me.

Looks like Molly is well on her way to a hangover.

I swivel in her arms to find a familiar face beaming back at me, but it's definitely not Molly's.

"Claire?"

"Blair," she corrects with a coy smile as if it really didn't matter.

A dark laugh gurgles through me.

"So what's the deal with you and Elton?" I ask. If I'm not getting lucky with Ally, I may as well settle a few mysteries.

"Cruise?" Her tiny nose scrunches up as if she had to guess which Elton. Something is definitely up. "He's just somebody that I used to know."

"Got it." Disgruntled ex. I can spot them a mile away. Blair here seems brutally bitter, and if I didn't know better she has me on the board for a little relationship revenge.

I take her in under this new light. Her lips are smeared with the blood of her latest victim, while her paper-white skin glows like a dying flashlight. There's something about her that screams vampire, and I'm betting it's the fact she bites—hard—in delicate places.

"So"—she gives a casual shrug—"did he mention anything?" The curiosity brews in her until her eyes look as if they're about to launch across the room like bottle rockets.

"He said to stay the hell away from you." I give a sly smile. "Rumor has it you're too hot to handle."

"Well. He was right. He should know—we dated for a small eternity."

Huh. I wonder if Kendall has anything to do with the bitter breakup. Not that I care. I have a feeling revenge sex with his ex is a great way to get under his skin. The way Kendall screams through those paper-thin walls makes me want to charge in with a shotgun and free her from his sexual dungeon. Turns out the room I'm in was *his* bedroom, which explains the chains and economy-size box of condoms in every drawer.

Blair dances into me, brushing her chest against mine with an invitation. Her blonde hair whips around to the music as she sways to the beat, taking me with her.

The music picks up pace, and Blair indulges in some hostile dry humping at my expense, but even with that raucous display of affection my dick chooses to lay low for the evening.

A familiar, beautiful face catches my attention from across the room.

"Ally," I whisper as elation washes through me. Some moron steps up and shoves his arm around her neck before swiveling his hands down her back and covering her ass like a baseball mitt. "Who in the hell is that guy?"

"What?" Blair pecks a string of kisses up my neck before biting down hard over my earlobe.

"Whoa." I pull her away gently, and she leeches right back where she came from.

The douche molesting Ally starts in on some hip-hop dance, twisting his wrist in the air like he's riding a freaking pony.

"Idiot," I say under my breath.

Blair pulls back and follows my gaze.

"Rutger?"

Rutger. Figures.

His hair is combed neatly to the side. He's wearing a light-blue sweater with a tie notched underneath, and he's got on a pair of bona fide penny loafers like some fugitive from Wall Street.

"He looks ancient," I muse. The guy's gotta be at least pushing forty.

"He's a grad student. A friend of Pen's"—she points over to some stoner dousing his insides with a beer bong under the careful supervision of his frat brothers—"that's Cruise's half-brother."

"Is that so?" I revert my eyes back to the wizard of Wall Street cutting loose like he's in training for a rodeo—as the clown. And somehow it doesn't surprise me that you can connect the douche dots all the way back to Cruise Elton.

He swings his hips into Ally's. He pushes into her like he's about to take her right here in the common room, and my blood pressure spikes to unnatural levels.

"Would you relax?" Blair tucks her finger under my chin and pulls me in. "Ally's a big girl—and I do mean *big.*"

I glance over at her. Ally's body is nothing short of perfection. I have no idea what the hell Blair is bitching about, but if she's talking boobs, I'm in agreement. God smiled on Ally—twice. That's for damn sure.

"I wouldn't worry about her. Rumor has it," Blair continues her tirade, "Ally can manhandle the best of them. Besides, you're *my* date. Remember?" Her hands find their way up my shirt as she backs me into the wall.

No, I don't remember.

I glance past her and meet Ally's gaze. She smiles and starts to wave, but her hand freezes midair and the smile melts from her lips. Her eyes widen as she checks out Blair.

A dull laugh rattles from me.

Looks like it's showtime.

"Come on, baby," I whisper. "Let's see some of those moves."

Blair slithers up and down my body like a seasoned stripper, giving Ally a run for her sixteen dollars.

It takes everything in me not to look over at Ally and break out in a shit-eating grin. Then again, if this goes on too much longer, Blair is going to have a lady boner she's going to want to put to rest, and I'm not going to want to have anything to do with it.

A pair of arms pull me to the side, and I glide over all too willingly.

"I thought you'd never show," I say, turning to find—Molly? Shit.

"Beer tastes like a skunk pissed in my mouth!" She spits just shy of my chest as Blair tries to bat her away.

"Beer *is* skunk piss. Welcome to the world, baby girl," I say, raking over the crowd in search for Ally. Her blonde flame of hair is still frozen as she gawks in this direction. And this time her jaw drops to the floor.

Looks like I've managed to get her attention—with two different girls.

Molly grabs me by the chin and forces me to look at her.

"I'm in love with you, Morgan Jordan." She plants a live one right on my lips, and her tongue pierces my mouth like a javelin.

"*Whoa.*" I try to pluck her off me, but she melts in my arms instead.

"*Molly.*" Blair snatches her up by the shirt. "What in the hell are you doing here?"

"He's my date." Molly gives Blair a decent shove and sends her tiny frame tumbling. "Back off, would you?"

I look over only to find that a crowd has migrated between Ally and me. Luckily I can still see the douche riding his invisible horse. Wish he'd ride it all the way back to the commerce corral.

Ally struts over with her fantastically long, svelte legs; a pair of silver heels glow on her feet, and her hair blows back as if she's in a movie scene. I guess the green-eyed monster showed up after all.

Blair hikes up on her heels, pushes her tongue in my ear, while Molly does her best to map out my abs with her hands, and Ally freezes. A hurt look sweeps across her face as she pivots for the door.

"Wait!" I try to free myself from the tangle of limbs coiling around me, but I get locked in a vise grip by Blair.

Rutger files out the door, and I catch him wrapping his arms around Ally as they head off into the night.

Looks like the green-eyed monster just gave me the finger.

———

By the time I drop Molly off, literally onto her mattress, it's well past one in the morning. I hung out at the party awhile, thinking Ally might change her mind and come running back, begging me to pleasure her in the closet, but no such luck. A part of me was afraid to head back to the house, afraid Ally *wouldn't* be here, that she was too busy having a sleepover at Rutger's seaside villa where they would have vanilla sex while rolling over a mountain of dollar bills. But I was wrong.

Ally greets me with a knowing smile as soon as I step through the door. She's sprawled out over the couch, flipping through some magazine with the tagline "How to please your man" scrawled across the front. I want to tell her she can throw that issue into the fire because she could have *written* that article, but I don't.

"Are the kids in bed?" I tease, nodding over to the torture chamber Kendall's holed up in.

She holds up three fingers before pitching her head back and having a mock orgasm. I watch mesmerized as her eyelids flutter and her mouth parts as she pants her way into ecstasy.

A silent laugh rumbles through me. I'd love to initiate the real deal in her, right here on the couch if she wants—put Cruise in my shoes and show him just how thin these walls really are.

"Are you hungry?" I point to the kitchen and she hops to her feet with a smile.

She's got on a leopard-print tank top that hugs her hips and not much else. Hot damn. Lucky for me, Ally forgot to put on her bottoms tonight.

"So, have you been home for a while?" I ask, trying not to look too overly excited about the fact she might have initiated a pair of blue balls in the future accountant she was hanging out with tonight.

"About an hour and a half." She shrugs.

Hour and a half? She must have come straight over.

My heart thumps, relieved to know she didn't clock any unnecessary alone time with the rebel-without-a-clue.

I open the fridge and break out the eggs and bacon.

"Looks like a grocery run is in my future," I say, staring at the beer and water bottles that take up most of the real estate on the shelves.

"If you want I'll go with you." Ally looks slightly hurt, saddened by something other than our nutrition-based conversation.

"Everything work out all right tonight?" I pull out the pan and break a half dozen eggs over the rim without looking at her. I'm afraid if I seem too interested I'll scare her off like a timid bird. And Lord knows I am way too interested in Ally to want to scatter her in the wrong direction.

"It was fine." She shakes her head. "I don't really want to talk about it." Her voice dissolves to a whisper. "But you looked like you had a good time." Her eyes land on mine and stay there as if demanding to know the truth.

"*Great* time," I correct. Nothing like prodding a little jealousy to spur things along. "Met a lot of friendly people—real friendly." I cut her a quick glance as I start the bacon.

"Yeah—that would be Blair . . ." Her voice trails off.

Knew it. She saw the whole show, front and center, while making it look as if she didn't even notice Blair and Molly pawing over me like a couple of bears on honey.

"Especially the blonde," I say. "I'm not too into the kid—but Blair—you know, she's all woman." The bacon sizzles right along with Ally. Steam comes from her ears. Her eyes light up like flames.

"Really?" She says it curtly, a little louder than necessary. It's obvious I've moved the boundary stone a little too far. "I'm sorry." Her shoulders sag. "I really can't stand her. She thinks just because she's rolling around in Daddy's money she can have whatever, *whoever* she pleases."

I switch off the eggs and turn up the heat on the bacon to move the party along.

I know just what she means. That idiot boy toy of hers with his upturned collar, his penny loafers filled with solid gold Krugerrands, didn't impress me much either. And he gets Ally just because he's got a fatter wallet? Please.

"Never mind." Ally shakes out her long, silken strands of hair, and my fingers demand to run through it. But I maintain my position and watch the bacon before the smoke alarm goes off. God forbid I disturb Cruise from his ever-present task of defiling my sister. On second thought I should burn the bacon—*often*.

"Blair is probably a good move," she continues. "She's definitely one to wine and refine you. And if you're really nice, she might even let you drive the Vette."

There's a Corvette involved?

The bacon starts in on its requisite charring, so I call it a day and scrape the food onto a couple of plates.

"For you," I say, setting it down before her and taking a seat.

"Wow, thank you." She says it sweetly, almost as if she's about to cry. "I've never had a guy cook for me before."

"Really? I'd think they'd be bowing at your feet fulfilling your every whim—starting with your stomach, then moving to far more interesting places." A smile plays on my lips, but I hold back long enough to watch her cheeks heat with color.

The night we shared runs through my mind—hot, mindless sex with no pretense, no *words* for that matter. This is exactly why one-night stands have a magnificent downside. You might be sleeping with a goddess and not even know it. If I could go back I would appreciate things a whole lot more, savor Ally's body like it was the most exotic fruit, the last bite of my entire existence.

"My stomach, huh? You're funny," she says it quietly, as if the idea were a joke. Ally sweeps the floor with her gaze, and I pop a piece of bacon in my mouth, studying the mystery of this forlorn girl in front of me.

Ally latches onto me with those lawn-green eyes, powerful and magnetic.

"Morgan?" She runs her tongue over her lips in one clean swipe and my crotch ticks to life like a bomb. "I hope you don't mind if I ask you something crazy."

"Go ahead." Damn—I fucking love crazy.

Ally picks up my hand and walks over, pressing her body tightly against mine.

She tilts into me with those glassy jade eyes. "Do you think you could love me tonight?"

4

BATTLE OF THE RATTLE

Ally

Morgan Jordan qualifies as a god on so many levels—the face, the dimples, eyes that shine like sapphires. But the truth is, we're cut from the same cloth, and I think the entire universe knows I'm no deity, no goddess in training, just a simple girl in blue jeans.

"Love you?" He takes another bite from the strip of bacon he's holding, slightly perplexed by my request.

"You know . . ." I pull him up to his feet and he tosses what's left of his food over his shoulder. "Love me with your body." I tick my head toward the bedroom. I'm too ashamed to tell him I was humiliated—that Rutger asked Jules Shaw to the Summer Splash down at the country club right in front of me because he knew I wouldn't be into "snooty stuff like that"—then he had the nerve to call me one of his favorite bad girls just before I detonated a slap across his cheek. I hope he's still nursing it—those fake veneers all popped off, exposing his rotten yellow teeth.

How could Rutger label me a bad girl if I've never so much as kissed him?

Morgan tilts his head back a notch while weighing the merit of my proposition.

"Ally"—his dimples go off and my heart detonates in my chest like a bomb—"I think we're having a miscommunication. And if we are, I'd really appreciate it if you were the one who broke it to my buddy." He glances down at the growing bulge in his jeans, and I swallow down a wicked laugh.

If I'm going to be a bad girl, then *I'll* choose who I will and won't be with—and tough luck for Rutger because I plan on being very, very bad. Besides, there's a sweetness to Morgan and everything in me is crying out for some of his affection.

I pull him in by the back of the neck and crash my lips against his to assure him that my indecent proposal was indeed the real deal.

His salty tongue sweeps over mine, and suddenly I'm hungry for far more than bacon.

We edge our way out of the kitchen. He walks me backward, slowly, through the hall, our mouths never surrendering their locked and loaded position.

Morgan interlaces our fingers and raises my hands over my shoulders as he backs me against a wall. He dives into an entire ocean of kisses with thoughtful, careful strokes that melt the pit of my stomach.

We stumble into the bedroom, and he closes the door with the light still on overhead.

I pluck off my T-shirt and bite down on a smile as he inspects me, his chest pumping like he's just moved a building.

"God, you're beautiful." He rides his gaze up and down my body, and I swell with excitement as he says those words. With Morgan it sounds genuine, not like the come-ons I've heard so many times as a means to an end.

I switch off the lights just as he presses a tender kiss over my temple.

I take off his shirt nice and slow, unbuckle his jeans, and he catches me by the wrist before any real progress can be made, pulling me gently down to the bed.

"Ally," he whispers as I pepper him with fevered kisses. It killed me to see Blair pawing all over him; Molly too, for that matter. I don't care if she is still in high school. Tess once told me younger girls are a threat you never outgrow. "What's going on?" He says it like he's honestly interested.

"This is going on." I slip my hand into his jeans and feel him grow from inside his boxers.

"I know," he whispers with a touch of sadness while securing his arms around my waist. He pulls back until we're lying on the pillow nose to nose. "Just tell me what happened. I could see the knife wounds as soon as I walked through the door. Do you want me to kill somebody?"

"No felonies." I press my body to his chest, skin over skin, and my stomach quivers from his touch. "See, that's why you're a bad boy. Normal people don't reach for the lethal solution. They sit down and have a conversation."

The moonlight streams in and colors him a pale stone-blue.

"Precisely why we're having a conversation." He pulls back with a naughty grin waiting to take over. It takes everything in me not to stop this "conversation" with my lips or with other body parts that are craving to have an intimate discussion with him right now. "This is different than the other night," he whispers, stroking his thumb gently over my cheek. "This isn't a one-night stand. I'm going to see you in the morning. You're Kendall's buddy. I'm not just some guy anymore. Sex will either get in the way or . . ."

He doesn't finish his sentence. Instead the words hang in the air while we try to decipher what exactly they might mean.

"I think for tonight"—I scoot in close—"I'd like to opt for door number two." I brush my lips against his dimple and feel it depress beneath me. Everything in me swims.

"Door number two," he repeats. "What's going to happen when we wake up and all those doors were just an illusion?"

"You always overanalyze things?" I reach into his boxers and glide my fingers over the one part of his body that's actually on the same page with me. He's long and strong, and I trace out the ridges with my finger as I glide from the base to the tip. Morgan is hard as Sheetrock, and he's burning with heat, all for me.

"I don't overanalyze, Ally"—he says it sweetly—"but I like to know my boundaries. I just want to be sure I'm not going to get my ass handed to me with a baseball bat."

I exhale into his neck, raking my lips across his five o'clock shadow. My mouth comes to life as I run my tongue along his sharp jawline. His words spin through me like a cyclone, and I know he's hinting at the fact this might not be the brightest idea. But then again, it just might be, and I'll go with that for now.

"I need you tonight." I sear the words over his ear. "Maybe at the end of the day all I really want is to go home with someone like you. Maybe that's the one thing the bad girl in me really craves. It can be our dirty little secret. No strings, just you and me, two birds cut from the same cloth, wrestling it out."

"Ally," he whispers just this side of sorrow. "Our dirty little secret?" His cheek flare with twin darts, no smile, just the resolute sadness that's taken over the mattress as a whole.

I refuse to participate in an all-out debate. Instead, I plunge his jeans down past his hips and he frees himself from them in seconds. Morgan collapses his warm skin over mine and it feels like a blessing. Some way, somehow this man—this virtual stranger—has harnessed the power to satiate me with the touch of his flesh alone.

His hand rides up and down my body as if he were mapping out the lay of the land. I create small circles over his chest with my fingers until my hands ride to the base of his hips and get lost in the soft curls that trace down to the most intimate part of him. My hand glides over his ridges and I latch on, pulling him in like a leash as my insides throb to have him.

Morgan reaches over and plucks a condom from the nightstand. He rolls onto his back as the pale strip of moonlight slices in from the blinds. He tears the package with his teeth and the sound of paper ripping stills the moment.

Here it is, my out if I want it. I'm sure a quick session in the shower could finish what I started, but I want to do this. Something warms in me at the idea of having Morgan this way, far more than it ever did at the thought of touching Rutger. I wonder if all I'm really doing tonight is giving Rutger and his high-society friends the big F.U. Maybe it has something to do with the fact that Morgan is the first guy I've ever shared Ruby with. Maybe it's because my body holds the memory of the other night close to the vest like a poker hand, and I want in on all those damn secrets—regardless, every ounce of my being craves to have him.

Morgan pulls me over him and my chest molds to his. His oven-heated kisses trace down my neck, lower, all the way to my chest as he covers his mouth over my nipple and I gasp as he warms me with his hungry mouth. He continues at a fevered pitch until his lips are buried right there, nestled in my chest like it is his favorite place in the world. I reach back and feel the length of him, my hand covered in the sticky goo from the condom, and instantly regret the move. I guide Morgan in and sit back with my neck arched as I ride him into a sexual oblivion that Rutger Crones only wishes he could experience with me or anybody else.

Rutger was right. I was the bad girl tonight—-on my terms, with my people. And being with Morgan doesn't feel bad at all.

The headboard knocks against the wall in rhythm to our bodies and breaks the spell for a moment. I give a dull laugh at the thought of Kendall and Cruise startling to attention at the sound of our hormonal surge. Truth be told, I really don't care. I'm tired of people like Kendall and Cruise and their perfect relationships while the rest of us are forced to listen to them, *watch*, even, on the rare occasion when I've happened to walk in on them in the bathroom that has no lock. Honestly? Maybe this will finally drive home the point that there are other people in the damn house. Not that I totally don't appreciate living in said damn house. I'm actually starting to love this damn house. A lot.

Morgan sits up and I wrap my legs around his back.

"Kiss me," he says it in a heated whisper as he plunges his tongue deep into my mouth and swipes it gently over mine. I let out a soft moan as I round out my hips over his.

A muffled giggle emits from the other side of the wall, followed by the sound of Cruise trying to quiet Kendall.

Nothing is going kill Morgan's hard-on faster than the sound of his sister's voice, so I intensify my efforts, pushing him in deeper, pulling him in with a fierce hunger, a primal purpose that far outweighs any familial concerns that might be brewing. I pant into his ear to quell any outside disturbance, and he gives a riotous groan of appreciation. Morgan seizes me by the hips and thrusts me down over him again and again. He pulls me in by the neck and my body inches toward its pleasure but stops short like it does every single time. Instead I feel a pinch deep in my belly, and I inhale sharply as he pushes in deep.

I don't know Morgan that well, or at all, but a part of me is dying to whisper something meaningful to him. I've never said "I love you" to anyone before, well, not of the male variety, and for some unknown reason the words want to form on my lips, they light me up like a flame on the inside, ready to climax out of me in a verbal eruption. There must be some reason they're pushing to the forefront; maybe all I really want is someone to love—for sex to mean something for once—and maybe a part of me sees a glimpse of that on the horizon with someone like Morgan.

Our bodies rock steadily as his hips move beneath mine. It feels anything but "dirty." For sure I don't feel like a bad girl. If anything I feel good, better than good. It feels perfect.

"I'm coming." He wrenches the words from the pit of his stomach, securing me down by the waist until I can feel his ceaseless throbbing inside me. "Shit." He gives a gentle laugh of exhaustion as he topples us back to the pillows. "You're a wild one, you know that? A spitfire, *hell*, a flamethrower."

"A sword swallower." I brush a finger against his cheek until his dimple ignites in a deep pool of black.

"I'll need a demonstration of that last one."

"I bet you will." I round my hands over his rock-hard bottom as he slides the condom off and tosses it square into the trashcan.

"I'm good for now." Morgan throbs a series of heated kisses up and down my chest until he reaches the nape of my neck. "I think it's time for me to show you a few good tricks." He strings his kisses all the way down to my hip before slipping his hand between my knees and pushing me open, exposing me wide for him to see.

"I'm good too," I say, trying to pull him back up to the pillow.

"Whoa." He holds out a hand. "Turnabout is fair play. I think if we're going to put on a show we owe it to the audience to provide a full-bodied performance." He runs his finger along the inside of my most intimate part, and I fold over him as if in agony, only there's no real pain—it's all one hundred percent pleasure.

"Morgan." His name cuts through me like a train pulling into the station. "Maybe some other time."

"What's wrong? Did I hurt you?" He springs back next to me with a genuine look of horror on his face.

"No, it's not that. It's just, I don't know." It's not like I'm going to fess up and fill him in on the fact I've never had the Big O. That the few times I have slept with a guy I've faked it because I felt sorry for their elusive and somewhat heroic efforts in trying to elicit one in me. It's not their fault I'm defective. And besides, something in me doesn't want to fake anything with Morgan, especially now that I know if it doesn't happen he'll be as disappointed as I am—and God forbid he feels inadequate. Morgan Jordan is anything but inadequate.

I press a heated kiss over his lips, soak in his sweet taste—memorize the soft velvet of his tongue, the framework of his teeth. I want to remember all of this, in the event it doesn't happen again. In the event he sees me for what I am, like the rest of the world, and reduces me to nothing more than a bad girl. Or worse, Blair hogties him and claims him for herself. At least I'll always know these intimate pleasures. Blair, or whoever Morgan ends up with in life, can never take that away from me.

Morgan

A blast of unholy light burns through my lids until they disintegrate. My body grinds and shakes, feeling as if it just stepped out of the microwave.

I let out a moan as the scene from the night before comes back to me in pieces. Bacon, Ally, and hot fucking sex equaled a trifecta of perfection.

"Hey." I reach over and try to hook onto her waist but an empty mattress greets me. My lids crack open, affirming the depressing theory. My dick and I were sort of hoping we could start the party all over again. Instead I find a note tucked under the pillow.

Spending the day with Tess. See you at the club tonight.
Thank you,
Ally

I stare at it a little longer than necessary, as if I'm hoping the tiny paper square will somehow morph into a pair of creamy smooth thighs, legs that stretch from here to Oregon.

A dissatisfied groan escapes me, and I'm suddenly unmotivated to get out of bed—especially knowing that Kendall is out there probably good and pissed at me for screwing her bestie. It's sort of her fault anyway, for trying to push us together in the first place. I could always throw it in her face since this is what she basically wanted. What did she think was going to happen, anyway? That Ally and I would hold hands and share ice-cream cones all summer? Besides, Kendall owes me a thank-you for exposing the fact these walls are made of onionskin. Maybe that perverted boyfriend of hers will spring for a muzzle since he's clearly into indecent bedroom toys.

I kick the cuffs at the end of the bed with my foot. Wish I'd thought of employing them last night. Maybe I can rough things up with Ally the next time she feels the need to get down and dirty. Every last part of her screamed there would definitely be a next time. At least there'd better be. I'm not done—not by a long shot.

A knock vibrates over the door and my brain jumps in my skull in rhythm.

"Dude, you up?" It's Cruise. He probably wants me to pack my shit and get the hell out for ruining his marathon fuckfest with my sister. I'm sure the libido killing works both ways.

"What?" I gravel it out, still worn out from the calisthenics. I could use another four or five hours of shut-eye; hell, it might take the entire day to recover.

"Kenny's out running some errands, so I thought I'd head over to the gym. You up for it?"

I push out a breath. "All right." I roll off the bed, landing my feet on the cold hard floor.

May as well get this over with.

⌒‿⌒

It takes about four minutes into the car ride for Cruise to clear his throat like some father figure about to gift me an unwanted lecture on waiting until both Ally and I are ready before diving into a carnal commitment.

"So"—Cruise shakes his head—"heard the fireworks. You initiate that?" He frowns into the road as if this were the last place he wanted to go with our nonexistent conversation, but I'm beginning to see the bigger picture—our playdate at the gym was arranged by none other than my little sis.

"Nope. Not me. I was happily chowing down on a midnight snack when she came at me locked and loaded and ready to blow." Well, not really blow, but it sounded good so I went with it. Besides, is it really Cruise Elton's business who I party with? I think not.

"Cool." He nods into the road, continuing to propagate his disinterest in my midnight mattress moves. "So, bottom line—Kenny doesn't think it's a good idea."

"Really? Could have sworn I saw *Kenny* in the cheering section." Knew it. I'm going to nail Kendall for not having the balls to tell me herself. Does she really think I'm going to let Cruise navigate the direction in which my balls move?

"She *was* in the cheering section," he says, stymied by this himself. "Look, she doesn't want Ally to get hurt. It's her friend. You moved a little fast, and I think it spooked her. Kenny says you're the love 'em and leave 'em type, and Ally needs someone who's willing to be a permanent fixture. She has a kid."

"Ruby." I nod, sinking in my seat a little, feeling like an ass. Not that I plan on loving and leaving Ally anytime soon. I'd be there for her twenty-four/seven if she wanted. Hell, I'd set up residency in her life if she let me.

"She told you about Ruby?" He looks stunned by this.

"Yup."

Cruise shuts the hell up from the apparent miracle of it all.

"Look"—I grind my palm into my eye, still trying to wake up for the day—"Ally doesn't want anything serious with me. She got all hot and bothered and asked me to do her a favor, nothing more, nothing less." Odd that she gave and yet didn't want to receive. Not sure what that was about. Never had a girl deflect my efforts that far into the game before.

He shakes his head as if he heard my thoughts and is as perplexed as I am.

"Ally's a funny one. I've known her for a good few years now, and have never seen her spend more than two minutes with a guy. I tried telling Kenny that it was probably mutual, but she was insistent that you clubbed her and dragged her to the room by the hair."

"Nice to know she thinks so highly of me."

"She does. That's the funny part. I think she's just as, if not more, worried about you getting hurt. But let's just keep that between us. I'd hate for Kenny to think I'm ratting her out." We pull into the gym parking lot and he finds a space near the front. Cruise looks over and socks me in the arm. "You're going to be my brother, dude. I don't want to see you getting hurt either."

"Ally couldn't hurt me if she tried." My chest cinches like it's calling bullshit. She could interrupt my midnight snack any damn time she pleases—Ally beats bacon any day. Not one part of my body can argue with that. I swing open the door and pause. "You know anything about Ruby's dad?"

"Nope. Lauren probably does. Kenny might, but I doubt it. Ally's pretty tight-lipped about her past. All I know is she's constantly broke, but join the club, right?" He holds up a finger and gives a small laugh. "She posed nude for Kenny's art class last semester, but the payout was great, so who could blame her?" He shakes his head as if he's reliving a memory.

"Well, if it's in the name of art." I can picture her sitting on a stool, her hair falling over her back. Her smooth skin exposed for the world to see. "I guess a person with Ally's body owes it as a debt to society."

He nods, his demeanor a little more serious than before. "Just watch what you're doing. Summer will be over before you know it, and I'd hate to be sweeping both your hearts off the floor when you break 'em."

Broken hearts.

Does Ally have the power to break my heart?

Something tells me she just might.

———

The gym is balmy as hell. It makes me want to stand in a fire just to cool off.

"No AC?" I ask Cruise as we head toward the weight room.

"Let's ask the douche himself." He slaps Cal some skin as he bumps into us. "Dude, this is Kenny's brother, Morgan. He's going to destroy those batting cages you got out back."

"Is that so?" He squeezes out a thin-lipped smile. Cal is bronzed, and 'roided out so bad he's got veins crawling all over his arms like garden snakes.

Cruise scans the vicinity. "So what's up with the private heat wave?"

"I've got two very erotic words for you boys—hot yoga." He tips his bald head in the opposite direction and we follow him down the hall where the humidity intensifies.

He gives a gentle pat over a narrow window. I can make out at least a half dozen girls bent over inside, with their bottoms pointed toward heaven.

"Hot damn."

"Would you stop?" Cal smacks me in the stomach to keep me from gaping. "Come here." We follow him through a door marked PRIVATE. "This is my personal office." It's dark as shit inside as we follow him to a large picture window leading into the hot yoga room. It affords me a better glimpse of the bodies in motion.

"Fuck, dude," Cruise spouts off. "You're breaking like ten different privacy laws. You're not going to get away with this. You know that, right?"

"What?" He shrugs into the glass. "Everyone knows two-way mirrors are for safety purposes. If one of those girls gets hurt, it's my ass on the line. It's my civic duty to serve and protect."

"Right." Cruise lets out a little laugh. "And I suppose you and Lauren take turns keeping watch."

"She's been apprised." Cal nods toward Cruise like a dare. "Besides, she's enrolled in one of these classes. We've got this thing, you know. She does special poses because she knows I'm watching."

"Speaking of special poses"—Cruise starts as we head out of the den of depravity—"Ally did a special pose for Morgan last night."

"Get *out*." Cal seems amazed. As he should be. If the downward dog floats Cal's boat then the acrobatic feats that went on in that bed last night would have Cal blushing like a nun. "That girl talks the talk but I've never heard of her walking the walk, or should I say riding the bull." He socks me in the stomach while belting out a laugh.

Geez.

I nurse my quasi wounds as I make my way back to the weight room, smacking into a soft body as I round the corner.

"Hey, handsome!" It's Molly. Her hair is pulled back in a ponytail, making her look all of twelve. Her hand glides down over my chest and dips into my boxers before I catch her. "Good morning to you too," she moans.

"Looks like I need to watch where I'm going." I glance back to find both Cal and Cruise are MIA.

"You know"— she bites down on her lips and looks up at me suggestively—"I have to move some really heavy boxes, but I hurt my back yesterday riding my bike. Do you think you could help me?" Her almond-shaped eyes recede just enough to plead in a way that only a woman can, or in Molly's case, a woman-in-training.

"Yeah, sure, why not."

"Great!" She takes up my hand and speeds me along until we hit the stairwell. I gently pull my hand away and secure it over the rail as a means of not giving her the wrong impression. I stuff my left hand in my pocket in the event she does the math and figures out I've got another free limb she can molest.

She leads us outside to the first floor in front of a Dumpster. We head down another set of stairs that lead to a darkened doorway and head inside.

It's cool in here, and the space is as wide and long as the eye can see. A hallway veers to the left, and I can make out a couple of doors.

"This place is huge." And empty, and I don't see a box in sight.

"It's the basement." She shrugs. "Cal doesn't really use it. I think it's nice." She licks her lips as she comes in close. "Don't you think it's nice? Lots of room to do things." She picks up my hands and rides my fingers up her ribcage. She's bony, a lot less curvy than Ally, that's for sure.

I gently pull back my hand. Molly's like a predator—move too quick and you're going to get bit. If it wasn't for Ally and her all-encompassing power over me, I'd more than likely yield to Molly and her boner-inducing antics. She's definitely got the looks, her body is budding nicely, and she seems like a sweet girl who very much wants to learn everything there is about life—right now—right here, in the basement. I'd better let her down easy. I'd hate to crush an ego and a fragile heart all at the same time.

"Look . . ." I swallow hard as she reaches for the bottom of her T-shirt and begins to pull it over her stomach. "No, no, don't do that. I think you're sweet, and pretty, and—"

"You think I'm pretty?" She perks to life as if I've just proposed.

"No, not like that."

Her face drops.

"I mean *yes* like that. It's just I'm not ready to go there with you."

"Then you like me and you just need time." She tilts her head and I get the distinct feeling I've succeeded in stringing her along.

Shit.

"I don't need time. I think you need to find yourself a guy more your age. Someone who's sweet just like you." And hopefully not horny as hell.

"I'm not interested in boys my age. I like older men." She cups her hand over my sweats and gives my dick a good squeeze.

"Shit." I pluck her off and take a breath, waiting for the dull ache to subside. "I'm sure there are a lot of older men out there who would be willing to come down to the basement with you and help you move some *boxes*." I raise my brows, calling her out on her little ruse.

"I get it." A smile twitches on her lips. "It's because of my brother. You think it's weird that your sister and he have this thing. And now your mom." It comes out bitter, as if somehow Mom and Kendall have managed to fuck things up between us—little does she know it's Ally who's the official cock block.

"Yeah." I go with it. "That's sort of a tough pill to swallow. Plus Cruise would kill me if he knew I was messing around with his baby sister."

Her eyes fill with fire. She's going to castrate him the next time she sees him. Already I'm liking the outcome here.

"I knew it," she seethes. "That bastard threatened you, didn't he?" She grunts in frustration. "He's such a controlling asshole." Her features soften almost instantly. "We won't tell him. We'll keep this a secret just between you and me, and no one will ever have to know. It can be our dirty little secret." She giggles into the idea.

"Our dirty little secret?" Carrington seems to be overrun with just those very things.

"*Yes.*" She throws her hands around my neck and jumps in the air like she just won the lottery. "We could come down here, or I can sneak you into my room!" She bops up and down as if it were the best idea in the world. But it's not. It's officially the worst idea in the world.

"I think I'll pass. You and me, Molly, we're going to be family whether we like it or not. Face it—once Kendall and Cruise tie the knot, I'll be nothing more than your big brother. If we let things get started, it's going to get weird, fast." I tick my head toward the exit. "Go on, get out of here. I gotta clear my head for a minute." I feign a look of disappointment. "I wanted this just as bad as you did." I hate dragging her down the path of deception, but the way her hips are grinding into mine I think siding with her is the only way to keep my balls safe.

"I'll accept that." Molly crushes her lips against mine, fighting to jam her tongue into my mouth until I pluck her off. "Just wanted to give you something to think about in case you change your mind." She bats those doe eyes up at me. "And I have a feeling you will." She swivels her hips all the way to the door before blowing me a kiss from over her shoulder.

Crap. Molly Elton is a spitfire from hell all right. Something tells me she has no intention of listening to a damn thing I just said.

I take in the open space around me and soak in the quiet, the solitude. It's a shame to have so much prime real estate go unused.

I walk in a small circle, scoping out the nooks and crannies, and an idea comes to mind.

"Hot damn, Ally," I whisper. "You are going to love this."

And so am I.

5

FLIRTING WITH DISASTER

Ally

The Pretty Girls Gentlemen's Club shines like a fallen star filled with demonic intent and idol worship, as it should because both are apparently good for business.

The club is hopping as girls make the rounds on the floor in their requisite G-strings, me included. Well, the G-string, not the rounds. I'm too busy breaking the first commandment for dancers that Dell carved out with his own finger: *"Thou shalt never stand alone in the presence of my customers."*

A pair of cold hands grip my ribcage, and I jump two feet in the air.

Tess laughs as she fans herself with an array of white feathers. She looks gorgeous tonight in her naughty bridal attire, a plumed tail for added effect.

"You scared the crap out of me," I say, trying to wedge myself back in the corner lest Dell become apprised of my fugitive-like status and fire me on the spot. I'm sure he wants to, but I bet Tess has made all his *Fan-tessys* come true to ensure that very thing won't happen. Tess is all about self-sacrifice, and she's never complained about paying in flesh to help out her family.

"Quit your bitchin' and get out there." She drives me from the corner, and an icy chill runs through me. "This place is packed with fat wallets tonight. You'll go home with *bags* of money. Remember, eye contact, make them feel like they're special. Really try to have that erotic connection. Nothing helps them part with their dollars faster than that." She pats me on the bottom and gives a little wink. "Keep your eye on the prize, girl—and I'll keep an eye on you." She mouths, "You'll be fine," then leaves, throwing her hands over her head and swiveling her hips until she disappears into the crowd.

The room sways around me. I try to catch my bearings in this sea of faceless people. This overcrowded floor, these floating nightgowns, the disembodied voices—men in all shapes and sizes who've come to worship at the feet of women primped to emulate blow-up dolls—it all makes me dizzy.

A warm body zips in from behind and I turn, trying to gyrate my hips to the music until I see an all-too-familiar face—Woody Bates, a guy I know from Garrison.

He's tall and muscular—not in a crazy beefcake way like Cal, but in a defined way. I'm not sure what it is, but he creeps me out just enough to send a red flag up every time I see him. Once in a while a guy will do that to me. There was William Howie, who I evaded my entire junior year of high school because he simply gave me hives when he looked at me, and then there was Rory, who hijacked my senior year and then my uterus. I shake the thought away before any unwanted imagery can surface. I hated just about everything about my senior year.

But at Garrison it's Bates who's taken the title of Campus Creeper, and now here he is, gawking at me in my pale-blue negligee with the peekaboo brassiere and the matching thong that leaves absolutely zero to the imagination.

"I was hoping to find you here." He looks serious as a bout of clap, and suddenly I'm willing to forfeit every dollar bill in the world to get away from him.

"Well, it's nice to see you. But I'm not allowed to hang out with anyone from school. You *know*, a girl's gotta work." I shrug as if I'd much rather bolt with him and head to Sigma Phi, but the truth is I'd rather stick my head under his tire as he backs out of the parking lot.

"So, maybe we can hang out afterward?" He comes in and wraps a hand around my waist uninvited, his thin-lipped smile pulling back as if it's a given I'm leaving with him. "I got a whole lot of dollars with your name on them, honey."

"Um, excuse me." I gently remove his wandering hands in lieu of squeezing the shit out of his balls. "The last thing I need is the *real* customers to think I'm unfriendly. I'm not exactly doing this for my health, and if the night progresses in this direction, my wealth won't be on the list either. So I'd better get back to work. I'm sure there are plenty of dancers here who would love to have some of your free time and money." I spin him into the crowd. "Oh, look, there's Kit from Tri Delta! She's always talking about how cute you are!" I shove him into the crowd and make a run for it in the opposite direction. I didn't really see Kit, but that's unimportant at the moment.

A couple of older men stand to my left, examining me like they might be interested, so I sashay over with the finesse of a drunk belly dancer. Obviously I don't have the skill set required for a seemingly innocent bump and grind. I look like I'm having seizures half the time.

The gentlemen are older, stately even. Swear to God I've seen the silver-haired one around town, most likely at the Bux while serving him a hot latte, only now I'm the hot latte in question, and I don't feel too hospitable about the arrangement. In fact, the only thing I'm feeling is light-headed, as if passing out is a real possibility. I would bet all the money I'm highly deficient in at the moment that one of these geezers has MD tacked onto the end of his moniker and is willing to conduct a rather thorough physical if I let him.

"What's your name, sweetie?" The elder of the two, sporting a white goatee, blasts the words over me in a Bacardi-scented heat wave.

"Angel—*Midnight* Angel." I try to keep my hips moving like I was spinning an invisible Hula-Hoop, only I'm not doing such a great job because my Hula-Hoop is threatening to fall.

"So what do you two do?" Oh shit. I'm pretty sure asking about occupations was straight off the red-light, do-not-pass-go list of conversations. Oh, who the hell knows? Tess gave me so many freaking rules, who could keep them straight?

The two of them look nervous, as if an entire army of soon-to-be ex-wives just stormed the facility, and they take off for the bar without so much as a "see you later."

Great. I knew this had crappy idea written all over it.

A familiar dark-haired god, otherwise known as Lord of the Ladies in these parts, gives a knowing smile from the foot of the stage and my insides cinch at the sight of him. Morgan's dimples go off and heat rises to my cheeks. A part of me wants to run and hide and another part of me thinks I should play it off as if our sexual sparring never happened last night. But God, did it ever happen. Last night was a dream within a dream. I can still feel Morgan's warm hands pouring over my body quick and furious as a waterfall.

I head on over, leading with my boobs, shaking my hair out, and the show is all for him. My hips swing side to side as I strut, teasing him, forcing him to replay those mattress moves that had the both of us groaning until the sun came up. Morgan lights a fire in me that no other man in this wayward establishment could ever hope to spark. Morgan Jordan has the power to make me feel sexy without even trying.

Morgan's got on a T-shirt that reads DIVE DEEPER, and I can't help but wonder if that's something pornographic that everyone except me understands. I come in close like I'm going to kiss him before shimmying down his waist and sprouting up again. A memory of last night sweeps through me, and my face, and other far more intimate places, floods with searing heat. My insides tingle, and I have the sudden urge to jump right out of my panties. I gift him a private smile because if we were alone, I might have done just that.

"Looking for company?" I almost said *looking for love,* and choked on that final word. Thankfully it incarnated into something else entirely before it flew from my lips. I was promised love once a long time ago but I learned my lesson: none of that is real. Love is nothing but made-for-TV bullshit that people wish for over mojitos and shooting stars.

"You're all the company I need." He brazenly pulls me in and steals a kiss off my lips, just a simple dot, nothing invasive, but my body explodes from the pleasure of his touch.

I take in a breath as his dimples dive in and out.

"Sorry," he whispers, "but I wanted to say thank you." There's a boyishness about him. Something soft under that tough-guy exterior that makes me melt just looking at him.

"You're welcome." I press my lips together. "But I think it's me who needs to be thanking *you.*" I lean in until we're a breath away. Morgan's storm-colored eyes grow all too serious as if he wants it, as if he's silently begging for one more kiss.

"Here you are." Tess pops in like an un-fairy godmother with all of the backward intentions only a Monroe can have.

"What the hell are you doing?" she hisses, shoving me back into circulation. "Do not fraternize with the help. Do you hear me? He's the *bouncer*, Ally. He's here to protect, not serve. You're working—remember? Now go make some money. I swear if I have to cover your house fees another night, I'll fire you myself."

I land in a pit of girls rounding out their moves in front of a group of men in business attire. The men taking in the spontaneous burlesque look like they're straight out of an insurance meeting, or car salesmen's convention. They hold out their whiskeys on the rocks as if they were a requirement to view the show, the ticket to the VIP room in the back.

I met a few of the dancers while I was getting dressed. They're just people like me, trying to get by. Some are trying to get high, but more than a few of them are mothers trying to make a living. It's just a job—a prison where they do voluntary time from when they're eighteen until they're thirty. Those are the peak years according to Tess, who is already on the descent at the tender age of twenty-six. For sure I don't want to see her here another four years. I want something more for her. I want something more for me.

I turn back and glance at Morgan. A beautiful brunette has cropped up by his side with boobs the size of cantaloupes. She offers him a drink that she's wedged between her cleavage, and he wisely declines. I've seen her in the back—perfect skin, killer smile. I don't know her name but she's doing her best to seduce him with her long, tan arms gliding over his chest like cobras. Where's Tess to enforce her anti-fraternizing rule when you need her?

My stomach squeezes with jealousy at the sight, and I dive deeper into the crowd. It's time to let my moneymakers shine and hopefully earn a few wrinkled dollars in the process.

———

Morgan follows me home from the club, and I can't help stealing glances in the rearview mirror. He gives a gentle wave as we stop at the long red light just shy of the bed-and-breakfast.

We drive down to the cabin and his truck slides in alongside my car. I get out just as he kills the engine, and he joins me as we make our way up the porch.

"We should drive together," he whispers, slightly out of breath. "You know, go green and all that good stuff."

"Oh, well, if it's for the planet then I'm totally on board." I bite down on a smile as we move closer to the door.

"So"—he swallows hard—"about last night."

My face lights up like a Christmas tree. "Don't worry about it. I was insane. I needed attention, and you were in the right place." I hear the words as they stream from my lips, but I don't believe them. I wonder if he does?

"Mr. Right Place, Right Time, huh?" His dark brows pitch low as if he were perplexed by the concept.

"I'm sorry." I shake my head. "In no way was I trying to lead you on. I don't know what came over me." I know exactly what came over me—*Rutger* came over me like a dump truck full of bricks, but I'll be the last person to admit it.

He tilts his head thoughtfully; his cheeks depress as though considering my words.

"I guess I needed to talk to someone." I bite down over my lip before I say anything else.

"Well"—he steps in close and the sweet scent of his cologne enlivens me, sends my thighs begging for a midnight reprisal—"it was a great conversation." He gives the hint of a smile as he draws in closer. His dimples swim in and out as if calling me out on the lie.

The door swings open and we both take a giant step back as if our mothers were congregating inside. But it's not some resurrected version of Mom, it's Kendall staring back at us. And a part of me very much wishes it were my mother. God, I miss Mom.

"We'd better get inside." It comes from me strained.

Morgan's eyes glow like sirens in the pressed night, giving him an air of mystery, an ethereal look altogether.

"Am I interrupting?" Kendall clasps her throat at the thought.

"No," I'm quick to offer. "We were just talking." I shoot a look to Morgan in the event he cracks one of his signature lewd grins.

"Anytime you feel the need to talk, you know where to find me," he whispers, his eyes locked with mine, and for a moment neither of us moves. Then he makes his way inside.

"Everything okay?" Kendall's eyes widen and retract, and I can see him there, mirrored in her eyes.

"Everything's great. Thanks for the clothes you lent me." If it weren't for Lauren's and Kendall's discards I'd be running around without much on.

"No biggy."

I take in a deep lungful of night air coated with the scent of pines and honeysuckle.

"Love summer," I say stupidly as I look around at the charred evergreens, their hooded tops, their fingerlike branches.

"You wanna take a walk?" She gives a tiny smile and nods out toward the dirt path that leads behind the bed-and-breakfast.

"Sure." Oh God, here we go. It's the *I know you fucked my brother* speech, most likely to be followed up with the *Why are you such a damn slut, Ally?* discussion.

We head over to the tiny stream that edges the property and slow to a plod. The boxwoods line the back of the cabin, continuing along the bed-and-breakfast with a border of Queen Anne's lace trimming the side.

"What's on your mind?" Kendall asks, quietly, as if afraid to break up the silence in this post-midnight world.

"I was just thinking about my mom. She loved the outdoors. She would point to a plant and teach us everything about it. There didn't seem to be a limit to what she knew." A small huff escapes my chest. "I sort of wish she left instructions on how to be a decent citizen before she died. I would have followed it to a T and not been such a screwup."

"Oh, stop." Kendall hooks her arm through mine and tilts her head over my shoulder a moment. "You're perfect and you know it. You've got it all: looks, personality, killer GPA, and apparently my brother's attention." She glances over at me waiting for me to admit it. "A little headboard whispered something to me last night." She says it low like a secret, and I wish to God it was.

"Okay, so your brother may have gotten my attention too." I swallow down a laugh as we come upon a stone bench overlooking the stream and take a seat. "Are you mad?"

"Why would I be mad?" She shrugs as if it were no big deal. "I mean, you're both old enough to make your own decisions." She shakes her head. "I just want you to be careful. I don't want him to hurt you."

"And you don't want me hurting him. I get it." I wonder if that's possible. If Morgan and I can walk away after what happened and just be friends. That's what this is about, right? Just something dirty to pass the time. But it didn't feel dirty. It felt beautiful.

"I can't imagine you hurting him." A tiny laugh bubbles from her. "He's got a reputation for having a heart of steel, or was that abs of steel? Anyway, I try not to keep track of my brother's hit list, if you know what I mean."

Hit list.

I cut a quick glance to the house.

"It's getting cold. We should probably get back." Kendall helps pull me to my feet and we head toward the tiny cabin. "So where were you tonight?"

"Oh, just here and there." I'm not quite ready to fess up and do the big dancer reveal just yet. I'm sure it'll come out sooner than later, and right about now I prefer later.

"Anyway, I think you and Morgan make a really cute couple. No pressure." She presses her hands out into the night and they glow like paper. "It's just, you know, fall will be here before you know it. I'd hate to see either of you dive in too hard, too fast."

"Too hard, too fast," I repeat mostly to myself.

God knows I've let that happen before and it didn't end well.

Fall will be here before we know it and I can't see this ending well, either.

⌢

The entire next week goes in that same direction sans the hot "conversation" I initiated last weekend. Down at the club it's all

the same, me with a different pastel negligee, and Morgan as the
happy bouncer who has unwittingly garnered a harem. It's safe
to say more than a few girls have taken to his drop-dead gorgeous features, those dimples that could each hold an ocean, his
rippling abs, the biceps that frame him out so fantastically. A
person might throw herself off the platform a time or two just
to have him catch her. And it's happened. The way the girls fly
into his arms after faking a shoe malfunction, you'd think there
was a bona fide mosh pit waiting below. I bet they all think I
was faking it that first night too.

He nods over to me through the throngs in thongs, and I
give a little wave. He hasn't made one move since that night we
were together, and I can't figure out why. Not that I mind too
much. Rutger and I are back on, sort of. He said he wanted to
catch a bite tonight, but I had to take a rain check. I told him
I had to tend to my "sick" sister, which isn't a far stretch from
the truth. I'm pretty sure telling him I'm a dancer will end it
for us on every level.

Woody Bates sweeps by and before I can stop him he wraps
his arms around my waist and gives me a twirl. He's made it
a regular practice to accost me just a little bit more each night
this week.

"Switching it up tonight?" I glance down at his beer. Usually
he relegates himself to the hard stuff, but tonight the only stiff
one he's sporting happens to be stashed in his chinos.

"That's right, baby." He lets out a riotous whoop. "Just like
I'm switching this up tonight." He plants a live one on my lips,
and I push at his chest to break free from his gorilla-like grip.

"Hey!" Morgan pops up from nowhere and plucks him off.
He decks him in the face so hard, blood shoots from his nose
like a faucet. "No touching the girls, asswipe."

Bates rolls around on the floor a moment before Dell shows up and helps him to his feet.

"Fuck." Dell's eyes bulge from his head, debuting those bullfrog genes I've always suspected he's had. Too bad for Tess; kissing this frog will only leave her with genital warts. The only Prince Charming I see around here is Morgan.

Morgan leans in, ready for a fight, but Dell holds him back from inflicting any more damage. Woody's nose hangs crooked as blood continues to trickle down the side of his face.

"Dude, you fucking *broke* it." Woody spits it out through his crimson-stained teeth. He cuts me a look as he makes his way past the bar. "You're going to pay for this."

Dell gives Morgan a firm shove into the stage. "You treat my customers like that? You can't go rearranging faces each time someone gets a little frisky. That's the name of the fucking game." Dell knots up Morgan's T-shirt and slams him against the wall. "Now get the hell out before the cops get here. I don't want any trouble. Consider it a night off." He shifts his gaze over to me, his greasy long hair falling in pieces over his eyes. "Control your boyfriend, would you?" He takes off in the direction of Woody, who deserved a broken nose to begin with.

"Boyfriend, huh?" Morgan's dimples dig in mockingly.

"He knows we commute." I shrug. And flirt, but I leave that part out.

"Anyway, I'm ready to call it a night." I reach down and pluck off my heels. "My feet are killing me."

"After you." He motions toward the door.

I run back and snatch my duffle bag from out of my locker. I don't dare try and change and glean the wrath of Tess for leaving early. There are at least a dozen extra girls on tonight, so it's not like anyone will ever notice I'm gone.

It's cool outside, with a warm wind that perks up every now and again to remind us it's the middle of July. The moon shines bright, bleaching the color right out of the world.

"You wanna go for a drive before heading home?" Morgan glows against the night sky like ivory, his eyes outshining the heavenly expanse, pale as pebbles. There's something pure about him, humble. Odd, I don't find those qualities in Rutger, and I don't know why. Maybe because he hasn't had the chance to wrestle me free from anaconda-like frat boys. If Morgan keeps saving me I'm going to believe he's my knight in shining armor. Already a part of me does.

"A drive sounds great," I say, glancing down at my non-accoutrements. "Hope you don't mind me in my PJs—less than my PJs, actually." I hold out my hands at the silver baby-doll negligee with the back fully exposed. I wish I could say I was ashamed, that I had the urge to cover myself up in a hurry, but Morgan has seen me in this same uniform for the past two weeks. I'm sure we're past the boner-inducing stage of our relationship.

"You can make a grown man cry in your PJs, darling." He gives the hint of a lewd grin. "If you're okay with it so am I."

We hop in his truck and drive down about two miles before he takes the turnoff to Charleston Beach. We descend the hillside to the parking lot and jump out of the truck into the salty breeze. The sand is so white it glows under the low lamp of the moon. The moonlight makes the beach look otherworldly, as if we were standing on another planet entirely.

"It's so beautiful here," I say, leaning into him. Morgan throws a beach towel over my shoulders as we make our way down to the waterline. The sound of the ocean lapping the shore crushes our eardrums with its constant thunder. It's barren here, just Morgan and me, the moon, and the incoming tide.

"How about here?" Morgan pulls me in, covering my back with his warm arms, and I sink into him, touching my hand to his blessed-by-God face.

"Here's perfect." I want to say *anywhere with you is perfect.* It's true. Morgan brightens my day whenever he's around. He's even made it a point to visit me at Starbucks a few times this week, though Blair tried to hijack him a time or two. I guess he's got to have a life too. My stomach boils, corrosive as battery acid at the thought of him having any kind of life with Blair Lancaster, of all people.

"So what's new?" he asks as we take a seat.

I adjust the towel under my bottom. I'm not too interested in digging sand out of places sand should never visit.

"What's new with you?" I shoulder bump him as we watch the surf foam up like a milk spilling over the sand.

"I asked first," he says. The words drum out of his chest and reverberate up my arm. The moon rains down its beams and bleaches all of the color from his face, giving him all of the sex appeal of an old-time movie star. It feels surreal to be at the beach like this with Morgan. We've become the stars of our own silent movie.

"I was thinking about Ruby a lot today." My heart sings just saying her name.

"I bet you miss her." He leans into me and touches his warm shoulder to mine. "Tell me about her." Morgan wraps an arm around my shoulder and shelters me from the breeze, from the biting sand needling against my flesh.

"She's amazing. She has the most vivid imagination. Everything is one ongoing story with her. One minute we're at the park and the next she has us surrounded with unicorns and fairies. She talks a mile a minute, but I never mind that. In fact, I welcome it. It sort of fills the void when we're apart."

His arm drops to my waist and he pulls me in, settling his face in my hair a moment.

"She sounds amazing." His breath heats my neck, and I sigh into him.

"She is. Maybe one day you can see for yourself." My heart races at the prospect of Morgan meeting Ruby. I don't tell him I've never brought anyone to meet her before. That our outings have always been exclusively relegated to Mommy-and-me dates. But then again, the Christies have always said anyone is welcome and Tess has come to every one of Ruby's birthday parties, mostly for moral support, but that's beside the point. Ruby loves Auntie Tess plenty too.

"I'd love to meet her." Morgan presses his lips into the side of my cheek, as naturally as the breeze licking the shore. I like it this way with Morgan. It feels comfortable, safe. "Maybe we can get some pictures of the two of you, enough to fill that album you're missing. We can make a day out of it." Everything in me warms at the thought of Morgan wanting to spend the day with me and Ruby.

"Really?" I fall back on my elbow and pull him down with me.

"Really." He reaches up and traces out the side of my face. "Don't look so surprised. I love spending time with you. You've made this summer totally worth the trip. If it wasn't for you I'd go batshit listening to the percussion going on next door. Not to mention my mom's been so busy with the wedding that I've hardly seen her." Morgan scoots in until the heat from his body sears over mine. He touches his hand to my hip and leans in further, his lips just a breath away from mine.

My heart pounds so hard I'm sure he can feel it, *hear* it. Why do I get the feeling Morgan and I just took a turn for the serious, or are about to?

His lips trace over mine, driving me insane the way they feather over my skin, and I give a heated breath.

"Um." I clear my throat and lean back a bit. "Tell me something about yourself."

Morgan shelters me from the wind as I nestle in his arms. It feels good like this with Morgan, safe.

"You know all of my secrets," I say, "and I don't know any of yours."

"Do I know all of your secrets?" He sweeps me with his gaze as if he suspects cobwebs hidden in the recesses of my past—that the closet of my life still has a corpse or two hanging from a noose.

"I do have a secret." He warms my cheek with his breath.

"Let me guess. You try on Kendall's high heels when she's not looking?" I tease, running my finger over his cheek, coarse as sandpaper.

"I wish it were that simple." His features darken. "Actually, Kendall doesn't know this and neither does my mom. I don't mind telling you, though."

I clasp the back of his neck and trace out small circles over the nape, encouraging him to go on. Morgan is all too serious and it frightens me on some level.

"Back home, in Oregon, there was this girl . . ." He pauses and my heart drops into the pit of my stomach. "We weren't serious or anything like that, but we were fooling around, and I may have gotten her pregnant. It's a mess. Right now she's engaged to someone else, and there are DNA tests waiting to be done. She swears I'm the only other option. I should get the results in a couple of weeks. She wants to wait until the baby's born, and deal with it then."

A breath gets caught in my throat.

"Oh my God." I wrap my arm around his neck. "I'm so sorry. I mean, I'm sorry you're going through this alone. I'm glad you told me. This must be so hard for you."

He looks down and shakes his head. "I feel like an ass for saying anything. She doesn't want me around. The idiot she's with even tried to buy me out of the picture. But if that baby's mine, I'm all in; there's no way they're keeping me from its life." His smile is layered with pain and my heart shatters for him.

"Morgan." I tighten my grip as he pulls me over to his lap. "I'm proud of you. You're a man for wanting to be in that baby's life." My lids grow heavy because he must think I'm inhuman for walking away from Ruby.

"Thank you." He bows his head a moment. "And"—the whites of his eyes expand—"in no way am I judging you for choosing adoption. In fact, I think you're a hero, Ally, and *I'm* proud of *you.*"

A line of fire burns through me as Morgan plants a careful kiss on my forehead. My eyes glitter up with tears, and I do my best to blink them away.

"You're going to make a great dad someday. I already know this."

He presses out a grin that ignites me like a flame and everything in me burns to have him.

"And you're an excellent mother, Ally. I can already see that."

"I haven't been able to give Ruby anything." I touch my cheek to his chest and look up.

"Life isn't about things, Ally." His eyes drill into mine as if he's speaking in far broader terms. "It's about love, about building relationships and helping people. You did a lot more for that little girl than buy her a swing set or a teddy bear, you gave her a life. And, you're lucky because you still get to be in it. That's pretty special."

There, he's done it. Morgan Jordan has galvanized himself over the framework of my life as a savior, a god, a counselor—all of the above. He's so much more than a friend, but I know that we can never be together. It would never work. The bouncer and the dancer—we're almost laughable to everyone in the free world, for sure to the people at Garrison if they ever found out. But they're not here tonight, and neither is anyone else.

"Morgan?"

"What's that?" He whispers it low, directly in my ear, and chills of excitement tingle up my spine.

"I think we should revisit our dirty little secret."

His dimples invert with approval. "I thought you'd never ask."

Morgan

The warm breeze feels downright tropical as I hold Ally in my arms on a white sandy beach at midnight. It would figure that the one time in weeks she suggests we replicate the mattress magic, I'm deficient a love glove.

Shit.

"Let's get back to the house." I rock her in my arms, trying to coax her into my line of thinking. "I've got ways to make our secret feel a hell of a lot dirtier." I whisper it hot in her ear and her neck arches back, driving me insane.

Actually, I don't have any new ideas but I predict I'll think up about a dozen on the drive home. I'd hate to miss out just because of some sophomoric blunder.

"I like it here." She bites down over her cherry lip, and my gut pinches tight. Her eyes sparkle in this dim light like embers. Ally sizzles right off the sand, hotter than a bonfire.

"Here?" Thought so. I pull her over me and ride my hand up her thigh. "I don't have anything with me," I confess. "Do you?" I doubt Ally routinely packs ammo for her night at the club. Deep down I know for a fact Ally Monroe is a good girl.

Her mouth rounds out in a perfect *0* as she catches on to our preventative predicament.

Ally reaches down and rides her hand over the bulge in my jeans as if to say, *procreation be damned.*

"Look"—I give a gentle laugh while tracing the outline of her features—"it's not like me to stop the train from pulling into the station, but I think maybe we've got too many offspring, or potential ones at best, floating around between us. There's no way I'm playing Russian roulette with my boys again."

A soft laugh bubbles from her. Her chest heaves in a series of intoxicating ripples, and I'm transfixed by her beauty. Ally lies over the beach like a fabled princess who has no idea she's royalty.

I press a kiss over her ear before running my tongue along the rim and she groans.

"There are a few other things I can think of to keep us entertained," I whisper, gently rolling her onto her back.

Ally gives an impish smile with her hair spilling around her like a lion's mane. She looks like a girl, a *teenager,* and for a minute I try to imagine that we're both in high school, innocent as the day is long, about to share our love with one another for the very first time.

I lean in and brush my lips over hers. Ally opens her mouth for me, but I stroke her lips with my breath until she reels from the effect. Ally pulls me down by the back of the neck and crushes into me with a mouthwatering kiss that makes my insides ache. I can't recall who I shared my first kiss with, but this one, this kiss has already bookmarked itself in my memory as an all-out fucking luxury that I can only hope to replicate time and time again. Ally is a rare treasure—one I'm not sure I'll be partaking in ever again. She's a take-it-or-leave-it kind of girl, and I'll take it every single time. I'm just afraid the invite might not be available in the future. I wish it were. I wish what we have could withstand the promise of a thousand tomorrows. I'd do anything to make that happen. That idea I had earlier while scoping out Cal's basement comes back full throttle, and I'm half tempted to bring it up, but not stupid enough to take a break in the action.

Nope. My ingenious idea will have to wait for later. Hell, I might even spring it on her last minute. I have a feeling it's going to take all of Garrison University by storm. We'll be swimming in dollar bills before summer is up. I'll make sure she has more than enough to pay for her fall semester and a new place to stay. Maybe then she'll take me seriously. Move me from the fuck-buddy shelf to the potential partner in lifelong crime arena. Although I'm pretty sure I need to cut the word "crime" from my lexicon whether it's a euphemism or not. It's baby steps with Ally, though, ironically, not when our bodies are involved.

I hike up on my elbow, and run my hand over her smooth-as-butter stomach. Slowly I inch my way north and she moans herself into a beautiful oblivion. Ally tries to pull me back down, her mouth open and waiting for mine, but I forgo the offer. I have a few other places I'd like to land my lips tonight, and I plan to explore them soon.

The ocean rushes the shore with its rocketing affection and touches the outer edge of our towel, but I ignore the threat for now. So the ocean's a little bit wet. Who the hell cares? I'm more into whether Ally is wet, and I'm determined to make sure the answer is hell fucking yes. I slip my hand beneath the split in the barely there lace number she's wearing and cup her breast in my hand, more than a handful and so fucking soft. It takes all of my restraint to not to bite down like I want to. Nope, this is all about her tonight.

Her smile fades. She runs her tongue over her bottom lip as if she's worked up an appetite. Ally glimpses up at me with her smoldering eyes. I don't think I've ever wanted anyone the way I want Ally. Maybe because deep inside I know I can never have her, that I'll never be good enough on an economic scale for her to consider me an option.

My hand rides down over her searing flesh and takes in the sting from her skin, like touching down on a hot iron skillet. My fingers create small circles over her stomach before dipping down to her panty line and slipping my fingers inside. I'd map her out with my mouth, but she protested the last time I tried. I know some girls have a hang-up about that. We'll get her there, just not tonight. Tonight we're traveling in the slow lane to ensure Ally Monroe gets an intoxicating rise out of the evening while using me as the fuel she needs.

"Come here." She tries to pull me down by the neck, but I don't budge.

"No thanks." I press out a smile. "I like the view."

"*Morgan.*" She averts her gaze a moment, and I take the opportunity to glide my fingers over her skin, tracing the shape of an *S*. I touch down over the coarse hair that lines the tender part of her body and my finger glides into the hot slick. Ally is well lubed for the night, and my ego would like to think I had more than a little something to do with it.

Her eyes close involuntarily as she catches her breath.

"*Morgan.*" She says it again as if pleading with me. Ally's chest rises and falls with the rhythm of my fingers. Her breathing becomes erratic, her shoulders flex in time as she writhes in the sand, her neck arches as if this is agonizing on some level. "Morgan, wait." She reaches down and secures her grip over my wrist.

"I'm good," I whisper. "I want to do this. I like watching you. You're beautiful, you know that?"

"Come here." She pulls me with the strength of a wrestler and dislodges my hand in the process.

"I want to finish. I want to do this for you," I say, running my hand back down to the heated slick I was enjoying before she stopped me. I open my mouth and trace her jawline with my lips.

"I don't want to disappoint you." She heaves the words in my ear as if she is a breath away from enjoying the hell out of herself.

"How—"

A wall of water collapses over our bodies and baptizes us with its icy brine.

Ally screams and laughs as the wave rolls back with ten times the ferocity it did coming in.

"Shit." I pluck at my T-shirt that's adhered to my flesh. I roll back over her and warm her lips with mine. I let my lips hover over her, waiting for her to want me, invite me in. Ally holds me down by the shoulders and dives her salty little tongue into my mouth. I gently catch it with my teeth, and my chest rumbles with a laugh. I swipe my tongue over hers, exploring slowly and methodically, as if I were setting up shop. Kissing Ally has quickly become my favorite pastime, kicking the old ball and stick out of the prime position they've held in my life since the day I was born. We kiss for what feels like hours, months. I soak in all of her moans, the sweet way her body writhes beneath me. I'm not ready to head back to the house, and for sure I'm not ready to ask her why the hell she thinks she could ever disappoint me. If anything, she's deprived me of witnessing one hell of an awesome sight. I think I've memorized her face, the way her body looks twisted in the sand, right down to the last molecule.

Nope, Ally Monroe doesn't disappoint on any level—never could, never will.

———

Once we arrive home, the rest of the night is uneventful. Ally takes a shower and crashes on the couch, falling asleep before I can beg her to help me out with the perpetual hard-on I've been nurturing since I arrived in Carrington.

Cruise's voice booms through the papier-mâché walls, barking out orders in his bedroom, and for the first time in my life I wish to God I were deaf. Between his sergeant-like commands and Kendall's high-pitched moans my hard-on has deteriorated all on its own.

It's becoming painfully clear that I've got to get the hell out of here. I'm pretty damn sure the seventh circle of hell has a lot to do with hearing your sister in the throes of passion, night after night. But it's not Kendall's pleasure threshold that has me worried, it's Ally's.

In the morning, Ally's taken off for Starbucks before I can get out of the shower. Kendall is nowhere to be found. I'll probably hit the batting cages in a few minutes. Stalk Ally on the way over—a man needs his coffee. God knows the brewed piss Cruise offers isn't going to help shape the day.

Speaking of the bed-and-breakfast bigwig, I find him hunched over his laptop in the kitchen, and thanks to sad mathematics I can deduce it's just Elton and me. He looks wrecked, like he partied all night and has a serious hangover to contend with, but in reality we both know it's because he doesn't get enough freaking sleep. Gyrating on your mattress all night will do that to a person. I should know. I used to live that way until Paige walked into my life and turned me into a genetic vending machine, a potential one at least.

That's precisely why I swore off random hookups. At least I did until I hit Carrington and Ally Monroe fell into my lap, literally.

My chest pumps with a failed laugh.

I was going to hold out for "true love," whatever the hell that might be. I think Ally and I can get to it. I think if she burns her illogical ideals to the ground, she might find something just beyond those ashes, preferably me.

And what's with denying herself the Big O? She saving that for Rutger or some other well-off douche? Sounds more like a punishment. If she keeps using my social standing as an excuse to cut off her good time, soon her entire body is going to subconsciously hate me.

Cruise springs up from the table and blinks a sarcastic smile.

"What's on your mind, doll face?" He dumps cereal into a bowl in haste, landing half of his not-so Lucky Charms all over the sink.

"Ally." My stomach clenches. I don't like how easily I admitted it. The next thing you know, I'll be drooling over how cute she is and crying like a schoolgirl over the fact she's just not that into me. Then, of course, Cruise and I will end the douchefest with a pillow fight and I'll have to beat the shit out of him for reducing me to the relevance of a seventh-grade girl. Funny how just about every mental scenario with Cruise ends with me beating the shit out of him. The first time he looks at Kendall crooked, that's exactly what's going to happen.

He plops down his bowl and a swig of milk slops onto the table. His eyes are nothing but a network of red wires, and he looks dulled out in general.

"Dude, you gotta get some sleep."

"Tell me about it," he gravels out. "At about three-thirty I had a plumbing backup next door that nearly washed away the entire second floor. I had to relocate three couples in the middle of the night, including my sister."

My gut tightens when he mentions his overly hormonal little sis. I cast a glance around the room, making sure she's not preparing to jump me from the corner. There's not a lot I wouldn't put past her.

"And now," he continues, "the rooms won't be available until God knows when. There goes any hope of ever getting into the black." He jabs his spoon into his food, and a handful of stale marshmallows confetti the table.

I don't say anything. Pretty much dealing with other people's shit at any hour of the day sucks, so there's nothing I can add to make this better.

"So tell me about Ally." He makes an effort to lift his lids. "You said you were thinking about her."

"It's nothing." I consider this a moment. Elton alluded to knowing something about her a couple of weeks ago, and maybe now, while his synapses are misfiring from a lousy night's sleep, is a great time to squeeze some info out of him. "So, how well do you know Ally?" Hell, maybe Cruise here did a little tour of duty with Ms. Monroe before Kenny popped on the scene. Not that I think of Ally that way—but for damn sure I think of *him* that way.

"Well enough." He pulls his cheek to the side with a sudden look of discontent. "Not like that."

"Got it." Thank God for small mercies.

"Why do you ask? Everything okay in that department?" He looks remorseful for even going there.

"I don't know." What the hell kind of answer is that? Unfortunately it's the truth. "She ever say anything about it?"

"You and her?" His eyes bulge a moment, disgusted by the prospect of Ally bringing up our sex life. "I'm not that close to her. Maybe she's said something to Kenny. Why? Are you into weird shit that freaks her out?"

Nice. He's suddenly good and pissed at my prospective perversion.

"You mean like those chains you've got dangling off the bed like a threat? Or that power motor I hear you running in the bedroom every now and again? What the hell is that, a weed whacker? Second thought, I really don't want to know." I sink down in my seat and thread my fingers behind my neck. "With Ally, it has nothing to do with anything extracurricular, just your run-of-the-mill stuff. Things you expect a girl to enjoy." I give a curt nod because that's as far as I'm willing to take it.

He shakes his head, stymied by what might pleasure the average girl. Crap. Maybe it's Kenny who's the pervert in this equation, but somehow I doubt that.

"Anyway, if you think of it, ask Kendall for me, would you? I'm pretty sure Ally wants me, she just doesn't . . . want to enjoy herself like you'd imagine she would." There—picture painted.

He lurches a little before diving into a dry laugh. "You don't know how to please her? Sounds like the problem is you, my friend."

"She won't let me."

"Again, you're the common denominator."

I shoot him a dirty look before changing the subject.

"What's Cal's number? I've got a business proposition for him."

Cruise huffs at the thought of me speaking to Cal regarding a business proposition of any kind.

"What?" I shrug as if I'm deeply offended. "It's legal." Mostly.

"Here." He messes with his phone before laying it on the table with Cal's ugly mug staring up at me, his number just below that.

"Do Ally a favor and watch some porn." Cruise gets up and starts heading down the hall. "Educate yourself, will you?" He shouts before shutting the door to his room.

Watch some porn.

I shake my head.

I couldn't log enough hours in front of the tube to answer the mystery to Ally Monroe, nor would I want to. I never want that image of Ally lying in the sand to erase itself from my mind—to pervert it with the image of someone else. I just wish I could have seen the rest of the night unfold the way it was supposed to. And I'm curious as hell as to why it didn't.

I punch a call into Cal.

It's time to turn things around financially for Ally and me. Maybe then she'll lose herself in ecstasy.

I give a little laugh.

It would figure.

6

LOVE BREWING

Ally

Starbucks is jumping, filled to the brim with Garrison defects happy to be free for eleven short weeks. It's nothing but a brown and green coffee-scented flurry from the moment I arrive. Gretchen, my least favorite shift supervisor, is on, adding to the increased shit factor of this stressed-out morning.

There's a line a mile long, right out the door, but I keep zoning out, losing myself while staring at the evergreens outside the window.

It's not really the evergreens clogging up my mind, or nature in general. Instead, last night's beach scene keeps replaying on a loop, and I feel lighter than air just thinking about it—just thinking about Morgan.

"Wake up!" Gretchen snaps, sharp and obtrusive like a hyena ready to attack. She looks like one too, with that large mouth and those long, hanging gums. Her blonde scraggly mane with a severe case of greying roots is enough to send anyone into hiding. Truthfully she scares the crap out of me. It wouldn't surprise me at all if she morphs into Bigfoot at night and terrorizes the region for the sheer joy of making people panic. She's that sadistic and weird.

I bolt to and fro, running myself ragged, trying to make coffee twelve different ways and systematically screwing up. Every. Single. Order.

"What the hell's the matter with you?" She leans in, and her onion breath accosts my olfactory receptacles.

"I don't know." Morgan bounces through my mind with those killer dimples, those glowing eyes, and my insides catch fire. "I must be tired." It's true. I kept thinking of Morgan and his magic fingers all night, wondering if I hadn't stopped him if he could have landed me in that mythical nirvana I've only read about in books. I swear he had the power to do it. I just didn't want to look like a fool when I couldn't get there and have to fake my way out of another situation. I really do want everything I share with Morgan to be real. I'd hate to lie about something so intimate.

"Tired?" Her face contorts into all kinds of crazy shapes, and I back into the stainless counter in fear she might explode and spew demonic confetti all over the place.

Blair steps up in line, and I make a face. Perfect. She's the icing on this craptastic morning.

"What's this?" Gretchen spins to gawk at the customers. "Relieve Penelope at the register." She presses into me with that salivating scowl. "*Smile,* Ally. Smile like your job depends on it!" She zips off to the back.

Like my job depends on it. I let out a breath.

I take over at the helm just as Blair steps up to the counter.

"Morning." I let out an exasperated sigh. "What can I get for you?"

Morgan strides in and bypasses the line.

"Well, look who's here!" Blair pulls him in by the waist, her thin lips curling at the corners. "Whatever you want, I'll do it for you—I mean, get it for you." A lazy smile slides up her cheek. She knew damn well what she was saying the first time.

"No, that's okay." He glances down at her arm and tries to step away but Blair's got him in a death grip. He reverts his attention to me, settling those steel-blue eyes over mine, and my insides pinch. "I just came by to see if you were on tonight."

I press my lips together in a panic. I'm not sure I've ever said anything to him about keeping my dance career under wraps for now. I'm not exactly ready to flaunt the pole in people's faces, especially not Blair's.

"No. Not on." I shake my head in a furtive manner.

"Good." His dimples go off. "Neither am I." Morgan's face softens into a smile, and suddenly it's just the two of us as the angry mob of caffeine-deprived plebeians starts to drift out of existence.

Blair puts in a double order, and I'm so nervous with the two of them watching me I punch the keys wrong, three times, before officially locking down the register.

"Shit," I whimper. "Gretchen?" I look back hesitantly.

"What?" she barks. She glances at the seized monitor and her face glazes over. "Now you've done it." She inserts her key, and starts hitting keys at random, which I'm positive will only make matters worse. "We'll have to call in for tech support, and do the rest of the orders manually." A fire blazes in her eyes as she grits out the words.

Crap. Functioning manually equals twice as slow.

I look up with heavy eyes, and Morgan gives a remorseful smile.

"I'll catch you later." He says it quietly, as if trying to preserve my fragile employment status. "I'll be at the batting cages the rest of the afternoon."

"Batting cages?" Blair dips her gaze to his crotch for a moment, quick to glom onto his balls and bat. "I was just heading to the gym, but my car is acting up. I'm supposed to meet up with my friend Erica. Do you think I can hitch a ride?"

"Sure." His brows narrow in for a moment as if he doubts her car is acting up as much as her hormones.

"We'll catch you later, Al." Blair winks over at me. Morgan raises his brows and they head out the door. Just perfect.

Lauren and Kendall waltz in and wave before heading to the back. Great. They can witness my bizarre coffee breakdown as I shove my head under the espresso maker.

"Ally," Gretchen barks in my face. "Those customers just walked right out on an order. I'll take the rest of your shift, since you're feeling a bit *sleepy* today." She draws her fists to her hips and squints her impossibly beady eyes over me. "In fact, you can turn in your apron and take that nap you so desperately need. I'm sick of all the excuses. I'm giving you the rest of your life off—you're *fired*."

"What?" I jump in horror at the thought of being canned. Stupid people get fired, thieves and people who are no-shows, not someone like me who's desperately undeserving of the unemployment line. "I want to work. I want to be here. I *love* my job."

"Sorry, sis. You're the reason for the backlog, and it's time to cut the weakest link. We need to *increase* productivity, not gift people replacement drinks all day long in order to rectify an error. Now go in peace or so help me God I will have you removed by security."

My fingers fly to my lips in horror.

Shit! I take my apron off and plop it onto the counter before making my way numbly into the seating area. My feet carry me over to Lauren and Kendall, even though hanging out with my friends might land me a day pass in the county jail. The way my morning has been going I'll probably score a life sentence while I'm at it.

"Hey," Lauren scolds. "Get back there and get that line under control. I'm not ordering until half those people disappear."

"I can't." The words barely eject themselves from my throat.

"*Honey*." Lauren picks up on my sudden state of despondency. "What happened?"

"Did you just get held up? Was there just a robbery?" Kendall looks completely freaked out, as though a coffee heist were a viable option.

I shake my head. "I think I just officially lost my job."

It all happens so fast. Kendall and Lauren shuttling me into the car while Lauren drives like a lunatic over to the gym. She hums on and on about having a spa day, steam rooms, and hot-stone massages, but I can't wrap my head around any of it. All I can think about is how I've managed to fuck up my employment record and now I'll be forced to wear a modern scarlet letter on my résumé—a big, fat *F* for *fired*. All I have left is Pretty Girls, and I can't even make enough on most nights to pay the damn house fee. Freaking Dell.

Once we arrive, the girls storm me off to the back where I'm stripped clean of my clothing in exchange for a thick white towel. We head into Hades, where it's so hot and smothering that the steam room replicates exactly how I feel.

A bunch of girls from Garrison are here, whispering as we walk by. I note Blair and her canine-faced friend sitting at one edge. Looks like Morgan landed her here in one unfortunate piece. But I try not to let my anger get the best of me, especially since she's the primary reason I've been relegated to a new level of financial paralysis.

"Everything is going to suck from now on," I groan, taking a seat on the surprisingly cool tile. God knows I'll never have enough cold hard cash to move out on my own. But I don't dare say that in front of Lauren. I'd hate for her to feel bad about living the dream with her new fiancé. Or, hey . . . maybe things aren't so hot between them, and it'll be like old times with Lauren and me. "How are things going with you and Cal?" I can't believe I've just sunk to an all-time low—digging for a fissure in my best friend's relationship.

"Things are still moving in the right direction." She makes a face. "The other day I brought a bridal magazine home. You'd think it was another man the way he completely freaked out." She turns to Kendall. "How about you? Cruise ever mention the wedding?"

Kendall considers it a moment. Kendall's dark hair and blue eyes send an image of Morgan searing through my stomach. God, why does he have to be so damn gorgeous? And so not right for me. But everything about him and that highway of tattoos trailing up his arms just complicates the issue.

"Cruise is all about the wedding night." Kendall leans in. "He's already planning a dozen different ways to surprise me in bed. He's not one to let things get boring. He's anti-vanilla." She darts a quick glance in Blair's direction for a moment.

The blonde bitch herself must have heard because her mouth just rooted itself to the floor. Serves her right. Although if memory is correct, Blair mentioned she and Cruise never did the deed—lucky for Cruise. Although I'm positive she'd jump into the sack with my Morgan if the opportunity presents itself.

Wait. Did I just call him *my* Morgan? What the hell is that about?

"Wedding night, huh?" Lauren purrs. "Cruise sounds like a wild one."

"Yeah, well, some guys like things a little untamed in the bedroom." She leans her head back against the wall and her chest rises as she takes a breath. "Some *girls* do too." She giggles it out.

I can totally vouch for that; Kendall is right there on the wild side with Cruise. I've heard at least a half dozen experimental noises stemming from their love nest night after night. I'm thinking Kendall and I need to develop a safe word in the event Cruise is about to delve into something alarmingly dangerous. Not that he would. He's a totally nice guy.

"How about you, Al?" Lauren kicks my foot a little. "Rumor has it you're hitting the sheets with someone tall, dark, and handsome." She and Kendall break out in titters.

A breath gets caught in my throat as I gape over at Kendall. Of course she told. Not that I blame her.

I bite down on my lip, unsure of how much I should divulge, especially since I've made it clear to Morgan that we're far from being a couple. I think I'm beginning to see why Kendall thought I might be trouble for him.

"Morgan and I . . ."

Blair clears her throat from across the room. "So Erica . . ." she says it a little louder than necessary. "About Pen's little get-together—of course I'll be there. I'm bringing *Morgan Jordan*. Have you seen him? He redefines the word *beefcake*. You should see the size of his—"

"So"—I clap my hands together and glare at the queen bee in question—"you know, Kendall," I whisper. "I don't believe

Blair was ever given the right amount of retribution for that stunt she pulled by getting Cruise tossed out of Garrison. We should totally take her down."

"You and me?" Her eyes widen, amused by the offer. "You're not thinking anything illegal, are you?" Her lips curve with approval as if she's already warming to the illegal implications of it all.

"No, I would never do that." Except on the rare occasion I feel the real me creeping out of my shell. A part of me wishes I could let down my guard around Kendall and Lauren, fill them in on my budding dancing career, even if it is temporary. I can't help but feel like I'm forever trying to be something I'm not.

Kendall leans in and we glare over at Blair together.

"Let's do this," she whispers.

"It's so on," I say, looking right at the wicked witch.

Blair Lancaster is about to go down in flames.

Now all I have to do is come up with a way to make it happen.

And I will.

———

Morgan and I are both off from the club tonight. Well, he's sort of on probation until next week, and Tess has removed me from the schedule until Dell cools off.

Rutger called and invited me to Pen's get-together later, so I'll have the misfortune of witnessing Blair trying to climb Mount Morgan.

"So . . ." I head over to the couch where the tattoo titan is reading a book. And dear God, there is nothing hotter than a boy and his book. I trace out the curves of his biceps with my eyes, the thick rope-like veins that thread just under his skin. I wish I could trace them out with my tongue. Given the next opportunity, I just might. "You read?" I'm actually caught off guard by this. I flip the cover back a little. It's some sci-fi thriller I've never heard of. Nevertheless, it's as thick as a Bible and no pictures, to boot.

"Yes, I read." His dimples flex as he presses out a wry smile.

"So, um"—I try to think of a million reasons to convince him we should both stay home tonight—"heard you were heading over to Pennington's." I'm not sure why I want him to say that he's not, that he's going to stay here with me. And if that were the case I'd call Rutger and tell him I'm too busy. I'd much rather stay in and read books with Morgan than hang out with Rutger and his snobby friends. That "bad girl" crack still has me pretty pissed. Besides, if Morgan and I get tired of reading we can always find something better to do—in the bedroom.

God, what am I saying? This is Morgan. He's practically the male version of me, and God knows I'm the worst thing that could ever happen to either of us.

"Are you going?" He squints at me with those delicious blueberry-pie eyes.

"Maybe." I bite down on my lip, not sure how to instigate a game of chicken with him. "I mean, Rutger asked."

"Mmm." He glances down at his book with a look of disappointment. "Blair asked." He shrugs. "So I guess I'll see you there."

"I guess you will." Crap. "Everything go okay on the drive to the gym?"

"It went great." He looks up at me from over his book. "Was something supposed to happen?" There's a curve on his lip just begging to break into an all-out grin but he won't give it.

"No, it's just—" My mouth stays open, wanting to protest the idea of him ever seeing her again, or fill him in on the fact that Blair is a grade A bitch who happened to get me fired this afternoon. Well, in a roundabout way. But then I remember her daddy's bank account could rival the US Treasury, and Blair would probably never set her designer stilettos in Pretty Girls, let alone work there. She has her own place, her own car, and for sure doesn't have a child she had to give up anywhere on the planet. "Blair is definitely someone who can pull you up in life." It comes from me weakly. I spring to my feet to ready myself for another date with Rutger. Rutger is okay—I glance back at the demigod taking up residency on the couch—but Rutger is no Morgan Jordan.

———

By the time I finish primping myself to perfection, Morgan has already taken off to pick up Blair. My stomach turns at the thought of the two of them having a good time together. I can just imagine her wrapping her skinny, pale arms around him, relaxing her skeletal frame against his tanned, well-hewn body.

A horn blares outside, quick and angry, and I snap to attention.

Rutger manages to show up a whole forty-five minutes late. It would figure, since I'm anxious as hell to get to the party.

"Hey, babe," he says in a bored way as I climb into the passenger seat. His hair is encrusted with gel, and some of his severely long bangs fall in his face. He's got on his signature polo in a mint green, and the collar is turned up the way he likes it. For the first time I notice his arms are neither tanned nor toned. They sort of straddle the wheel like pale noodles.

"So where were you?" I ask, buckling up as he tears down the road at breakneck speed. "You were a little late."

"Enough with the bitching. I'll get you to the ball, Cinderella." He rolls down the window and hawks a live one right out onto the street.

Eww, seriously? Ten years in the finest boarding schools and he has the nerve to talk to me that way *and* hawk a loogie in my presence? Nice.

Rutger drives us to Pen's palatial estate in his father's antique roadster. He rattles on and on about how he's taking it to a car show this weekend at the country club, where there will be a bevy of other boys showing off their daddies' classic rides.

I give a complacent smile since I can't get a word in edgewise. So this is what it would be like with Rutger: car shows and country clubs, lots of silence and tolerance on my part, and—holy shit—trips to fantastic houses like the one we just pulled up in front of.

"Geez." I try to sound underwhelmed but my heart just jumped in my throat at the sight of the opulent estate. I knew Pen came from money, but I never imagined him living in style like a king. This mega-mansion is ripped straight from the pages of one of those oversized real-estate magazines you see at the doctor's office. It's almost hard to believe that only one family lives there. Well, *did* live there. Pen's mother is in Europe, and his dad is at the bed-and-breakfast, although I have no idea why. "This place is magnificent."

Rutger looks out at it through the windshield, his face frowning at the estate as if it freshly insulted him. "It's okay. New money. What are you going to do, right?" He barks out a laugh and slaps me on the back.

We stride up the stairs and Rutger's hand fondles my ass all the way to the door.

"Rutger, *stop*," I say, gently placing his roving digits back to his side.

"What? You're my bad girl. You like that kind of stuff, remember?"

"No, I don't remember," I whisper, mostly to myself as we head inside.

A breath gets caught in my throat at the sight of it. I can't help but take pause at the sheer extravagance that went into this place—crystal chandelier in the entry, marble staircase. The room just off the entry is the size of a warehouse. A monolithic oil painting hangs in the oversized sitting area to my right. It's of Pen and his parents in happier times. I gravitate over and spot an entire herd of people I know from Garrison.

"Odd, isn't it?" Kendall pops up beside me, and we take in the painting.

"I think it's totally cool. I'd love to do that one day. Wouldn't you? Of course I'd need the mega-mansion to go with it."

"I don't know." She makes a face. "I don't think a painting like that would fit in the bed-and-breakfast." She wrinkles her nose. "Maybe a scaled-down version—something more down to earth. I don't think I could ever live in a mausoleum like this."

"Are you kidding? Look at this place. It's gorgeous. It screams that the people who live here never have to work a day in their lives. It's everything I'd ever want."

"Really?" She looks perplexed by my statement.

"Yes, really. You have to be nuts not to want this."

"Well, the fact the people who are supposed to be living here have decided to vacate the premises should clue you in that this isn't all that it's cracked up to be. In the meantime, Pen is using it as his palace of perversion. It's not *things* or fancy houses that make the world go around, Ally, it's love—and it just so happened this place didn't have any." She shrugs.

Blair cackles like a witch from across the room, and both Kendall and I twist in that direction.

Morgan says something to her and she continues to guffaw like an idiot at whatever spews from his mouth. Blair has on a red satin dress that hugs her nonexistent curves, but her hair is curled super cute in long luscious waves and her bright-red lips give her that old Hollywood feel. And unfortunately for me, she looks glamorous. She looks like she belongs in a place exactly like this. Morgan looks pretty dapper himself, all decked out in a pale-blue button-down and a pair of chocolate chinos. Oddly enough, he too looks like he could take up residency here.

"I look like crap." I take a step back and the buckle breaks on my strappy heels. "Perfect." I reach down and confirm the fact it's ripped right from the seam. "I'm so tired of running to the thrift store for anything I put on this body." I pluck at the floral dress I picked out of a bargain bin. "I swear I thought this looked good when I picked it out. And now I feel hideous."

"Are you high?" Kendall averts her eyes as if it were ridiculous. "You look fantastic. And if Rutger doesn't think so he can roll up his thesis and smoke it."

"Right, Rutger can smoke it." I say it low but I can't seem to take my gaze off Morgan. He's perfectly attentive to whatever the hell bullshit is streaming from Blair's nonexistent lips, and I can't help but feel a tiny bit jealous. Rutger didn't let me get two words in on the way over. Come to think of it—ever. "Well"—I let out a depressed sigh—"I better go find him."

"He's with Cruise and Pen." She nods behind me.

We strut off together, and I swivel my hips a little rounder than usual in the event Morgan happens to look my way.

By the time we hit the sofa, Blair and Morgan have joined our circle.

"Hey." I smile at Rutger as I fall into the seat beside him. His cologne is so strong it nearly bowls me over. Doesn't that stuff dissipate after a while? Then again it's probably the good stuff, and rumor has it the only way you can get rid of the stench is to rub yourself silly with dollar bills.

"Hey yourself, doll." He wraps an arm around me and gives my right boob a hard squeeze. Instinctually I glace up to see if Morgan saw the bawdy exchange.

Morgan raises his brows and frowns at me before shooting Rutger some serious lasers of hatred. Morgan is just on auto-pilot. He's still playing the part of the bouncer, thinking he needs to protect me from roving hands. Although in this case I wouldn't really mind.

I nestle into Rutger to give Morgan the impression that I'm totally fine with the pervert next to me molesting my nipple in public, which I'm not.

The vicinity lights up with laughter at something Pen just said; I missed the punch line but I nod as if I totally didn't.

"Hey, babe." Rutger slaps his hand over my knee a couple of times before finding a home for his fingers on my inner thigh. "Why don't you get us a drink?"

"Oh, sure." I glance up at Morgan like a reflex before returning my attention to Rutger and his roaming digits. "Not a problem."

Pen lets out an egregious belch that should come with a decibel warning, and Erica laughs as if it were the cutest thing ever.

Gross. Leave it to Blair's skanky bestie to appreciate the crude and the lewd.

"Girls love that shit." Pen espouses his not-so-sage wisdom without provocation.

"I'll have to try that out." Rutger nods at Pen's stupidity, only I don't think he's finding him so stupid. "In *bed*." He gives a riotous laugh while exchanging high fives with the oafish offender.

Rutger swims his hand deep up my thigh and gives me a not so gentle smack on the ass as I get up.

"Get one for all the boys, would you?" he crows.

"Oh, I'm fine." Cruise is quick to refuse Rutger's offer.

Blair raises a finger in the air. "I'll take something. A venti caramel frap and make it soy, milk tends to hurt my stomach." She lets out a cackle and high-fives Erica. A small bout of laughter filters through the room, and suddenly I want to be anywhere but here.

"Double espresso, please." Erica flashes her fangs in my direction. "Nonfat, no sugar. And don't worry, honey, we tip your kind well."

"You're like our own personal little barista!" Blair squeals with false enthusiasm. "Gee, Ally, you're really going to come in handy at parties this summer. Isn't that right, Rutger? You'll never have to hire a waitstaff with her around. In fact, I bet she's a full-service kind of gal." She pulls Morgan's hand to her chest and presses a kiss over his knuckle.

Rutger gives a quick squeeze to my bottom. "That's why I keep her around."

"Hey, make it quick and I'll double your tip!" Erica claps like a seal. "We should call you Servant Sally!" Both she and Blair explode into a fit of laughter.

"It's *Ally*," I correct, rather stupidly.

Morgan catches my gaze and holds it. He's got a fire in his eyes, and he looks as if he's about to explode.

"Anyway," I whisper. "I'd better get those."

Kendall starts to get up. "I'll help."

"No, it's okay," I say, speeding toward the back where Pen hitched his thumb. "I can handle this on my own." I brisk past Blair, past Erica and all that fake overprocessed crap she calls hair, which, by the way, is balding in patches.

"Of course you can!" Blair shouts over the hum of the party. "You're a pro—literally."

Her cackles follow me all the way down the corridor and into an oversized stainless wonder that doubles as a kitchen. Thanks to Blair I'm no pro. In fact, I would be *lucky* to work one of their "parties" but unfortunately tonight I'm the butt of all their jokes. Tears spring to my eyes, and I try to blink them away.

The sting of their words, of Rutger's unwanted advances, replay again and again. The worst part is that Morgan was front and center to witness the horror.

A heated body appears next to me as I grab onto the long steel handle of the fridge. That woodsy cologne, that shock of dark hair, hovers in the periphery of my vision. He presses his body against my back. I'd know that wall of Sheetrock anywhere—Morgan.

"Hey, beautiful," he whispers hot in my ear, and a series of shivers runs up my spine. Morgan warms his chest against my back as he dusts my neck with barely there kisses. "Let me get this for you." He whispers it hot over my skin, and I melt into him.

I twist in his arms and bury my face in the heat of his neck.

"Hey"—he smooths back my hair and a shiver runs through me—"it's okay."

"It's not okay. I'm a joke."

"You're not a joke, Ally. Not to anybody, least of all me."

I blink back tears and take him in—tall, dark, and inked beyond handsome. There's a sincerity in Morgan that I haven't found in anyone else—for sure not in Rutger.

"Thank you," I whisper.

He latches onto me with a tender gaze. Morgan Jordan exudes an inextinguishable fire from those steel-blue eyes. It makes everything in me quiver to have him.

His mouth edges in, ever so close to mine, and a breath gets caught in my throat at what might come next.

My lips part in anticipation. His granite-like chest presses tight against me as my thigh slips between his legs.

"You're welcome." He digs a smile into the side of his cheek.

I turn back around with a new sense of resolve and pluck a few beers from the fridge.

"You don't have to do that. They're assholes."

"It's not a big deal. It's just a couple of beers," I say, handing the bottles to Morgan. Before the oversized stainless door shuts, I spot a few iced coffees in the back. "Looky here," I say, snapping them up. "Looks like I get to play barista one last time."

"What do you mean, one last time?" His brows dip down in a V, and my panties beg to fall off in his presence.

"I was fired." I make a face. "It's safe to say it's been a pretty shit day all around."

Morgan wraps his arms around my waist and presses the sweetest kiss over my lips. He pulls back with his eyes rounding out as if to gauge whether or not it was okay. I pull him down and crash our lips together, and as I swipe my tongue softly over his, my insides ache to have him. A tiny moan gets locked in my throat and he gurgles out a laugh.

"You've got the best damn set of lips on the planet, you know that?" he whispers, tracing out my lips with his. "And as for Starbucks, it's their loss." He pulls back and his dimples press in deep as the ocean. Morgan has the power to melt me with just a barely there smile.

"You think so?"

"Yes, I think so. I think any employer would be happy to have you. In fact, a little bird told me there's a brand-new night-club opening soon and the owner needs a right-hand man, or in your case, woman."

"Really? That's so cool!"

"Really." He presses his lips together and eyes the coffee in my hands. "Now let's get you some glasses so you can serve those the right way."

Morgan pours the coffee into tall crystal goblets to better suit the bitch brigade. He carries out the beer, and I have the honor of giving Blair and Erica exactly what they deserve.

We enter the giant room, and I give a private smile over to Kendall.

"Brews for my bros." Morgan is quick to pass out the long-neck bottles.

"Here we go, girls!" Thankfully both Erica and Blair have paired themselves over a leather ottoman. "One for you and one for you!" I say, holding them up in tandem.

"Wow, Ally, you're so good at this." Blair openly mocks me. "It's like you were *born* to serve coffee."

Erica holds back a laugh. "You're impossibly talented."

"And you're both impossibly stupid," I say, dumping the goblets over their heads.

Blair and Erica leap up and scream as if a knifing just took place.

"You bitch!" Blair seethes, extending her arms as milky rivers drip from her fingers. "This is an eight-hundred-dollar dress!"

Erica brings her fingers to her lips. "You got that on sale?"

I don't wait for the Pretentious Princess to answer. Instead, I stride toward the door. This is the part where I probably should have an exit plan in place. I'm pretty sure walking back to the bed-and-breakfast in a pair of broken heels is a great way to abuse my feet.

"Ally, wait," Kendall calls after me.

"I'll get her." I hear Rutger call out. He appears by my side before I can reach the entry and pulls me back by the elbow. "What the fuck was that little stunt about?" His nostrils flare as he slams me against the wall.

"Let go." I snatch my arm back. "In the event you didn't notice, they made me feel like a cheap piece of trash."

"Way to go," he snipes. "Because you acted exactly like that." He slams my shoulders against the wall once again before he's plucked away rather violently.

Morgan lands his fist hard over Rutger's jaw, and I hear a distinctive pop over the murmur of the gathering crowd.

I bolt out the door and into the night.

I'm done with Rutger.

I'm done with pretending to be someone I'm not. There's no point. They saw right through me anyway.

Footsteps dash up from behind—Morgan strides up next to me, beaming that irresistible smile.

"Heard you needed a ride."

"You going to give it to me?" I give an impish grin. Somehow having Morgan by my side makes everything okay.

He wraps his arms around my waist and brushes a tender kiss just below my ear.

"I'll give you whatever you need for as long as you want it."

"Sounds almost too good to be true." I catch his gaze and hold it.

"Sometimes good things are true, Ally. And sometimes you find them in your own backyard."

My own backyard. I bite down over my lip at the prospect.

Morgan Jordan owns me in the worst way, and he knows it.

But we could never work.

Could we?

Morgan

We fly through the night, back to the house while Ally looks out the window dazed, most likely reliving the scene that just took place.

I let us in, and Ally is quick to pluck off her heels.

"You okay?" I ask, taking her in. Her gorgeous hair falls over her shoulder in perfect lemony waves; her breasts ripple from the low-cut dress that clings to the curves that bless her body.

"Of course I'm okay." She gives a sad smile. "You're with me." She motions me back toward the bedroom, and I dutifully follow. I'd ask if she's hungry, but don't want to throw a wrench in whatever she's got planned.

Ally tosses her purse in the corner of the room before switching off the lights. I kick the door shut and step in to her as the moonlight bleaches the walls a pale shade of grey.

"Why are you so nice to me?" she asks, picking up my hands and giving them a gentle swing.

"Because you deserve people to be nice to you. And, by the way, you're nice." A dark laugh rumbles through me. "The girls you dunked in java juice might beg to differ. But it's true. Their opinions don't matter anyway."

She wraps her hands around my waist and leads us back to the bed.

"Would you hold me tonight, Morgan?" Her voice sounds fragile, like she's just this side of tears.

"Your wish is my command." I peel my shirt off, hoping she'll want more than a quick embrace.

Ally glides up to the pillow and pulls back the sheets. I wrap my arms around her until we're spooning, and I brush her hair with my lips.

"When I was little"—she says, nestling her bottom into my stomach—"sometimes when things bothered me, my mom would hold me like this until I fell asleep."

"Mmm." I try not to let my disappointment shine through. I'm pretty sure putting me in the same category as her mom earned me a fuck-free evening. "That's nice."

"She made me feel safe like you do."

My heart swims when she says it. I want to make Ally feel safe, feel *loved*. That's exactly what I'm feeling for her, love. I wonder what Ally would do if she knew how I felt. I wonder if a lecture would follow on how two people like us could never truly experience that emotion together because we don't have enough dollar bills piled in the bank to back it. I hope what happened tonight opened her eyes—showed her that just because you have a few dollars to your name, doesn't mean you can buy a heart, empathy, compassion, or class. Who the hell treats someone the way they treated Ally tonight? Rutger is lucky if he didn't go home with a busted jaw. I might still arrange it if I didn't break it already.

"I always want to make you feel safe, Ally." I press a kiss in over her ear. "Tell me about your mom. What's she up to?"

"Wish I knew. She died when I was fifteen."

My body goes rigid. Shit. I hadn't even considered that option.

"I'm sorry." I tighten my grip around her waist and draw her in.

"No, it's okay. It was such a long time ago. That's right around when I let loose and sort of stepped out of my skin for a while. I spent every waking minute in the library up until then, and when she died I hit the party scene and never looked back." She lets out a sigh, hooking her leg around mine.

"That's got to be tough." Tears pool in my eyes, and I blink them away. "Tell me something about her."

She gives a hard sniff, and for a moment I wonder if I should have said anything.

"She was so wonderful. She had a smile that made you feel special. She had this amazing way to lift you out of any funk. The best part was she always knew the right thing to say." She jostles my arm. "Kind of like you."

A dull laugh rolls through me.

"Can I ask what happened?" I'm pretty sure it's painful to relive, but I get the feeling Ally wants to go there. And so do I. I want to know everything about Ally. I want to make all the hurt go away.

"Cancer. It was late in the game when we found out. She went pretty quickly." Her back shivers. "I wish you could have met her. She was pretty great." A ragged breath rattles from her chest. "Her name was Ruby."

Sadness vibrates through me like a tuning fork.

"Ruby," I say softly as I touch my cheek to hers.

"Ruby," she repeats quietly as if her ghost were right here in this room, and she didn't want to wake her.

"I'm sure she'd be proud of you." I pull her in until she's fully adhered to my body. I want to take all of the pain, the hurt, the rejection she's ever felt and make it go away.

"Maybe," she whispers before falling asleep in my arms.

I hold Ally all night long thinking of all the different ways I'd like to tell her how I feel. I'm pretty sure we've reached that bridge and I'm ready to cross it.

I hope she is too.

The next morning a stream of summer sunshine cuts through the curtains and rouses the two of us at an ungodly hour that actually still has the letters A.M. attached to it.

"You're still here," I marvel.

She rolls over and looks up at me with the touch of a sexy smile on her lips, her mascara slightly smeared.

"Was I supposed to go somewhere?" She spreads her warm fingers over my chest like a fan.

"Never." I bring her hand to my lips and kiss it. "You feeling better?"

"Of course I am." She presses a heated kiss over my mouth. "You always make me feel better. You're magic that way."

We cling onto one another for a very long time until Ally decides to hop in the shower, and I head off to make her breakfast.

Kendall is already at the table wearing nothing but an oversized T-shirt, her bare legs hiked up on the chair.

"Morning, sis." I stroll past her and pop open the fridge.

"You're chipper." She repositions herself until one of her legs kicks beneath her like a swing. "That was really nice of you to bring Ally home last night."

"Yeah, well, I don't like to see people get bullied." I pluck the eggs and bacon out and rummage through the cabinets for the frying pan.

"That's what makes you such a great knight in shining armor." She makes a face as if she is in full agreement with what just flew from her lips.

"What is it? Spill," I say, cracking egg after egg into the pan.

"Do you have feelings for her?"

"Yes." I shoot a quick glance down the hall.

"Do you think she has feelings for you?" Kendall looks at me with a level of concern I've never seen from her before.

I don't say anything right away. "Look at this face." I blink a smile. "How could she resist?"

"Morgan," she chides as if I should get serious.

"*Kenny*," I tease.

"Come on. Do you think she's just messing with you?" She jumps to her feet and scuttles over.

"Not unless you know something I don't. Look, we're pretty much no strings attached. And that's her thing, not mine."

Kendall wraps her arms around me and gives a brief hug.

"I just don't want to see my big brother get hurt, that's all. Summer will be over soon. School starts in just a few weeks— we both know you need to get back. And I don't want to see Ally get hurt either. Although, the entire time I've known her she hasn't really taken any guy seriously." Kendall looks up at me with a wide-eyed expression. "Do you think she's going to start with you?"

I gaze out the window at the pines that trail down as far as the eye can see and take a deep breath.

"God, I hope she starts with me."

7

YOU AND ME

Ally

The sun eludes Carrington this afternoon as a strangling mass of charcoal clouds streak across the sky. I stare at my in-box full of rejection letters, feeling like the dumbass I am for even putting myself in front of not-so-corporate America.

Kendall slides a cup of coffee over to me. "Any luck?"

"Three strikes, I'm out." I give a wry smile.

"Gosh, Ally, I'm so sorry." She hitches her glossy hair behind her ear, her eyes wide with shock, most likely because she finally sees that dark cloud hovering over my head. It's the same one that's been pissing over me since my mother died. "I'd offer you a job at the bed-and-breakfast, but we're strapped. Cruise is there now, trying to salvage what he can after that plumbing disaster. In fact, I'd better get going and join him."

"Don't worry about it." I flex a grim smile. "Something always seems to come up for me." Dell's stripper pole comes to mind like some giant stainless-steel erection. I don't dare tell Kendall I've got something to keep the financial cogs turning just a little bit longer.

"Hey, good looking." Morgan pops up from behind me and touches down a kiss on my cheek. His hair is still dripping wet from the shower, and he holds a strong soapy scent that makes me want to drag him back to the bedroom. There's nothing like a freshly scrubbed Morgan Jordan to start the day off right.

"Get a room." Kendall laughs as she heads down the hall.

"I can't afford a room," I whisper.

"What's going on?" Morgan leans over my shoulder and I snap the laptop shut.

"You up for a walk?"

Morgan is kind enough to make me breakfast before we take a stroll on the property. We follow the stream out as far as it'll let us before we even say a word. I feel good like this with Morgan—safe, comfortable.

"You're a master chef, you know that? And I'm not being sarcastic," I say. "You have a real way with bacon." I slide my shoulder against his, and he wraps an arm around my waist—easy and right.

"Yeah, well, I just did it so I could watch you eat."

"So that's what gets you going? The way I chew my food? Boy, you're easy to please." I give his chest a playful scratch as we take in the sharp scent of the pines.

"I don't think you could ever not please me." He lands a solid kiss on my forehead, and my muscles tense up. Little does Morgan know I specialize in letting people down. That's one job the universe will never fire me from—the CEO of disappointments. "I'm on tonight," I whisper. He knows I mean Pretty Girls. "It's going to be weird not having you there. You want me to talk to Dell?" I'm sure I could convince Tess to do a little persuading of the sexual variety or at least threaten to cut him off—either, or *both* if needed.

"Don't worry about it. Dell's an ass. He'll probably say no anyway. Besides"—he takes up my hand—"you couldn't keep me away if you tried."

His dimples dig in so deep I swear jumping into one would be like taking a cliff-side plunge.

"Good"—I squeeze him tight—"because Tess is giving me some serious pointers on the pole later, and I'd hate for you to miss the acrobatics. I'm sure the moves I'll be doing will be illegal in ten different states and quite possibly land me in traction."

"Ally Monroe engaging in illegal activity? I might have to conduct a citizen's arrest."

I belt out a laugh. "Right. I'm sure I'll fall on my head so that won't be necessary. Although, if you feel the need to play doctor again—I might be up for some of your alternative treatments. In fact, I feel a dull ache coming on that only you can cure."

"You won't fall, Ally. And if you do, I'll be there to catch you." Morgan pulls me in just as the sky darkens overhead.

The moment grows altogether serious as a light rain starts to fall.

"You're always there to catch me, Morgan. Why is that?" Maybe he'll say it—give me the words full strength, those very words I've longed to hear since my mother passed away, but that no one has said, not even Ruby.

"Because you fall a lot." He pulls his cheek to the side and his dimple winks at me.

"Are you always such a wise ass?" I press my chest against his and tip my neck back to look straight at him.

"I learned from the master. You have much to teach."

"You're welcome, grasshopper. I find my black belt in sarcasm is both cathartic and catty. What more can you ask for?" Plus it masks a thousand feelings. I like the mask. I like the way it bandages up the wound so the world can never see it.

"Yeah, well, sometimes things get serious." He leans in like he's about to kiss me, and pauses. Morgan locks his steel gaze over mine. "That's when you use heartfelt words to express how you really feel. Those are the important ones."

The rain falls in long, silver slats, cutting across our bodies sideways at an aggressive pace. It's so loud, as if someone turned up nature's volume all the way, stealing the moment from Morgan and me. And now, we'll never know what those important words were or who was going to say them first.

—⁓—

That night, at the Pretty Girls Gentlemen's Club, I hang out with Tess in the love shack she shares with Dell and his unholy harem while she teaches me the fine art of pole dancing. Tess said she had to pull a few "strings" so Dell would give me another chance at the club. I don't even want to know what the details of said "strings" were. I'm sure it involved a flesh exchange. And, considering Dell was at the receiving end, it more than makes me want to hurl. Speaking of the club, Morgan is there now, probably getting accosted by an entire bevy of underdressed girls. Not that I can blame them for trying to have their way with him. I just don't want them to.

"Make love to the pole, Ally," Tess commands as she jumps up onto it and points her toe toward heaven. "See how easy it is?" She twirls down with the grace of a ballerina.

"Nice." I go up and hop onto the metallic structure just the way Tess demonstrated and actually end up sticking until I slowly release and edge my way down in short staccato jerks. "Ha! That was easy." I flex my foot in the air, and land on my head with a thump.

"That's a great way to throw out your back." Tess claps her hands as if ordering me back on my feet. "Come on! Let's see that again."

I give it another go like a seasoned showgirl and jump on the pole as if it were Morgan. I caress its cool steel exterior and slide down with ease this time, finishing it off with a little twirl. It takes about a dozen more tries before I feel confident that I can tackle the phallic lightning rod in the big room, but I'm starting to get good vibes about the entire situation. Maybe this whole dancer thing will really work out for me? I mean, if Morgan's okay with me showing off my goods, minus providing services, I don't see what's wrong with turning a few bucks by way of my body.

"Look at you!" Tess beams with a streak of red lipstick smeared over her teeth. "You did it! I knew you were a natural. You're destined to knock 'em dead."

"Maybe I am. I got fired from Starbucks. And God knows I don't have enough to pay for my own place *and* books next semester. I'll have to take out a monster loan just to graduate." I sit on the floor with my back against the pole. "Worst of all—" I'm going to say it. I can feel it bubbling from my lips like a volcanic eruption. "I'm going to miss Morgan. He goes home in a few weeks. So there's that."

"Morgan?" Her face knots up in confusion. "Are you talking about that guy who gave you a ride?" She points in the direction of the club. "The *bouncer*?"

"Yes." I nod, shocked by her apparent dismissal. "The *bouncer*. He's nice. He makes me feel special, and safe—and I'm going to cry rivers and flood this whole damn place when he leaves." I press my lips together as tears make their appearance a little sooner than expected.

"Oh, honey!" She lands next to me soft as a whisper. "You love him, don't you?"

Love?

I shrug, still not sure she pegged the right emotion.

"I don't know." I take the tissue she's manufactured from thin air and blow my nose. "I'm not sure I've ever loved a boy before. I mean, how would I know? How does anyone know?" Is there some relational juxtaposition I'm supposed to conduct? Do I hold our relationship up to Kendall and Cruise's? Lauren and Cal's? God forbid I use Tess and Dell as a measuring stick, but if we're just passing time together, how are we any different?

Tess pulls me in. A faraway look takes over as she considers this.

"Oh, Ally. When you think of that person, and your heart is so full that you can't take it anymore, that's when you know," she says sweetly while brushing the hair from my forehead. "You'll want to spend every waking hour together, and he'll occupy your thoughts from sunup until sundown. There won't be anything you won't want to share with him. I think when all of those things fall in line, that's when you can really be sure you're in love." She presses a soft kiss over my temple.

"Thank you, Tess."

I think I'm already sure.

———

The club is filled to maximum capacity tonight as I peer from behind the thick velvet curtain. The smell of smoke and whiskey lights up the air as music pulsates from the speakers.

Tess convinced me to step into a pair of long white boots that crest my thighs, a metallic G-string with a bona fide chain that rubs me the wrong way, and a hot-pink bra encrusted with an illegal amount of rhinestones that bejewels my chest.

I'm on after Cinnamon and Spice—a duo that wows the crowd by indulging in one another's hips and lips.

Once they boogie on down into the crowd, Tess gives me a gentle shove.

"Remember—eye contact. Choose a customer and focus. Make him feel like the only man in the room. You've got this, girl!"

"I've got this," I repeat, stepping out onto the stage. I've been relegated to the dance floor since that first night I took a tumble. Well, it was mostly a self-imposed sanction. But tonight I'm conquering my fears, walking the catwalk like a big girl and rubbing up against some serious stainless steel. The pole catches my attention. It's not at all like the flimsy, thin stick Dell had installed in his living room. This one has the girth of a telephone pole.

My palms sweat at the sight of it. My stomach does a revolution, and it's only then that I remember I haven't eaten a thing since Morgan made breakfast.

Shit. This is totally throwing me off my game.

Okay, don't panic. A slight roll of nausea cycles through me.

The catcalls begin as the music slows to a ridiculous pace.

Choose your get.

I scan the crowd for a friendly face to latch onto until this fiasco passes but I have a hard time looking at any of them.

Then, buried in the haze, I see him—Morgan. He's got his hair slicked back. His T-shirt looks two sizes too small, causing his biceps to bulge like hillsides. His rippling abs contour through the fabric, and I smile, big and bright in his direction.

Morgan widens his grin. His dimples explode, taking my insides down with them.

Something deep inside me solidifies as I take him in. It's as if a spotlight had fallen over Morgan and assured me of everything I already knew deep down. My heart feels full, like it's ready to burst, and for damn sure I don't think I can take it anymore. Morgan locks eyes with me, and I'm mesmerized. He's everything I've ever wanted in a guy. And more than anything, I want to spend every waking hour with him. He occupies my thoughts from sunup until sundown. There isn't a thing in the world I don't want to share with Morgan Jordan.

Everything in me swims with relief. There's not a doubt in my mind—I'm in *love* with him, and I want the whole world to know it.

My hips swivel as I strut down the illuminated catwalk, ready to throw all caution to the wind and give everything up for the one I love.

I quickly approach the pole in all its vertical glory.

I take a running leap and land midway up with my leg wrapped around it for dear life. Holy shit! This is so not like the pole I spent hours perfecting my routine on. Again, I'm going to strangle Tess once I get backstage. Thoughts of Morgan flood to the forefront of my mind, and I mold my body over the pole as if it were the dark knight himself. Then something strange happens and my limbs contour over the iced steel. I release my upper body and fall backward, my hair sweeping over the platform below. It feels empowering, gratifying—dangerously sexy. I twirl my way down with my leg still pointed skyward.

I did it!

I bounce to my feet before strutting to the edge of the stage to do what I had planned on all night: swan-diving right into Morgan Jordan's arms. The crowd goes wild as I fall, weightless, light as a feather.

"Damn, you were hot." He lands a searing kiss right over my lips.

I hold him by the neck and moan into him. I never want this feeling to end.

"Thanks for catching me," I say breathless as I spring to my feet.

"Thanks for falling in the right direction." He gives a quick wink.

Kit is already on stage replicating my efforts on the pole, although she happens to look like a butterfly floating up and down its shaft. I doubt she'll be tumbling off stage anytime soon, by accident or on purpose.

I wrap my arms around Morgan and pull him in.

"There's something I have to tell you," I whisper.

"What's that?" He squints in an effort to make out what I'm saying over the blaring music. The thick cigarette smoke generates a toxic haze between us.

Just as I'm about to harness all of the power my vocal cords can muster, a strong pair of arms yank me away—Woody Bates.

"Hey, sugar." His breath creates a nuclear wind of liquid courage as it sears over my face. His eyes are partway closed, and he's drifting in a circular pattern, clearly wasted out of his mind.

"Hey, you." I try to play along while gently removing his roving appendages the way Tess taught me.

Morgan pops up over my shoulder.

"This guy giving you trouble?" he seethes.

"Nope, got it handled. I'll see you in a bit. I have a lot I want to say." I bite down over my lip a moment before reverting my attention to Woody. Then a thought comes to me. I've got the perfect revenge for Woody Bates's oddball behavior both on and off campus. It's called Operation Clean Out His Wallet one last time.

"So are you ready to party?" I swing my hips into his and his beady little eyes widen a notch. I glance back and Dell is speaking with Morgan, probably telling him not to catch flying girls. Dell's a moron that way.

I turn back to Woody. He and his banknotes are about to go down.

"I'm ready if you are." He slurs it out with a greasy smile.

I do a little private show, nothing too overtly sexual, just rotating my hips like a hula girl and holding out my hands with a smile, ready for an honest wage earned.

"It's payday, Woody," I say, glaring right at him. I'm tired of him getting all of the show and me getting none of the dough.

He licks his lips and breaks out in a smile that reeks of sexual elation. Woody wraps his arms around my bare waist and his fingers travel south making themselves at home in the crevice where my G-string resides.

"You can't do that!" I try to pluck him off, but his arms have rooted to me like a vine.

Morgan blows him backward onto the floor. He thrashes Woody around with the strength of a lion.

"God! He's going for the jugular!" I scream.

Morgan throws a couple of wild punches and Woody gets in a few good kicks to the nuts.

Shit! He's going to take a perfectly good Morgan Jordan and castrate him. This is all my fault.

The room lights up with screams. Woody's face bloats as bright as a cherry while Dell and the bartender try to stop Morgan from attaining a lengthy prison stay.

"Morgan," I scream as Tess comes and holds me by the shoulders.

I hate this.

Morgan gets up and holds his hands back as if he's leaving voluntarily. He gives Woody one last swift kick in the ass before turning to me.

"Are you okay?" he asks, cupping my face with his hands.

My insides melt as he examines me with such careful attention. Morgan sets my skin on fire when he looks at me this way.

"I'm fine," I say. "Are *you* okay is the question?" I dip my gaze to his Levi's.

"I'm more than okay now that he's not giving you a physical."

"He's just wasted. Woody's a goof." I wrap my arms around Morgan and help him along. He's hobbling, wincing with every other step, and it's safe to say Woody left his indelible footprint over his ball sack. I bet Woody was looking forward to crunching my boyfriend's jewels ever since the day Morgan added a new hump to his nose.

Did I just call Morgan my *boyfriend*?

Dell and Tess stomp their way over with stern looks.

"You know what this means, right?" Dell grits it through his chipped teeth.

"It means he's a hero." I glare at the two of them. They have a lot of audacity to bust his balls when clearly someone beat them to it.

Morgan groans as he leans against the wall. "You want to sign me up for your fight club?"

"*No*. It means take your white-trash ass the hell out of here and don't look back," Dell barks. "I don't want any more trouble at my club. And you're more trouble than I've had to deal with in years."

Morgan looks at me and offers an apologetic smile.

"That's it," I say, siding myself with Morgan. "He is neither trash nor trouble. You'd be *lucky* to have an ounce of what makes him tick." I stab my finger in Dell's scrawny chest. "It's you who's trash for not having the balls to tie yourself to one woman."

"Ally!" Tess tries to pull me back by the shoulder, but I yank myself free.

"It's true, Tess. You deserve someone who treats you better than this. Does he make your heart feel full? Do you think about Dell sunup until sundown? I seriously doubt it because he's too damn busy entertaining six other girls on the side." I revert my rage back where it belongs. "You're the one who's trash, Dell. You're nothing but trouble for leading my sister on. I hope she leaves you, and I hope this dive of yours tanks."

I whisk my way over to the lockers and throw my T-shirt on, tearing off the bejeweled bra like a magician through my sleeve. I jump into my sweats, freeing myself of the chastity belt chained to my ass, and step out of the overglorified waders.

"Let's get out of here," I say, taking up Morgan's hand and speeding us out the exit.

"Call me!" Tess waves after me as Morgan and I make our way into the dark, cool night.

"You were fantastic." He pulls me in and gives a sad smile.

"On the pole?"

"Nope. Just now, telling everyone how you really feel."

"I think that's exactly what I should do next." I take a breath. "Tell you how I really feel."

Morgan

Ally decides to wait until we're somewhere more memorable than the parking lot at Pretty Girls to clue me in on her feelings.

"Sounds romantic," I say, trying not to come off like some sarcastic douche. As soon as the *R* word sprung from my lips, a dopey grin lit up my face.

I can feel it coming. Tonight's the night. Ally is going to share her feelings and for damn sure I'm going to do the same. Although, I'm half afraid my feelings have evolved a little too quickly and the emotion that best describes them begins with an *L*. Ally is much more reserved. She's probably going to tell me she thinks I'm a "nice guy" for removing the parasite that attached himself to her body.

"So"—I start, unsure of how to do this—"you want to head to the beach?"

Her lips curve with devilish intent and she shakes her head.

"I was thinking . . ." It comes out breathy and my dick perks to attention in hope that the rest of her musings have a clear role for it. "We should just go home." She bats her lashes at me before biting down over her cherry-stained lip.

Hot damn. The entire fucking night just exploded with promise, sort of like my body is begging to do.

We hop in the truck, and I drive like I'm auditioning for NASCAR as I land us in front of Cruise's place in record time, only there's a car parked in my usual spot.

"Cal and Lauren are over." Ally chews on the inside of her cheek while rethinking the situation. "Let's just go in." She wrinkles her nose at me as if plan B is well under way.

"Suit yourself," I say as make our way inside.

All heads turn in our direction as soon as we step through the door.

I spot Cruise's little sister taking up real estate on the couch. Her bare legs are slung over the side, already parting like a promise.

Crap—just what I needed.

Molly delivers a lewd grin in my direction, and I pretend not to notice.

Kendall, Cruise, Cal, and Lauren are seated over at the kitchen table, locked in a heated poker game. The girls look bored out of their minds.

"You wanna play?" Kendall directs the question to me, but Ally's the one who shakes her head, refusing the offer. Kendall cuts a hard look to Cruise. "I told you we should have played truth or dare."

Ally rides her hands in the air and stretches. "I'm so exhausted. I think I'll just turn in for the night."

Every pair of eyes shifts in my direction as if expecting me to parrot her excuse.

"Where were you two?" Lauren develops a slight tick in her cheek as she takes me in with suspicion.

Ally says *beach* and I blurt out *movies*.

We exchange a private smile as the color rises to Ally's cheeks. Looks like I was right and she's still keeping the dancing gig under wraps for now.

The table seizes up with an unnatural silence. Molly's face contorts with hurt, as if Ally and I just announced we'd eloped.

"To a movie, then the beach." Ally shrugs it off as if it were the truth. "Now if you'll excuse me, I've got a mattress calling my name." She leans in. "I'll take a quick shower. I smell like someone put a cigarette out in my hair." She swipes the bottom of my chin before waltzing down the hall.

Lauren breaks out in a choir of *oohs* and *ahhs,* making me want to vacate the premises permanently. I should get my own place so Ally and I can shower in peace—preferably together. Then it hits me like a Mack truck. School starts in just a few weeks, clear across the country.

"Well, good night, folks." I start heading down the hall.

"Wait a minute, lover boy." Cal gets up and motions me over. He's got a wifebeater on, and his muscles bulge out like someone blew him up with a hose. "I need to talk to you outside a minute."

"Sure."

Molly licks her lips as I walk by, and I pretend not to notice. Molly is trouble. If ever there was a snake in the grass it's her.

Cal and I step out into the cool night air, shutting the door behind us.

"I thought about what you said." He gives a nod in the direction of the gym. "I'll let you have the place as long as you give me half."

"Half?" I balk. "I thought we agreed to twenty percent?" Shit. Cal is going to suck the life out of the club before it ever opens its doors.

"All right." He smooths his hand over his dome for a moment. "Look, I'll give you the good-guy discount. Forty percent but that's my last offer." His eyes bulge as if calling his bluff.

I'd love to sit out all night and negotiate, but I've got Ally ready and raring to go, with *feelings* no less.

"Forty percent." I seal the deal with a knuckle bump. Shit. I'll have to make sure to skim off the top. The last person I'm doing this for is good old Cal.

"So when's opening night?"

Seeing that both Ally and I are currently unemployed, "Tomorrow."

"What are you going to call it?" He slaps me on the shoulder as we head inside.

"Rock Bottom." The exact place my ass seems to land time after time.

But not tonight.

Tonight the only bottom I'll be landing on will be Ally's.

———

Lauren and Kendall are busy hugging out a long good-bye as I trek my way down to the bedroom. It's dark inside, just the way I like it.

I close the door behind me and lock it in the event someone loses their way to the restroom.

"Ally?" I whisper in hopes she didn't sneak out the back.

She slips something cool across my eyes and ties it from behind.

"Nice," I whisper. "It looks like we're kicking our dirty little secret up a notch tonight."

She giggles up a storm like it's the funniest thing on the planet and something about her laugh sounds buoyant, girlish. For damn sure Ally Monroe is the happiest girl in the world right now, and I'm about to take her on a sexual adventure that's going to make her a hell of a lot happier.

A brisk knock vibrates over the door.

"Go away!" I shout in an effort to make it loud and clear. "We don't want any."

Ally ignites in another giggle fit as she gropes her way down my body. She snatches my hand and leads me to the bed like the sultry vixen she is.

"I thought you said you wanted to talk?" I tease. It's clear to me Ally has rearranged the agenda to fall in my dick's favor. Although, something in me is dying to hear what she has to say. I'm hoping for the right words—the words that have the power to change everything. Those are the ones I'm planning to use. If I play my cards right, Ally and I could get to that place I've only heard about. *Love* wasn't exactly a word we kicked around growing up.

"Shh . . ." She presses a finger to my lips and takes off my T-shirt slowly and methodically. Her fingers fumble with my jeans like they've never been there before so I help out with the endeavor by hopping out of them and my boxers in record time. She runs her hands over my chest with enough pressure to claw right through me.

"Whoa. I see you like it rough." I pull her in by the back of her head, and her hair is dry. She must have skipped the dip. Can't say I blame her. There's nothing like cutting right to the chase.

She moans as I run my hand over her curves. She's got her sweats on, catching me off guard.

Her cool hands run down and grab ahold of my dick like she's getting ready to take a dog for a walk.

"Whoa, baby. It's not a leash," I whisper. "I got an idea." I touch my cheek to her head a moment. "Why don't you spill out the feelings like we planned, then I'll treat you to a night of loving that will brand itself over every single one of your tomorrows."

"Uh-uh." Ally leans in like a bear going after its prey and delivers a sloppy, heated kiss that makes me wonder if I'll need a life preserver to make it through the night.

"Okay, you want to play. I get it." I land a tender kiss to her forehead as we land soft on the mattress. I firm my arms around her and can't help but notice Ally feels lankier, more sinewy than usual. I'd mention it but I happen to know better than to focus on a girl's weight in bed. Ally is perfect, and I don't need her thinking she's not. "Tell you what. I won't give you any of this"—I grind my hard-on into her thigh—"until you give in and tell me exactly what you were going to say." I hate to admit that I'm dying to hear how she feels. Hell, I think I need to hear it. I want it, that's for sure.

Ally lets out a heavy sigh and turns over until we're spooning.

"Let's spill a few feelings," I whisper, tracing my fingers over the curve of her thigh and she quivers. "I want to watch you move beneath me. I want to help you with that little problem you're having." I give it as a heated whisper in her ear, and she groans as if she's already there. "I have things planned for your body that are illegal in forty-eight different countries." I tease her with a kiss over her neck but Ally doesn't say a word. "I want to bury myself inside you and stay there all night—all *year*." I give her shoulders a quick massage and she moans, deep and guttural. "Do you want that?"

"Mmm-hmm." It comes from her tight-lipped, but Ms. Monroe continues with the silent routine so I don't give in.

"Have it your way. I can hold out as long as you can." Not really, but it's worth a shot.

Ally grinds her bottom into me, and I pull her in tight.

"Change your mind, sweetie." I brush her hair with a kiss. "You can have all this and more."

But Ally doesn't change her mind. Instead, we fall asleep just as frustrated as when the night began.

———

In the morning a streak of Massachusetts sunshine cuts across my lids, annoying the hell out of me. I reach over and Ally's gone, nothing but wrinkled sheets left in her wake.

I don't really get what happened last night. She seemed adamant to tell me something when we left the club, then as soon as we hit the mattress she clammed up.

It takes all of my willpower to roll out of bed.

Maybe she changed her mind about me, or worse—whatever she was going to say last night wasn't the big deal I thought it was.

The strong smell of bacon emanates from the kitchen so naturally I migrate in that direction. Ally's reading at the table with her lids heavily hooded as if she had an equally lousy night's sleep.

"Morning, sunshine." I give a sideways grin because I think we both know it's not as great as it could have been.

Ally dips her nose back in her book without saying a word.

"Morning!" A high-pitched voice bleats from over by the stove. I glance up to find an overtly perky She-Elton wearing sweats and a severely undersized T-shirt.

"Molly?" I glance back at Ally for explanation, but she just continues to scowl into her novel. "Morning." I omit the word "good" because it doesn't feel genuine at the moment.

Kendall speeds over with a look of hellfire embedded in her eyes.

"You asshole!" she hisses in my ear.

"What the fuck?" I whisper, annoyed with my underdressed sister who took a page out of Molly's playbook and opted for the barely there T and not much else. I glance over at Ally and she's still in the same jeans and tank top from last night. Odd.

"You're lucky Cruise isn't here." Kendall's voice strains as if I'm in deep shit with the ringmaster who lays down the law in her bedroom. "When he finds out about this, he's going to kick your ass all the way back to Oregon. If you're smart you'll leave before he gets home."

"What?" I squint at her. She's all riled up about God knows what. "Did Cal tell you what I plan on doing?"

"You strategized this with *Cal*?" She gags as she tries to get her next sentence out. "It would figure." She stalks off and lands next to Ally at the table as if they've sided against me.

What the hell?

Molly heads over with a plate of eggs and bacon.

"There's enough for all of us," she sings. "Even you, *Ally*. I would never leave you out." Her lips pinch as if withholding a smile.

Ally shoots up like a bullet and heads to the sink so I follow.

"What's she doing here?" I don't remember Molly joining us at this early hour before and what's with the gloating?

"She spent the night." Ally cuts my balls off with her words. Her eyes are red as tomatoes and her face is blotchy, like she's been crying for hours.

"Hey, what's going on?" I go to wrap my arm around her and she jumps back, livid that I even tried. "Wait . . ." Everything in me freezes. "Where did Molly spend the night?" I whisper it so low I'm not sure she heard. "On the couch?" Please, God, let it be the couch.

"Nope." Ally presses out a depleted smile. "That's where *I* spent the night."

"Shit!" My hands gravitate to my temples as I spin into the sink.

"Everything okay?" Molly bounces her leg off her knee like a schoolgirl.

"Everything's great." Ally snarls it out like a war is about to erupt. "So"—Ally whispers without making eye contact with me—"did you enjoy yourself?"

"No, I did not *enjoy* myself." Fuck.

Ally huffs at my statement as if I've somehow managed to insult her in the process.

"We didn't do anything," I plead. A visual of Molly pulling on my dick like she was trying to pluck a carrot out of the ground comes to mind. Shit. "I told you—I mean *her*—to fill me in on all those feelings or there wouldn't be any action, and she opted for no action. And, for the record, I thought it was *you*."

"You *thought* it was me?" Ally bites down on her bottom lip and her features soften.

"*Yes*." I shoot her a wild-eyed look. "What the hell were you not doing in that bedroom last night?"

"Oh, so this is my fault?" She jabs a finger into her chest.

"No. That's not what I'm saying." Shit. "I'm not saying this is anybody's fault." Least of all mine.

"Oh, it's somebody's fault." She glares over at the sexual serpent in our midst. "I knocked but you said you were 'busy'— that you didn't *want* any."

"What the hell did you knock for?"

"Because it was *locked!*" Her lips tremble, and for a minute tears seem imminent. "Besides, I heard giggling and it sounded like a good time was being had by all. I thought maybe I missed some big cue and . . ."

She shakes her head, unable to finish her thought.

"Shit," I mutter. Kendall shoots spears of hatred at me from the table. Molly turns and openly licks her lips in my direction as if we were the real deal. Kendall busies her in conversation about school—about *high school,* no less. I bet good old Cruise will have the local authorities alerted once he finds out I almost banged his sister. "How do we get rid of her?" I fold my arms and lean into the sink while Molly scarfs down half the food by herself as if she's worked up an appetite.

Crap.

"Are you sure you didn't do anything?" Ally's lids hood over, and she looks hurt beyond repair.

"No. Thank God." I almost caved. I almost disregarded any constraints I may have placed on the two of us last night and bent her over the mattress. I bet that's what she wanted. Something tells me what Molly wants Molly gets, and last night I was at the top of her hit list. "Look, we need to talk." I say it low, so Molly doesn't jump on the offer. I'm so pissed. I have no intention of giving Molly another second of my time.

"I know you're talking about me." Molly averts her eyes as if this were high school. "Look"—she seethes in Ally's direction— "you're going to have to get used to seeing us together. This isn't something that's just going to go away. Morgan has feelings for me, and I have feelings for him. It's going to be Morgan and Molly in the end. Our names even sound good together." She says that last bit with an unexpected burst of enthusiasm.

Her phone vibrates and she snatches it up from the table.

"It's my mom. I gotta go." She hops over and dots my cheek with a kiss. "We can't tell her or she'll shit a brick. I'll catch you later, 'kay?" She skips all the way to the door.

Ally leans into me. "Sounds like you've got more than one dirty little secret."

I glance down at her. Her eyes are still burning from the pain I've inadvertently caused.

I have a feeling Molly's mom and brother are the least of my worries.

8

THE DO-OVER

Ally

Morgan is insistent on making everything up to me.

After the fiasco with Molly-the-Manhandling-Menace he took a scalding shower, which exuded steam well into the hallway for a half hour straight. Who knows what communicable diseases Molly has managed to collect now that her hormones have run amuck. Everybody knows high school is a petri dish of sexual plagues that are constantly mutating into treatment-resistant strains. I wouldn't be surprised at all if she was playing host to all sorts of hybrid STDs. It's becoming more than clear that she and Cruise are victim to some mutated genetic disorder that's marked them for a life of carnal catastrophes. I can hardly wait to see the power tools she'll amass before she's thirty.

Morgan gets dressed and comes back out to the living room, his eyes still filled with remorse. He has that dripping with hotness, fresh from the shower appeal, and instinctually my panties demand to fall off. Lucky for me I know better. What happened last night may have been an accident, but it still weighs on me like a lead coat.

He cups my face in his hands before bowing into a tender kiss.

"Ally, in no way am I remotely interested in Molly. I swear to you, you're all I think about." He traces my lips with his, warm and inviting. "You're all I need."

My insides quiver. A searing heat rips through the most intimate part of me, and I desperately want to drag him back into the bedroom, but I've yet to delouse the sheets.

Tears blue my vision, and I try to blink them away. An entire dam of words tries to break through my vocal cords at once.

"It's okay." He presses a finger tenderly over my lips and I kiss it. "You wanna take a ride?" he asks sweetly.

I press my lips together in hesitation because I know what's about to bubble out. "I'd go just about anywhere with you." It's true, and I can't seem to fight it.

We hop in his truck and take in the haze-filled day with the heat sealing over us like a blanket fresh from the dryer.

"If you don't mind"—Morgan ticks his head toward several bloated grocery bags in the backseat—"we're going to run a few errands real quick."

"What are the bags for? To hold the loot?" I wish. All those credit-card late fees are really adding up. Derek and his "liquor store runs" bolt through my mind and suddenly a first-degree robbery doesn't sound that unappealing.

"More like *create* the loot." He reaches back and hands me a bright-orange flyer that has all the appeal of a HAZMAT scene marker.

ROCK BOTTOM OVER-21 CLUB

GRAND OPENING *TONIGHT!*

$20 COVER

HALF OFF ALL DRINKS, *UNLIMITED*

"What the hell is this?" I study the map printed on the back until I realize I'm staring at the fitness front Cal uses to visually defile unsuspecting women. "The gym?" I over enunciate as I often do when I smell a poorly hatched scheme on the horizon. "You're never going to get people to pay this kind of cover."

"Of course we will." His dimples ignite as he gloats about said poorly hatched scheme.

"*We?*" I'm not sure whether I should be flattered or afraid. "Oh no."

"Oh yes. We'll run it together, side by side, from setup to cleanup. It'll be a joint venture." He glances over, clearly shocked by my resistance. "There are three universities and four junior colleges we can hit this afternoon."

"What?" I stare at him in disbelief. "I thought we were headed to some romantic getaway at the beach and all of a sudden we're opening a nightclub?" I squawk, staring down at my cutoffs and flip-flops with a newfound level of remorse. I wore the red string bikini that acts more as a nipple shield just to impress the hell out of his penis, although he sort of had me at "a joint venture."

"It'll be fun. I'll buy you lunch." He nods over at Johnny Burger's, and I'm quick to shoot him down. "Or, I can speed like hell, and we can get it over with quickly as possible."

The truck slides out from under us, and I smack him in the shoulder before he slows back down. Dell was right, Morgan Jordan is trouble. My cheeks flush just thinking about all the ways he's wrong for me and yet, a part of him has already settled in that sweet spot in my heart.

A stunted silence fills the space between us.

"I'm seeing Ruby in a few days," I whisper.

"That's great." Morgan looks over and gives a tender smile. "What's on the agenda? Mani, pedi—mall?"

"No, but that's an awesome lineup. You'd make a great dad."

"I don't know about that."

"I was thinking more movie and ice cream."

"Even better. I like a woman who's smarter than me."

Another beat of silence strokes by.

"Come on." He ticks his head to the side. "I set you up for a good one. Hit me with your best shot. I say, *I like a woman who's smarter than me* and you say—*that's not hard to find.*" He shakes his head. "I'm sure you could do better."

"No, I can't do better because I don't think it's true. You're one of the kindest, most intelligent, crafty"—I hold up the flyer as evidence—"guys I know. And I think you're damn good-looking to boot—so there. Theory refuted. Intelligence and hotness verified."

He looks over at me and studies me with serious intent.

"If you say so. You're the boss." His dimples dart in and out as if they agree. "So is that what you were going to tell me last night before we got interrupted?"

"Um . . ." I bite down on my lip. I'm pretty sure telling someone you love him for the first time shouldn't be done on the interstate when he's driving a robust twenty miles over the speed limit. "I'll hold off until all possibilities of vehicular homicide have been extinguished." Heat rises to my cheeks. It was sort of a lame thing to say in lieu of "I love you." "Besides, I don't want to think about what happened last night. What the hell kind of lunatic is Molly anyway?"

"She's determined, that's for sure."

"Spoiled little rich girl." I lean back into my seat.

"I don't know about that. Cruise doesn't exactly look like he's rolling in it."

"Okay, so she's just a spoiled little girl minus the rich. I don't really care what she is, but if she thinks she's going to pull another stunt like that she's got another think coming. I think it's time I have a little conversation with her." I'd better sharpen my claws first.

"Be careful." He twists his lips to the side. "I'm guessing Molly has a nasty sting that neither of us wants anything to do with."

I wish I could say it was Molly who had better be careful, but in all honesty, it's not like I'm going to pull her into some knock 'em down, drag it out catfight. I've always looked at her like some kid, not some boyfriend-stealing tramp. I cut a sideways glance at Morgan. I guess in a roundabout way he is my boyfriend. A wave of heat pulses over me at the idea. I haven't had a boyfriend in forever. Well, not unless you count Rory, and that was a federal catastrophe that an entire legal team could attest to. I shake the thought out of my mind. "Anyway, as far as Molly goes, I'll simply shoo her away and hope she finds another drop-dead gorgeous boy to sneak into bed with." I reach over and spin a soft circle over his knee. Morgan catches my hand and buries a kiss in my palm. "So you were really going to withhold that rock-hard body until I told you how I feel?" It comes from me weak, as if I regretted the words as they flew from my lips.

"I was and thankfully did." His eyes widen at what might have been if he didn't. "And, by the way, from now on we'll be conducting our dirty little secret with the lights on just to be safe."

"Duly noted." My insides burn at the thought of Morgan seeing me splayed out like that. I try to imagine Morgan watching me, expecting things that my body seems to have the inability to produce. A breath escapes me as the heated visual bounces through my mind.

Once we arrive in front of Garrison, Morgan takes a turn onto the side streets.

"You'll have to hit Greek row." I guide him until we land on the street with oversized boxy houses the size of apartment buildings. "So how do I do this?" I reach back and pick up a stack. "Do you want me to run up and ask if they want to come?"

"Nah. Here." He doubles the stack in my hands and pulls slowly in front of Alpha Sigma. We're just going to crop-dust the shit out of the neighborhood."

The flyers flutter from my hand like leaves in the fall. Morgan honks his way up and down the street until a crowd has amassed and people are scooping up the orange papers like they contain some nuclear doomsday warning.

I laugh as we hightail it out of there and head back onto the highway.

"Hey, you know what?" I say, startled by my own revelation. "If we can get a bunch of people to show up, we can make some serious money."

"That's what I'm talking about, baby." He holds out his hand, and I slap him some skin.

Money. The thought of having *any* sweeps over me like my own private summer.

"We could be sitting on a gold mine. I could pay off my credit cards, and even buy a few books next semester." A breath gets caught in my throat. "You think we can move out on our own?" Even if it were temporary, it'd be amazing to be alone with Morgan.

"Gee, I don't know if Mom and Dad will let us." He jostles my knee and a line of fire rips up my thigh from his simple touch. "That's the plan, girl." He touches his finger to my cheek. "That is the plan."

I take him in. Mr. Gorgeous, Mr. All-Around Perfect—and I do believe Morgan Jordan is my Mr. Right.

"Thank you," I say a little quieter than necessary.

And, later tonight, I plan on thanking him in an entire catalog of unforgettable ways.

We spend all afternoon littering the neighborhoods of anyone we think might be a potential customer to our new joint venture that involves dancing and debauchery. And unfortunately, much of the evening is spent maxing out Morgan's credit cards while driving down the inventory of every liquor store in a ten-mile radius.

By the time the club opens at 10 P.M., we've gone home and changed. I'm in my requisite or, more to the point, one and only little black dress, and Morgan is in his usual uniform of jeans and a T-shirt. But, I must say, Morgan Jordan glows hotter than a firebrand with his hair slicked back, the shadow of stubble on his face, and those electric-blue eyes that seem to be backlit. I can feel a serious meltdown taking place in my panties, and I'm pretty sure he'd solve my problems in the pleasure domain, right here if I wanted.

He sears me with a heated kiss and my insides quiver. Morgan holds the scent of soap and mouthwash, his high-octane cologne that has the ability to intoxicate me all on its own.

"You ready to do this?" he shouts above the music streaming from the speakers he's deposited all over the place—another hit to his seemingly bottomless credit card.

Cal is out front collecting the cover charge, and already there's a steady stream of bodies filtering in.

"I think we're already doing it." I bite down on a smile as I run my fingers over his bristled cheek, the hard curve of his neck. I look around at the basement with its strange low lighting, the bar tucked in the corner, and not much else other than a span of space that opens up to a few rooms off the back. "Do you know how to tend bar? Because if you're counting on me to do it, the only things we'll be serving are wine coolers and beer."

"It's Steven's day off." He winks.

"Steven?" Then it hits me. Steven is the bartender from Pretty Girls. "Dell is *so* going to kill you." And perhaps me in the process.

"For that? I doubt it." He shakes his head and nods toward the entrance as bodies begin streaming in. "But for *that*, just maybe."

I turn back and gasp. Six girls from the Gentlemen's Club stride in with their five-inch FM heels, and their questionable attire, which is definitely not intended as street wear, and for damn sure shouldn't be legal.

"This way, ladies." He herds them over before leaning into me. "It's for the Exotic Room. Unlike some people, I don't charge a house fee. They keep every dime they make. It's win-win all the way around."

"Exotic Room?" It gulps from me like the civil offense it's panning out to be. Shit. Something tells me everything about this place is going to be replete with illegal escapades in less than ten minutes. "We are all *so* going to fry!"

"Relax." Morgan rubs my shoulders and peppers the side of my face with kisses. "It'll be okay. I've got it all handled."

Every muscle in my body freezes when he says those words. I swear he just repeated verbatim the exact words Rory whispered the last fated night of his freedom.

"Handled?" I cock my head, expecting a full explanation.

"I promise you we're not breaking the law." His lips press into a line. "We might be skirting it—but trust me, it's not a big deal."

Skirting?

"This is temporary," he continues. "It's not like we're setting up shop for years. Let me get these ladies settled, and I'll be back." He dots my lips with a kiss before speeding the small harem down the hall.

Shit, shit, *shit*!

Lauren strides over with a spring in her step. "This is freaking fantastic!"

"You think?" I pan the vicinity, half-afraid I'll spot ten different felonies in the making. I'm pretty sure Ruby won't be allowed to visit me in the big house, where I will be sporting an orange jumpsuit—two fashion blunders that are a punishment unto themselves.

"Loosen up, would you?" Her overglossed lips widen into a cherry-stained grin. "Cal says you've already raked in *two* grand. If they keep coming in like this you're looking at a small fortune. He's just pissed he didn't think of it."

"Two grand? I didn't hear a thing after that but who the hell cares, because two freaking grand!"

A pair of arms circle my waist, and a warm kiss heats my neck. I turn to find Morgan wearing his deliciously wicked grin, sans the bevy of strippers he's solicited for the night.

"I'll be in the middle of a winning poker hand if you need me," he growls hot and sexy into my ear.

"Poker?" My stomach explodes in a vat of acid. The felonies are quickly piling up to the ceiling, and I've moved well past wondering *if* we'll be detained by law enforcement to *when*. "Good luck?" I don't know whether to be ticked or proud that he's thrown in some illegal gambling for good measure. If we're going down it might as well be in a brilliant shock of flames. "If you win big I'll reward you." I crush my lips against his and plunge my tongue into his mouth like an assurance of things to come, hopefully me.

"I've already won big. I've got you, don't I?" Morgan dots my lips with a kiss before melting back into the crowd.

"Well, *hello*?" Lauren teases. "Things are really heating up between the two of you." Her demeanor changes on a dime and suddenly she looks horrified. "Don't fall too far, too fast. He's Oregon-bound in just a couple of weeks. Remember?"

Crap. I do remember. I was just doing an excellent job of pushing it to the back of my mind.

That horrible feeling of foreboding takes over once again, and my heart plummets through the floor, straight to middle earth. I hate the thought of Morgan taking off for greener scholastic pastures sooner than later.

"Right." I try to shake it off. "We're just messing around. Nothing too serious."

Stupid, stupid Oregon for being on the other side of the fucking country. Maybe we'll have one of those long-distance relationships? We can Skype and everything. Or maybe I can move to Oregon? But that's too far from Ruby. Stupid Massachusetts for being so damn far from the West Coast.

Then, quick as a blade, reality sets in. A god like Morgan Jordan needs a warm body next to his at night, or at least he deserves it, and I won't be anywhere near the vicinity.

"Oh, no." Lauren looks like she's about to be sick. "Ally!" She doesn't bother to hide the fact she's über disappointed in me and my man-lust for all things Morgan.

Kendall steps up, looking like a knockout with her long, dark tresses perfectly framing her face and her blue eyes shining bright as her brother's. My insides pinch. Once Morgan leaves I'll have a hard time being near Kendall in general.

"What's going on?" Kendall looks to Lauren for answers.

"She's fallen in love with your brother, and now she's contemplating whether or not a long-distance relationship will ever work out."

"You always know what I'm thinking." I mean for it to come out far more sarcastic than it does.

"I can read your mind," she assures. "Besides, the answer is no. Long-distance relationships never work out. Look at me and Cal. He started to get wishy-washy once he graduated, and he was less than a few blocks away. Face it, men need leashes, and they don't make them that long."

Shit. Lauren is always right. I seriously hate that about her.

"Do you really feel that way about Morgy?" Kendall touches her chest as if I've delivered a lethal blow.

"*Yes.*" My eyes widen with panic because for one, I haven't shared this little tidbit with "Morgy" yet. "I'm in love with him. There, I said it. But it's totally your fault." I drill a finger in Kendall's pillowy chest. "You practically pushed us together. You *knew* he couldn't sleep on the couch. That could have ruined his entire baseball career." I chew on the inside of my cheek in the event other ludicrous theories on how Morgan

Jordan's penis happened to find its way into my vagina decide to pop out.

"He *is* gorgeous." Lauren shrugs, as if consoling me on some level.

"And he's generous to a fault," Kendall adds.

"Is he good in bed?" Lauren is ready and willing to get the sexual lowdown right here in front of four hundred of our closest friends.

"We are so not going there." Kendall slaps her hands over her ears to avert the sibling-based trauma.

"Oh, look," Lauren says, giving Kendall a shove into the crowd. "I think I see Cruise, and he's got a new toy just for you! It buzzes, and vibrates, and glows in the dark, oh my!"

Lucky for Kendall that Cruise—the Wizard of *Ahhs*—is there, albeit sans the sex toy.

With Kendall out of the way, Lauren digs in. "Dish!" Her eyes get all wide and swirly like a pair of pinwheels at the prospect of titillating details. "Did he help you solve your *problem?*" She drags out the word *problem* like it's code for something, and we both know it is.

I sigh and my entire body sags at the thought of even verbalizing my sexual faux pas.

"He didn't?" She shrieks over the music. "Are you sure? Have you *seen* him? *My* underwear melt each time he walks in the room. Geez, Ally, you have some serious issues."

I open my mouth to let her know I'm just about ready to resolve them once and for all when I spot Molly and Blair by the entrance.

"What are they doing here?"

"Who cares?" Lauren says, maneuvering me toward the bar. "They just gave you forty bucks."

"Maybe I can turn around and hire a hit on Blair with the money."

"She's not in your league, Ally. Morgan is all yours. Trust me, I've seen the way he looks at you. If I didn't know better I'd swear that boy was in love."

Morgan, in love? With *me*?

A fire spreads through my body at the thought of Morgan feeling that way.

This is huge. If he feels for me anything close to what I'm starting to feel for him—what I've *felt* for him, deep down inside, right from the beginning—then we could have something spectacular in store for the two of us.

Too bad fall semester is breathing down our necks. Too bad Oregon is about as far away as you can get from Massachusetts in this country.

Damn it all to hell, why did I have to fall so hard, so fast?

Morgan

"Eight fucking thousand dollars—*profit*," I say while driving Ally to the most extravagant hotel Carrington has to offer, and for damn sure it's not at the Elton House wade-through-your-own-shit-because-I-can't-fix-the-plumbing Bed and Breakfast. Nope. This place is about as far away from Calamity Cruise as you can get. I checked it out on the Internet before reserving the room this afternoon—a honeymoon suite that overlooks the water.

"Eight grand?" Ally grips her throat like she might choke herself to death. "And what are we doing *here?*" She leans out the window, and takes in the elegant building lit up like a woman in a glittering dress.

"*We* can do anything we like." Considering it's three-thirty in the morning, I'm betting sleep is a high probability, but my dick is amped and severely hopeful that it too can find a nice warm place to stay. "Remember, the money got split with Cal. But we still got forty-eight hundred and he took thirty-two. Twenty-four hundred for each of us, sound good?"

"Sounds *too* good." She licks her lips like a promise as we get out of the truck.

It's cool out, unnaturally quiet here compared to the riot streaming out of control back at the club. The place looked like shit when we left, and the liquor sold out an hour before closing. Those alone are pretty good signs of things to come, but for now the only thing I want to come is Ally.

We take the elevator up and it opens with a quiet whoosh to a well-carpeted floor that deafens me with its silence as we step into the hall.

"Last room on the right." I press a kiss in just under her neck. She holds the scent of strawberries, and her neck tastes like cotton candy. Every last part of me is dying to devour her.

"God, it feels like prom." She giggles a little too long, and I can easily surmise she has a few good drinks under her belt—not so much that she can't walk a line but just enough to have fun.

I let us into the palatial suite, and Ally sucks in an audible breath at the luxurious accommodations I managed to score. I opted for the full honeymoon package, which included enough candles to burn down half the state, not to mention an explosion of red and pink flower petals. Looks like those pricy rose grenades I threw in as an impulse buy went off as planned.

"Oh my God!" She tosses down her purse and runs to the oversized bed with petals strewn over it in the shape of a heart. She tosses a handful in the air and petals rise around her like confetti. I want to remember her this way, beautiful, happier than I've ever seen her, with flowers magically floating around her.

A wall of windows with a view of the Atlantic extends in front of the bed. I'm looking forward to seeing the view in the morning while holding Ally in my arms.

"We don't have to do anything you don't want." I stride over and dot a kiss on her forehead. "We can crash if that's what you're up for. Or, we can pick up where we left off last night and see where words can take us."

"I'd like that," she whispers, pressing into me. Her heart races out of control, palpating over my chest like a promise of things to come, hopefully her. "I mean, I like that second part." She glances down a moment. "I have a confession to make."

I swallow hard. I've always felt there was something she's been holding back, something lurking just beneath the surface, but I didn't think she'd give it as bonus material in the heart-to-heart we're about to have.

"The things I'm going to say"—she gives a series of rapid blinks as if fighting back tears—"I've never said to any other guy before. I've never wanted to."

I ride my hands up over her back until our stomachs press tight, and my lips curve because I like where she's going.

"Morgan"—she strengthens her grip around my waist—"ever since I laid eyes on you, that first night, you've had this strange power over my world. In the beginning, you annoyed the living hell out of me, but I soon forgave you because—you were a force to be reckoned with beneath the sheets."

I tuck a hellish smile into the side of my cheek.

"And now . . ." She hikes her shoulders up to her chin and holds them there. Her eyes sparkle in this dim light like shards of broken glass. Ally is so damn beautiful I can't help but openly stare. "You're all I can think about. I don't think I've met a single guy who's showered me with so much careful attention, so much kindness, and, well—love." She lowers her gaze a moment. "Which brings me to my next point. Morgan"—her eyes bear into mine as if she's just had a tragic realization—"I've fallen in love with you."

A groan of approval vibrates through me as I peel a heated kiss off her lips.

"I love you too, Ally Monroe. Swear to God you're all I think about. Just being near you drives me insane."

"You love me?"

She says it so sweetly, seemingly amazed that anyone could feel that way about her. A part of me hurts just hearing her ask the question.

"Yes." I can barely push the word out. "You're beautiful, both inside and out. You hold the world in your eyes when you smile—the entire universe is brighter because you're in it. And, I swear to you, I've never said those words to another woman, not even my mother." I huff a quiet laugh. "We weren't too quick to throw the *L* word around the house growing up." I take in a breath and hold it before I drill my point home. "You're special, Ally. And there's no one for me but you."

Her mouth falls open and she runs her fingers through my hair, looking at me as if seeing me for the very first time.

"Morgan." She hums my name over her lips and my insides quake.

My mouth covers hers with a heated explosion, and our tongues meet up in a wrestling match that fires up my hard-on with a bionic blast.

Ally gives a gentle tug at my shirt before pulling it off alarmingly slowly, as if she were teasing me. I let her fingers reach down to my buckle, and she works her magic until my jeans fall to the floor. I step out of them and pull off her dress, watching her body as it stretches to the ceiling. I take her in with her sexy-as-hell lace bra, memorizing her beauty.

"You're amazing," I say, gliding my hands over her hips, dipping my fingers in the lip of her underwear. I lean my head back a moment. It takes everything in me not to turn the party into overdrive and attack her, animal-style.

Ally pulls me down by the neck and kisses me as if her life depended on it—deep-throated, aggressive kisses that assure me sleep is nowhere on the agenda tonight. She swipes her tongue over mine and moans as if doing that alone would be enough for now and forever. Her fingers tug at my boxers until they're history, and I implement a little trick I learned in high school, causing her bra to fly off her body and shoot clear across the room like a rubber band.

"*Morgan.*" The smile on her face says she's clearly impressed, but I'm about to excite Ms. Monroe in far more interesting ways with my tongue.

I bend over to retrieve a condom from my jeans and have a change of plans. "While I'm down here." I press out a dry grin as I drop to my knees and venerate her beauty as she hovers above.

Her jaw goes slack. She's about to protest, but I flex her panties down past her thighs before she can put up a fight.

"House rules." I run my hands from her ankles to her thighs in one fell swoop. I press a kiss in just under her belly and trail on down until I hit her moist, wet slick and she gasps. "Ladies first tonight."

She shakes her head just barely as I plunge a finger deep inside her.

Her neck arches back and her breathing becomes erratic as if she were already there. If nothing happens for her tonight I'm going to have to turn in my man card.

Damn, I want to watch. I touch my thumb to her pleasure zone, and Ally bucks as if I've just lit the fuse.

"There you go," I whisper, my heart jackhammering out of my chest as if it wanted to witness the event itself. "Let's finish you off, girl. Open for me," I command as I gently guide her thighs apart. I wrap my arms around her legs and cover her with my mouth.

Oh shit. She's so fucking sweet—so fucking wet I'd be a lunatic not to have her like this every single night.

Ally grabs ahold of my hair and gives a hard tug, letting me know things are moving in the right direction. I ride my tongue over her—roll her sweet flesh around in my mouth while savoring this moment for later. I ride her faster, stronger until it feels as if I'm about to swallow her whole.

"*Morgan.*" She lets out a series of elongated gasps and scratches the hell out of my scalp in the process. Ally trembles above me, a strangled cry escaping her throat. I keep at it long after her knees lock together and she tries to pry me off. Ally jumps back and falls on the bed in exhaustion.

I crawl up and pull her over me.

"Was that good?" I wrap her legs around me and hold her tight.

"Better than good." She gives a little laugh. "I've never had that happen before."

"Standing up?" I dip my tongue in her mouth so she can taste how sweet she is.

"Gross." She laughs. "And no, the event in general."

"*The* event?" I pull back to get a better look at her.

"Yes, the *main* event." She lowers her lids as if she's embarrassed by the fact. "I was an orgasm virgin, well on my way to the Guinness books, and you rudely derailed my world record.

Now I'll forever be after you to repeat the effort." She runs her fingers through my hair and slips a kiss over each of my eyelids.

"Repeat the effort, I will." I run my hand down her back and glide over to my favorite spot until I feel her wet slick overflow like a fountain.

"Except not now." She cinches her legs again. "Right now, I want to return the favor." Her lips curl to the side. "I wish I knew of something outrageous to do to your body to really make your head spin. I'm sort of low on tricks and treats."

"You're all the treat I need."

Ally slides down my body and runs her finger along the entire length of my dick, and I want to scream because her touch alone has the power to drive me insane. Her warm breath falls over my cock, and I tense with anticipation.

She covers me with her mouth and rides me up and down, wrenching a groan from my gut that aches for miles. Her hair splays over my body, and I reach down and grip my fingers into the length of it. Ally glides a hand around my balls and massages me into a pitch-perfect nirvana. My enthusiasm for her efforts is about to explode in a biological fucking good way.

"Holy shit," I hiss, tipping my head back for a moment. It hasn't even been a minute and I'm ready to blow sky high from the insanity she's inspired. "Ally." I try to pull her off but she won't relent. "Ally, you can stop." I snatch the condom up and tear it open with my teeth. I pull back and put it on before rolling her onto her back. "This is what I want," I pant as I climb over her. "I want you. I want to be inside you."

She gives a little grin as she calls me down with her curled finger. Ally grabs ahold of me and guides me in.

"Morgan." She gives it in a heated whisper.

"I'm right here, babe." I singe her lips with a kiss. "Do you want this?" I ask as I press into her body. She lets out a groan that's far more effective than words.

"Yes," she whispers. "I want this." She looks up at me with those lawn-green eyes. "I want *us*."

Us. And there it is. Ally wants us. If she wants us as much as I do, I'd say we're in a really good place, at least until fall rolls around, but I'm not giving that buzz kill another single thought. Nope. Instead I press in and my dick throbs from pleasure. "You're so fucking tight." The words tremble out of me. I push in deep inside of her and watch as her lips part in ecstasy. Her eyelids flutter as I glide in and out, slow and easy, as if I were trying to kill us both from anticipation. "I love you so much it hurts," I whisper in her ear as I lose myself in the assault.

It hurts to love her because in a few short weeks this very simple act will be near impossible to replicate. I reach down and lash my tongue over her neck, riding it in one hot slick all the way to her ear. Ally writhes beneath me. Her hips press in against mine as if she's coming along for the ride.

I heave over her in a fit of delirium. There's no way in hell I can ever leave Ally. She needs me, and I need her in the worst fucking way.

I peak deep inside her body and tremble in a perfect moment that turns this bed, this entire damn hotel into the type of paradise I've only dreamed about. I don't think I've ever felt this impossibly satisfied before. I think those three magic words took us to a whole new level that neither of us expected.

"That was great," she bleats as I collapse over her.

"That was fucking fantastic," I pant.

Nope. I can't leave Ally Monroe.

We're going to make this work. I can feel it.

I just haven't figured out how.

———

A splash of uninvited sunshine penetrates the honeymoon suite where Ally and I unofficially moved our Facebook status to "in a relationship."

I groan and pull the sheets up over our heads.

"You're still here." I say it groggily, trying to sound sarcastic, but it comes out just this side of an insult.

"You sound disappointed, Mr. Jordan." Ally glows like a soft peach as she gives an impish grin. Her mascara is smudged to the point of igniting another boner in me before I have the chance to stretch into a new day.

"Nope, not disappointed. It's just this is the part where you usually morph into Molly."

She gives a playful slap to my chest as she laughs. Ally rips the sheet off of us in the event I was having difficulty identifying her.

"But I'm glad you're you." I pull her in tightly and land a playful kiss over her lips. My hands ride lower between her thighs until my fingers land in the warmth of her body. Ally bends her neck back. Her mouth opens with a gasp.

Her hair is wet, and tiny beads of water run down her back.

"You took a shower?" I dip my hand between her legs, working my thumb over her slick folds until she groans.

"Had to." She pants, brushing over my ear with her teeth. "You defiled me."

"Trying to show me up in the hygiene department?" I run my hand up until I'm cupping her soft tit. I dip down and land my mouth on her quivering flesh, running my tongue over her sugared nipple until she's nice and hard. "I'm going to bite you." I graze her with my teeth and pull at her until she's stretched beneath me at least an inch.

"Ouch," she says softly. "And, oddly, it kind of feels good."

"I think you're going to like all the ways I plan on hurting you." I gently flip her onto her stomach and ride my finger down her backside before slowly inserting it into her bottom. She's so tight, I'm pretty sure there's no hope of my plan taking flight.

"Out, *now.*" She says it sternly, like she might rip my balls off if I don't comply. She turns her head slightly to look at me. "That's a no-fly zone, buddy."

"Got it." I prop her up on her knees and take a seat behind her to enjoy the view. Ally's pink folds glisten in the morning light, calling out to me like candy.

"What now?" She sounds less than slightly amused.

"I'm in the mood for breakfast." I land a soft kiss over the most intimate part of her, and her body writhes with pleasure. I raise her even higher and indulge in another series of clean sweeps with my tongue that leave her audibly moaning like a dove. "Is this a no-fly zone, Ally?" I plunge my tongue deep inside her, and she lets out a strangled cry. "Do you like this?" I glance over at her with her lips scraping against the pillow as if she were in pain. "I can't hear you." I touch my lips to her moist flesh and she flexes as if she's just about there. "I can hold out like this all day if you want. What's the magic word, Ally?"

"Please," she whispers into the pillow.

I trace my lips over her thighs. "I'm sorry. I didn't hear you."

"Yes, dammit, *please.*" She gives a hard twist, and I almost drop her. I land her softly on the bed and turn her around—the look of disappointment rife on her face.

ADDISON MOORE

"You *did* say please." I give a wicked grin as I push her knees apart and swim down toward her thighs once again. "Get up on your elbows." I instruct and she's quick to comply; her chest rises and falls like a catastrophic event is about to unfold. "You're going to watch, Ally. And if you don't, I'm going to enter the no-fly zone, and I'm betting you'll like it."

"Right." She squints as if calling out my bluff. "You need safe words for places like that, and we don't even have a safe word," she says, looking cute as hell, and it takes everything in me not to laugh.

"The safe word is *faster.*"

"Faster?" Her eyes widen. "That doesn't sound like a safe word."

"No it doesn't, so I suggest you do as you're told." I dip my mouth down over her belly, dropping down past her soft curls before hitting the slick I've been craving to get back to. I glance up and her eyes enlarge as if shocked to see me. My tongue finds a home over her, and I roll her around in my mouth, never wanting to stop. Her hips swivel as she moans with a satisfying rhythm.

I glance up and she's right there at full attention, unable to take her eyes off mine.

"Faster?" I ask, holding back a smile.

"Faster?" She looks perplexed. "No, *no*, not faster." She intensifies her gaze just this side of a glare. "Jordan, you are going to pay for this."

"I hope so." I push in with a heated kiss before flicking my tongue over her until she lets out a scream that sounds like an entire choir has been waiting to erupt from her vocal cords since the beginning of time.

"Morgan." She groans, putting me in a headlock with her knees.

She turns to the side, and I swim up beside her.

"You did good." I melt a kiss over her lips and die a little.

Ally Monroe.

The breakfast of champions.

9

ROCK BOTTOM

Ally

To say that Morgan and I have taken flight on a shooting star that burns with passion would be propagating a lie. We are so much more than that, bolstering ourselves higher and higher, and for sure neither of us ever wants to come back down to earth.

On Thursday night, Rock Bottom is pumping like a hot New York nightclub that people actually fly in to visit. Morgan tried to lure me back to the honeymoon suite the last few nights, but I assured him I'd rather save the money and give Kendall and Cruise a run for theirs. Suffice it to say, we've tested the mattress springs back at the cabin and created our own heartbeat into the night with the clatter of the headboard.

I'm chatting it up with Steven at the bar when I spot Tess barreling toward me, her blonde hair whipping through the establishment like a flame.

"Here we go," I whisper. This can't be good.

"Well, hello there, *sis!*" She says it with a bitchy smile on her face like she's about to impale me with one of the whiskey bottles within reach. I scuttle away from the bar. "Leaving so soon? Aren't you going to give me a warm welcome? Perhaps a guided tour?" Her eyes widen as she pulls me in by the elbow.

"Kit was nice enough to let me in on your little secret when I asked why we had eight different girls call in sick on the same night."

"Eight?" I press my lips together because I know I've got a lot of explaining to do.

Her gaze wanders for a moment as she squints over at the bartender himself.

"Steven?" She screeches it out in a fit of disbelief. "What have you done, Ally?" Tess clamps her hands to her hips as she sweeps the room with an interrogating gaze. "Oh, hon, Dell is going to *kill* you. And I mean that literally. You need to stop right this minute and send everybody back to Pretty Girls where they belong."

"This isn't a hostage situation, Tess. They're here because the pay is better. Plus there's no house fee."

Her mouth drops to the floor, and for a moment I think she's considering her options.

"Look, I'm warning you, Dell isn't going to sit around with his thumb up his ass once he finds out what's happening here."

"Please don't tell." An image of her moronic boyfriend mowing Morgan down with his Camaro bounces through my mind. "Morgan is leaving soon. His mom's wedding is next weekend. It'd be sacrilegious to slaughter him before then."

"Relax, I'm not telling, Ally." She rolls her eyes at the idea. "Dell's got his ways of finding out on his own. Believe me, that man knows everything. And if *you* know what's good for you, you'll leave town right along with your newfound boy toy." She pulls me in gently by the neck and sighs. "Are we still on for Ruby's birthday?"

"Of course." I shake my head at her. "I'd never deny you that. You and Ruby are the only real family I have." I hate to relegate Derek to the realm of distant other, but he sort of did that to himself when he harvested his own pharmaceuticals. Of course, Morgan feels like family too.

She leans in and presses a tender kiss just above my cheek.

"Be careful, okay?" Her blonde locks are swept to one side, hiding her eye in a sexy way. I wish to God Tess wasn't chained to Dell like some kind of explosive device. Too bad she can't see he's ready to blow and take her with him. "I love you, sweetie."

My heart thumps unnaturally when she says those words. I don't believe Tess and I have ever said *I love you* to one another.

"I love you too, Tess." I pull her in and offer a death grip of a hug. Something huge is about to happen in our lives, but I can't pinpoint what. I just hope somehow we both get our happy endings.

Tess runs out of the club as if it were on fire, and I shudder thinking about her cryptic words. If Dell finds out, both Morgan and I will have a demon by the tail.

"Hey, bitch." A female voice booms as she twists me around by the elbow. It's Molly. Her lipstick is smeared, and her hair looks as if she's been dancing on her head all night. "I heard you've been screwing around with my boyfriend."

"And who would that be?" God, she's tanked. Where's Cruise when you need him?

A hard slap ignites over my cheek, and I feel the sting long after she's distributed it.

I touch my fingers to my numb face. It feels raw as a steak—already swelling. Just past her shoulder I spot Blair. I think I know who lit Molly up like a stick of dynamite. Lighting the fuse is Blair's favorite sport.

"What the hell?" Kendall appears and helps support Molly, to keep her from falling flat on her drunk ass.

"Looks like our favorite power bitch is up to her old tricks again."

"*Molly.*" Cruise pops up, pissed as hell at his sister's state of unsober being.

"Get her home," Kendall snaps. "I'll wait here with Ally." A touch of an evil smile twitches on her lips.

Cruise doesn't protest the idea and hauls Molly's slaphappy ass right off the premises. I think I'll tell Cal she's no longer welcome. I'm pretty sure Cruise won't fight me on it since she's underage. Chalk another one up on the felony scoreboard.

"What has she done?" Kendall asks me, shaking with anger while glaring at Blair.

"What hasn't she done? She tried to destroy you and Cruise, and now she's after Morgan."

"Poor under-laid Blair." Kendall feigns pity. "I think maybe *we* should show her a good time instead."

"*Kendall.*"

"Not like that." She averts her gaze. "Follow me."

Kendall is a woman on a mission, and judging by the way she's stomping over to Blair, I'd bet a serious ass-kicking was about to start. Blair is going to require tons of pain meds and years of psychiatric treatment to recover from the surprise this evening is about to produce.

Kendall links her arm through Blair's, and I do the same on the other side as we sweep her off toward the back.

"Okay, I get it, you're pissed," Blair says, shuffling her feet in the air because we've resorted to airlifting her to our final destination. I'm hoping an incinerator is involved. If I'm going to fry, it might as well be for something big and, in Blair's case, totally worth it.

Kendall swings open the door to the Exotic Room and speeds us inside.

A red light strobes through the darkened environment, tinting the room and everyone in it a sultry shade of sin. I spot Rutger and Woody Bates—an appropriate pairing when you consider this very room is a magnet for assholes. Bates gives a slight wave as if he's still got a chance. Creepy.

"Attention, everybody!" Kendall's voice shrills high like a whistle, and the girls slow their movements to a crawl. "My friend here would like to strut her stuff, but she's feeling a little shy, so I thought maybe you could help her out?"

Help her?

"What's her name?" Cinnamon, one of the girls from the club, belts it out like a song.

"Blair." Kendall is quick to divulge her victim's name.

"Bodacious Blair," I add, and the room lights up with laughter because, well, the irony is evident.

So that's it? Kendall's big revenge is making Blair swivel her hips in front of a couple dozen wasted men—maybe scoring some loose bills in the process? Unimpressive. I doubt this will shred the fiber of her rotten being. Most likely it'll just breed the need to delve further into exhibitionism.

The girls break out in a choir of "Go, Blair, go Blair," and it all sounds a little too cheerful, like this is some sorority event engineered to bolster her morale instead of ushering her into public humiliation as intended. Kendall obviously needs some assistance in this department so I gladly step in.

Kendall braces Blair by the shoulders, ready to launch her into the growing circle of bikini-clad dancers, and the only thing I can think to do is pants her. Only she's not wearing any, so I opt for the next logical solution. I pull her dress off over her shoulders so fast that Blair is clear across the room before she notices it's missing.

"Oh my God," I gasp. Not only did Blair go commando, but she seems to be deficient in the boulder-holder department as well. Not that it matters much because honestly? What's there to hold?

"Our work here is done," Kendall hisses as she speeds us out of the Exotic Room and deep into the mix of bodies clear across the club.

We laugh our asses off for the next twenty minutes straight. It was a thing of beauty watching Blair flail and gyrate while trying to cover her bits and pieces, and I do mean bits.

But I have a feeling our little act of revenge is going to be reciprocated, sooner than later. Blair Lancaster doesn't go down easy. Nor does she fight a fair fight. Boyfriends and doctoral degrees have been known to vanish under her wrath, but I say bring it. I'll expect anything and everything. She's out for a hell of a lot more than simply humiliating us. She's out to snake our boyfriends from underneath us—at least one of them, and I'm betting that one is mine.

But one thing I know for sure: Morgan Jordan isn't going anywhere.

Except of course to Oregon.

———

Saturday, I set off for my playdate with Ruby. I'm so grateful the Christies don't mind me spending time with her that I hug Janice, her mother, to death each time I see her.

The Christies live in Farmington, about a two-and-a-half-hour drive away. Nothing but country roads stretch out before me, like silver snakes that slither on for miles. I never seem to mind the drive because every minute brings me that much closer to seeing my sweet rose-faced cherub.

Ruby has an adoptive older sister named Merrill and a younger sister named Kayla. Janice asked if we could all hang out together because Ruby's sisters were jealous she was getting her nails done, so of course I said yes. I opted for Morgan's genius suggestion of a mani-pedi playdate along with my equally genius plan of sneaking in some ice cream and a movie.

Morgan. I can't seem to get him off my mind, and with each passing mile my heart aches just a little bit more knowing I'm that much farther from him. Funny, the only one who's ever elicited those feelings in me before was Ruby. It's as if Morgan has managed to graft himself over my heart almost as firmly as my own flesh and blood. For a moment I fantasize that Ruby was ours, mine and Morgan's—that she lived with us in married housing over at Garrison. Then in a viral assault on my emotions I remember that he's leaving in less than two weeks and all of the good times, the club, the way he rocks that damn bed, will up and leave with him, right along with my heart.

I arrive at the oversized house with its proverbial white picket fence and stretch my limbs before heading toward the porch.

Ruby runs out at top speed, laughing and clapping her hands, happy to see me.

Her hair is entwined in an intricate French braid, and she's sporting a touch of a summer tan. Her lips are a testament to her name.

"My beautiful girl." I pick her up and offer a spin before planting a big wet kiss on her cheek. "Are you ready to get pretty-pretty?" That's what she calls going to the salon, getting *pretty-pretty*.

She holds out her nails and waves them through the air as if they were already drying.

Janice comes out with the girls, and we pile in her minivan and head into town.

I always let Ruby pick her color first, and then I use it too. At least that way I can look down at my nails and know she's wearing the same shade. Sometimes just looking at my hands is enough to make me want to cry. It's a visceral pain, being away from her, but one I've learned to live with because each passing day brings me that much closer to seeing her again, then it all starts again on a loop. I steal glances at Ruby, who's seated to my right with her hands extended for the manicurist to tend to. I try to memorize every bit for later but these warm fuzzy feelings rarely last until next time. I spend way too many nights crying myself to sleep because I desperately miss her. Speaking of crying myself to sleep, that's exactly what I'll be doing once Morgan goes back home. And, if Morgan did manage to knock up some girl back in Oregon, I doubt he'd want to make the move in this direction at any point in time. Not that we've even broached the topic of what to do when the new school year begins.

"You're quiet," Janice says as we soak our nails side by side. "How are things going?"

"Better than ever," I blurt. Really? Are they? It seems like an odd thing to say after contemplating my relationship's impending demise.

"Judging by that goofy grin that hasn't left your face, I'm betting there's a boy involved." She tilts her head to the side as if chiding for me to agree. Janice is sweet and cute. She's at least fifteen years my senior. She wears her hair in a blonde pixie and miraculously manages to keep her figure lean even though I've seen her pound the all-you-can-eat buffet at the Chinese restaurant more than half a dozen times.

"Okay," I whisper. "So there might be a boy." I bite down on the goofy grin threatening to permanently etch itself onto my face.

"Well, don't just sit there." She bounces her leg off her knee. "Come on, dish."

"His name is Morgan." Just verbalizing his name—feeling it tumble from my lips—excites me in places that shouldn't be excited in a nail salon. "He's got this amazing jet-black hair and dimples you could curl up and *nap* in. And his smile, well, it lights up the night clear to the space station."

"Whoa!" Janice breaks out in a spontaneous laugh that makes all three girls look up with their full attention. "You had me at dimples." She lets her enthusiasm settle for a minute before prodding on. "So, where are things headed? Is this a summer romance or something that has the potential to last?"

I heave a giant sigh. "I wish I knew. He goes to school way out in Oregon. He's just out for the summer for his mother's wedding." I give a sheepish grin. "I said the *L* word for the very first time."

Her eyes widen with a smile all their own. "Okay—so, did he say it back?"

"Yes." I can feel my cheeks turning ten shades of crimson.

"Look, Mommy!" Ruby calls and holds out her bright-pink fingers. It takes a minute for me to notice she's looking at Janice, not me. Of course she is. I'm "Mama," and I think it's way nice of Janice to allow her to call me that. It's amazing Janice doesn't feel threatened or worried about letting me visit. Not that she should, but when we established this arrangement four years ago, under the guidance of her legal team, I had every worry filtering through my brain. Fear was my middle name. Still is. Ruby's father blinks through my mind, and I push him away. Thank God he's not Ruby's "daddy," her "dada," or her anything. Janice married a good man. She knows how to pick 'em, unlike me—well, except for Morgan.

"Hey"—I turn to her—"I just thought of something."

"What's that?"

"You're a sane person with a great track record in the relationship department, so you must know a thing or two about sifting the wheat from the douche. Would you mind meeting Morgan and telling me what you think?" I already know Morgan Jordan is no douchebag but, in a small way, I want Janice's approval. Hell, I think I need it.

She blinks back in surprise.

"Oh, Ally"—her face crumbles just enough to worry me—"I'm no judge. If this guy makes you happy, then that's good enough for me and it should be good enough for you too."

"I suppose you're right." I just can't afford another mistake. I'm damn lucky I'm not sitting in a prison cell somewhere. One wrong person—one wrong move—can equal a lethal combination and take freedom out of the equation when it comes to your future. I of all people should know.

"You're still so afraid of what almost happened," she says it sweetly. Her heart breaks for me. I can see it in her face. "Honey, you're a different person now. You know deep down inside what makes someone a moral and upstanding citizen. And if that's the type of man Morgan is, then, sweetie, you've already got it all. Of course, you'll have to figure out the distance thing, but in college that's no big deal. Angus and I went to schools on opposite coasts, and look at us, we turned out just fine. I promise you, if this is meant to be, ain't nobody or no amount of land going to stop it from happening." She gives a little wink.

God, I hope she's right.

I glance over at Ruby and her porcelain-doll face, the piercing green eyes that make the summer grass jealous of their color, and my heart melts.

Lord knows I can't afford to make another mistake in love.

"Tell you what." Janice pulls me from my trance. "Ruby's birthday is coming up—if he's still in town, bring him by."

"Really?" I wanted Janice to meet him, but for it to be on Ruby's birthday seems like a dream. I'd love to have Morgan there to share that special day with me.

"Yes. That way I can meet this dark-haired god who stole your heart. I promise I won't judge him. I just want to see those dimples for myself."

"Fair enough."

My hearts beats erratically.

Morgan is about to venture into the final frontier in my life—Ruby.

This is going to be big.

And now, suddenly, Morgan Jordan feels a lot more like family than ever before.

Morgan

Garrison University is oversized and pretentious. It screams *we engineer the future assholes of America.*

I shake my head as I take in the sights. How the hell did Ally end up here anyway? *Why* the hell did Ally end up here? Everyone knows state schools are more fun. Not that I should talk. I don't go to a state school, and come to think of it my own mother went to Garrison. And, of course, Kendall, who I've always admired for having her head screwed on straight, attends this wayward establishment and claims to like it.

The grounds are mostly empty with nothing but a stray bicycle here and there. A few skateboards whiz by as I make my way through campus. I didn't want to tell Kendall what I was up to in fear she'd leak it to Ally and ruin the surprise.

The sun straddles high above as I race up the steps to the administration building and head inside. A blast of air-conditioning greets me as a modern amenity but the pale limestone floors make it feel as though I've just entered some seventeenth-century castle. I kind of like the idea because Ally is every bit a princess. Although, ironically in this fairy tale, Ally doesn't need saving. She's no damsel in distress. She's a kick-ass, take 'em by the balls and ask questions later type, which is what attracted me to her in the first place. Plus she's got a smart mouth, and I can appreciate a girl who can put me in my place once in a while.

A young girl, with a dark mop of a head, sits behind the only desk in sight so I make my way over, locked and loaded, with a million questions ready to blow.

"Excuse me?"

She glances up, sans the smile. Obviously they don't pay her enough to want to be here on a perfect summer's day.

"Hi." I tap my knuckles over the counter. "Are you guys still accepting applications for the fall?"

"Of next year?" She reaches for a stack of brochures.

"No. Actually, I was thinking more like this year." My heart sinks like a lead weight because I know where this is going.

"Oh, no." She looks at me like I just crop-dusted the vicinity with a foul stench. "Fall semester starts in just a couple of weeks. It's closed to new applicants. You could apply for *next* fall." Her eyes widen as she pushes a glossy brochure in my direction, hoping I'll take this ray of trifolded sunshine and fuck the hell off.

"Got it. How about spring?" I can lose a semester if I have to. Worse things have happened.

"They've already recruited for that too. Enrollment for next fall opens in late October and ends right after Thanksgiving. You should hear back from the university around April or May."

"Got it." Crap. "So, what's the tuition?" I think I know. Kendall is on scholarship and has private loans, so it's got to be in the stratosphere.

"It's twenty-one thousand for twelve to eighteen units a semester." She doesn't even blink at the honest-to-God horror that just spewed from her lips. "If you need assistance we have a great financial aid office. They've got every grant, loan, and, scholarship you could think of."

Fuck.

"I'm sure they do." It feels like a twenty-one-thousand-dollar bullet just sailed through my heart. There's no way I can entertain going here. My grades aren't as stellar as Kendall's and for sure no one is going to gift me a scholarship for anything but baseball.

Baseball.

"You wouldn't happen to know the name of the baseball coach, would you?"

———

Ally and I drive up to the cabin at the same time.

I don't dare tell her about my adventures at Garrison. Or how I was invited to try out as a walk-on next week, not that it would instantly cure the tuition problem, but it couldn't hurt.

"Did you enjoy your Ruby Tuesday?" I tease as I pull her into a hug.

"Ha, ha. I get it. Ruby and it's Tuesday." She bites down gently on my lower lip and my dick tries its hardest to stand at attention. It's taking everything I've got to control the budding excitement. "It went terrific. In fact, I have a little surprise for you, but it's for another day." She tips her head playfully and her eyes siren out at me like a pair of key-lime pies.

"Well, I have a surprise for *you*," I say. "But it's for another day."

"Really?" She squeals and jumps on the balls of her feet.

"No, not really—well, maybe," I murmur, grazing her gently over the ear. "You're so fucking cute, you know that?"

"You have a dirty mouth—you know that?" She flirts when she says it. She makes a face as she looks through the tiny window of the cabin. "Kendall and Cruise are home."

"Let's go somewhere." I spin her in the direction of my truck. "We've got a little bit before the club opens, and I've got Cal doing the liquor run. I don't have to be anywhere until at least ten o'clock."

"That makes two of us. Let me get out of these jeans. You want to hit the beach?"

"If it means staring at you in a bikini, hell yes I want to hit the beach." The beach, the sheets, *both*.

We head inside to do a quick change and find Kendall and Cruise knotted up in one another's arms watching a movie.

It takes less than five minutes for me to throw on my swim trunks so I hang out with the lovebirds for a second while Ally gets ready.

"You guys heading out?" Cruise asks, nodding at the towel thrown over my shoulder.

"I thought we'd check out the ocean—see if it's still wet and salty like they say it is."

"You should head over to Pine Tree Cove," Cruise whispers, glancing toward the hall as if he doesn't want Ally to hear. "It's private. If you go to Charleston you'll be surrounded by soccer moms and teenagers." He nods as if this were a part of some bro code. "Just saying."

"Pine Tree Cove." I nod. That should be easy enough to remember. If I forget I'll just smack into one.

Ally comes out with her hair pulled back in a ponytail, her face scrubbed fresh. Ally's so beautiful all on her own she doesn't need anything from a bottle to make her pretty.

"Catch you two later," I say as we head out the door.

"Morgan?" Kendall glances back at me. "Rehearsal dinner is Thursday, don't forget."

"Got it," I say as Ally and I head outside. "You'd think by the fifth go-around there wouldn't be much to rehearse." Actually, it might be Mom's sixth march down the aisle. I stopped keeping track.

"That's a lot of wedding dresses to buy." Ally wraps her arms around my waist as we step out into the sunshine. "I plan on doing it once and getting it right the first time." Her mouth opens with surprise as if she just realized she said that out loud.

"No, it's okay. I agree. I think something like that should be entered into carefully—done once and done right."

"Carefully." She smiles. "That's my new favorite word." Her gaze drifts for a moment before settling in the direction of her car. "Oh no."

The front tire is flat on the passenger's side, and her Honda looks like it's taking a nap. Hell, it looks like it needs one.

"Don't worry." I press a kiss in over her temple. "I'll throw on the spare in the morning, and we can head into town and get it fixed."

She pulls me in by the chin and sears a kiss over my lips that takes the breath right out of my lungs.

"You're always saving me—you know that?" Ally holds my gaze as if those words were gospel.

"You don't need saving, darlin'. You're strong enough on your own. Besides, we're a team." I give her shoulders a little squeeze. "Teammates help each other out."

"Well then"—she runs her tongue over her lips and they shine like glass under the sun—"I feel damn lucky to be on your team."

"I'm damn lucky to have you." Now if only I can think of a way to keep the team within kissing distance next semester.

But I'm on it.

And I never let my teammates down.

———

Pine Tree Cove is about seven miles up the coast, and thanks to my good sense of direction, and even better GPS, we manage not to miss the turnoff.

PINE TREE COVE. Ally reads the sign while gliding her long, tan legs over one another.

Ally Monroe has been doing her best to elicit a boner in me all the way over, and with nothing but my swim trunks on there isn't a lot of room to hide the evidence.

Cruise mentioned this place was private and both my hard-on and I are hoping he's right.

Sure enough, the parking lot is bare as my ass in the shower. It's *free* too, which is another point I'd like to award him since I'm running low on quarters, but thankfully not on cash. The nightclub business is apparently where it's at because for the first time in my life I've got more than two dimes to rub together. I could get used to this, that's for sure. But it's for a limited time so I appreciate the fact I've got to make every last penny count.

A layer of salted air clings to our skin as we get out of the truck.

"It's not this humid back home," I say without thinking as we walk down a small hill on our way to the beach.

Perfect. Remind her you're leaving in a couple weeks. Shit.

"Oh"—she wraps her arm tight around my waist—"it's not like this all year." My body goes weak thinking we might be able to count on one hand how many more times we can do this. "Fall is my favorite time of year," she says. "The colors are outrageous, and the air goes cold right after Labor Day. It's amazing the way nature just knows to do that." She says that last part quietly, drawing it out, as we walk down to the brown, sugary sand.

"I like fall too." I say it quiet, somber as a eulogy as we stroll through the warm sand.

A set of boulders sits near the hillside. A few pepper trees offer the area shade, so we migrate over. I lay out the blanket, and we toss our stuff down. My wallet has a condom snug inside in the event we decide to get enthusiastic with our bodies.

Ally tilts her head seductively and smiles with those strawberry-colored lips. Her eyes lower to slits as she reaches down and pulls off her T-shirt, revealing a barely there red string bikini. She peels off her shorts, and my dick pulsates just taking in the bandage of a bottom held together with a few measly strings. Suddenly I'm overcome with the urge to unwrap her like a present. I'm enjoying the hell out of the fact her bottoms are equally as pleasantly scant as the top.

"Hot damn, girl," I say, pulling her in by the waist.

"Your turn." She plucks my shirt off and runs her hands over my chest in a series of achingly slow circles.

"You're pretty good at that," I say, picking up her hand and kissing each of her fingertips.

"Stripping?" Her eyes widen as if a slap is next on the agenda.

"No." I push out a little laugh. "Taking *my* clothes off." I gently pull her in by the face and give a playful bite to her bottom lip. "I'm going to have to keep you around, Ally." Shit. Did I just go there again? Is there any way to get through this afternoon and not depress the hell out of us by bringing up the not-so-distant future? I mean, it's obvious Ally and I have a future, right? What the hell am I saying? Of course we do, a brilliantly long one—paved with happiness and hot sex right through to our golden years and beyond.

"Are you going to keep me around?" Her features soften as if she had started it out as a smart-ass remark, then it became a general-interest question that directly affects her well-being.

"Hell, yes." My lungs pump out some serious steam as if I ran all the way here from Cruise's cabin. "You're all I've ever wanted."

"And, you're"—a smile twitches on her lips—"*it!*" she screams, slapping me on the chest and taking off toward the waterline.

"*Hey*"—I shout, taking off after her—"that hurt, Ally. You're going to have to kiss it to make it feel better."

Laughter bubbles from her as she streaks across the sand. Her ponytail whips around her shoulders like a white flame.

"You'll have to catch me first!" she shouts as she races down the waterline.

"Sweetie, if I catch you, you're going to have to kiss a few other body parts as well." I come up on her in less than five seconds, dive for her ankle, and miss.

"Morgan." The smile melts from her face as she looks over my shoulder.

A wall of water collapses over me like an avalanche before yanking me back, trying to drag my sorry ass right into the Atlantic with it.

"Well played, Monroe." I roll onto my back and feel the sun warming my skin.

"It's going to happen again if you're not careful." She strolls forward, and I pretend not to notice.

"Careful is my middle name."

"Yeah, right." Her foot swoops just shy of my hip and this time I snatch it, pulling her down to the damp sand right along with me.

Ally falls to her knees in a fit of laughter.

"Let go! A wave is going to come and—"

"And what?" I reel her in until she's lying next to me.

"You're getting me wet."

"Now who's the one with a dirty mouth?" I slip my hand down over her bottom and circle around to the front.

"Morgan!" She laughs, squirming and biting down over my ear.

I run my finger along the lips of her bathing suit bottom before dipping my hand in. I can feel her warm slick, wet just like she promised in a roundabout way. Ally bites down over that bright pink lip approvingly as I slip my finger deep inside her. Sure enough, Ally Monroe is warmer and wetter than the big blue sea.

A wave starts to crest in the distance, and I wrap my arms around her.

"It looks like we're going under, babe."

Ally turns to look just as the powerful blast detonates over us. The water retracts, and I shake my hair out.

"Morgan!" she screams, staggering to her feet.

"That's the second time you shouted my name, and I'm still not getting any action." Any sane man in her presence would be begging by now.

She kicks the damp sand over my stomach and takes off for the shade.

"Was that an invitation?" I scramble up and give chase until I land next to her on the warm blanket.

"Everything's an invitation to you." She reaches over and scratches at my chest, so I catch her hand and kiss it. "You're a perv."

"Yeah, well, you're a tease."

The sunlight hits her just right, lighting her up from the back like an angel. The water beads over her skin and glows like a thousand fallen stars.

Her features grow serious. She reaches forward and plays with a loose strand from the blanket as if trying to deflect her thoughts.

Shit. She's feeling it. Thinking it. All that talk about back home—*fall*—it sunk into her bones and now I've dragged her into the funk I've been trapped in all week.

"Come here." It slips from me sadly, far too quietly to match the light banter we've volleyed back and forth for the better part of an hour. Ally conforms to my chest, and I press a kiss into the back of her hair. The dark cloud of uncertainty has squatted over us, already pissing on our parade whether we like it or not. The fall semester has become the nine-hundred-pound gorilla looming over us with a sickle. Long-distance relationships suck and we both know it. The first mile I'm away from her I'm going to want to turn back. I'll probably cry like a pussy as soon as I hit the state line.

Ally reaches down and dips her hand into my shorts, her cool fingers finding me and my seaside shrinkage.

A dry laugh rumbles from me as I pull her over me and indulge in a deep-throated kiss. The heat of her mouth pushes me out of sanity's bounds while her tongue strokes me into a rush of excitement. I pluck off my shorts and Ally glides over me, kissing my stomach, my happy trail, all the way down south. She wraps her lips around me and encourages me to grow in her mouth.

A heated breath rips from me. I reach over and fumble for the condom I packed with a seed of hope and tear into the package.

I pull her toward me and slip it on.

"Looks like you're ready this time." She smiles but it looks sad, lonely.

"I may not be the brightest, but I learn from my mistakes." Mostly.

I dip back over her with a kiss wetter and hotter than the sea and the sun. I don't want to think of the past. And I'm pretty sure the future has the capability to kill my hard-on just as fast.

I pluck at Ally's string bikini like I've been dying to do ever since we arrived. I give a slow, methodical pull until both her top and bottom come apart in pieces.

"I dressed for the occasion," she whispers, running her tongue over my neck.

"Honey, you are the occasion." I lay her back and roll on top of her. Her legs rise over my ribcage and I hike them back before plunging deep inside her. "Fuck, Ally." I give a heated whisper right in her ear. "You're going to be the death of me."

This is the moment I want to remember. This is the moment I want to relive over and over again. Right here at Pine Tree Cove, buried in the only girl I have ever wanted to spend my life with.

"I love you," I whisper, rocking in and out of her as achingly slow as possible.

"Morgan." She lets out a series of soft groans, and I'm about to lose it. "I love you forever."

"Forever," I whisper.

10

SCARE TACTICS

Ally

Thursday morning, Kendall and I decide to run out and pick up flowers for the rehearsal dinner.

"I'll drive," I offer as we head out into the overbright day. The sweet scent of pines perfumes the air as the heat expels their oils into the air. I soak it in because it just so happens to be one of those last, magical days of summer.

We step over to the Honda and a scream gets locked in my throat as I take in a bloodied mess sitting on the hood. Kendall shrieks to high heaven, sending both Cruise and Morgan flooding out the door.

"What the hell happened?" Cruise hooks an arm around Kendall's waist, trying to calm her.

"Shit." Morgan steps over and peers at the carcass lying over my car. "It's just a rat." He picks a stick off the ground and flicks it off. "Looks like a bird lost its breakfast. Either that or a stray cat has one mean crush on you." His dimples wink in and out. "Go shopping." He touches his lips over mine with a cool, minty kiss. "Drama's over. You okay?" Morgan wraps his arms around my waist and offers a gentle smile.

"Mmm-hmm," I whisper as Kendall says good-bye to Cruise and gets in the passenger's seat. I glance back over at the rat with half its body bashed in. "Do you really think it was from a bird?"

"Yes. You're safe." He leans in and his lips find a home just over my ear. "I'll always keep you safe, Ally. I promise."

⌒

Lauren meets up with us at the flower market, and we walk up and down the multicolored aisles perfumed with an abundance of all the things that make my allergies sing.

I shuffle from the poppies, red as a blood let, to the black-eyed Susans. A smattering of stargazer lilies catches my attention and I linger. I sit mesmerized by their long purple tongues, freckled and soft as velvet—their pollen-coated tips, delicate and powdery as cinnamon.

I wish Morgan were here. But more importantly, I'm dying over the fact Morgan is just a hair away from packing his suitcase and driving right out of Carrington for a good long while. I thought for sure he would have brought it up by now—that he would have mentioned it in some small way—but it's like it doesn't even matter. It's as if he can just as easily lure me to his bed as he can kiss me good-bye. Or maybe, like me—he's afraid to go there. I mean, he said he loved me, and that's got to count for something. Tess once said that boys only say "I love you" if they think a blow job is on the horizon, and at the time I believed her. But a lot of things have changed since then, and now I'm not so sure.

"Hey, girl." Lauren speeds over and wraps an arm around my shoulder. Her strong, musky perfume envelops me like a cloud—all business, no sweetness, much like Lauren herself. "Who the hell shit on your rose parade?"

I shake my head, blinking back tears.

"Hey!" Kendall swoops in from behind and sucks in a breath. "It's my brother, isn't it? Did he do something stupid? I'm so going to kill him if he did something stupid."

"No." I shake my head. I'm deathly afraid to confess anything to Kendall because it will undoubtedly get back to Morgan. "I swear it's not him. Really it's not. It's me. I'm the one who's paranoid about things I can't control. Morgan is far more mellow." Too mellow, but I keep the commentary to myself. "You know, he goes with the flow. I bet he doesn't even think about *tomorrow*, let alone next week. I'm just overreacting." I pluck a dahlia from the bucket and press my nose deep into its cushioned leaves. No scent, just beauty. I squeeze my eyes tight to stop the tears from flowing.

"Maybe Morgan didn't *do* anything"—Lauren rattles my shoulder until I glance up at her—"but does this have anything to do with him?"

A tiny squeal escapes my throat. I never could lie to Lauren.

"Knew it." Kendall looks pissed to hell and ready to rip his balls off. "Is this because he slept with Molly?"

"Holy shit!" Lauren screams so loud that ten different cashiers run in our direction.

"It's okay." I'm quick to wave them off, and then tip my head toward Lauren. "She doesn't get out much. The flowers are beautiful." I make crazy eyes at Lauren until she settles back into her skin.

"He *slept* with Molly?" she says, looking like she's ready to eviscerate him with her teeth. She's a good friend in that respect. Lauren wouldn't hesitate with a homicide if the need arose.

"He did *not* sleep with Molly." I over enunciate in an effort to drill home the carnal correction. "Well, technically he did, but that's not the point. He didn't have his way with her." He kept his penis tucked safely in its holster. That's one weapon he's only allowed to use with me.

"And did Molly have *her* way with *him?*" Kendall asks, careful and slow, as if I might not have considered this option yet.

"*No.* Thank God nothing happened that night. And, by the way, Molly is a piranha. I don't care how close the two of you are to being related. She's cutthroat when it comes to getting what she wants. I'm just glad Morgan escaped with his man parts intact." I open my mouth to continue my tramp-inspired tirade but Lauren accosts Kendall with her purse before I can get a word out.

"You *pushed* Ally and Morgan together." Lauren finishes off by smacking her in the arm.

Kendall tries to respond, flustered, and nothing but air comes out. Lauren seems to have that effect on a lot of people.

"Stop it, both of you." I toss the flower back into the bucket. "Kendall didn't push us together. In fact, if you want to get technical, it was all some weird coincidence concocted by the universe." I flail my hand through the air, at a loss for down-to-earth descriptives. "Do you remember me telling you about that one-night stand that left me high and dry at the beginning of summer?" I stare at them, half afraid to offer up any more info—like the fact sixteen US dollars were exchanged. Or rather, left behind. Nevertheless, a few lattes came from the bonus.

Kendall jumps in horror and presses her hand to her chest. Lauren spends another ten seconds paying tribute to dumbasses everywhere before she, too, lets out a harrowing moan.

"*No!*" Kendall seems shocked at the prospect of her brother treading into manwhore territory so soon on his visit, and with me of all people.

"Yes," I assure her. "Most definitely, yes. I was shocked to hell the next day when you brought him over to help me move. Anyway, it's ancient history." I chew on my nails for a second. Then without warning I open my mouth and vomit out the entire story—how he caught me when I fell off the stage at Pretty Girls, how infatuated I was with this amazing creature who was like no other man I had ever seen, and then the sixteen dollars he mistakenly left on the table and what I thought it meant.

"Get *out!*" Lauren shouts. She's laughing so damn hard she has to cross her legs to keep her bladder from joining in on the funfest. Lauren has a history of pissing her pants on my behalf and for far less humiliating infractions.

"Morgan?" Kendall's face pales at the thought of our chance encounter. "What the hell possessed you to do that?"

Both she and Lauren stare at me expectantly as they await the dirty deets.

"As soon as I saw all those tats I knew he'd fuck me like a boss." I avert my eyes at the thought. Okay, so maybe there's a little truth to that.

They gasp in turn—Lauren far more amused than Kendall.

"Relax. That's not how it went." I give a long blink. "Besides, he's a god, Kendall. A million different women would give their right boob to bed him for a lot less than sixteen dollars."

"She's right." Lauren shakes her head before reverting back to me "He's a fine specimen and certainly no one is going to fault you for dragging him to the nearest mattress. One-night stands work out all the time." She gives a circular nod into her lunacy, and it takes a minute for me to deduce that she's mocking me.

Kendall bites down on her lip. "Well, I *almost* had a one-night stand with Cruise."

"And . . ." Lauren waves her hand in the air as if searching for words. Swear to God if she says she had a one-night stand with Cal I'll run up and down the aisles and start overturning these happy little flower buckets. I know for a fact she cast one of her dry spells on that poor baldheaded tribute to steroids for a good six months after they met. "I almost had a one-night stand with Cruise," she teases.

I decide to leave out the part about nearly throwing my own hat into the Elton mattress ring, but that was long before Kendall and well after Blair. "All right"—I link arms with Kendall and Lauren—"so you both almost had a one-night stand with Cruise." I dab the tears from my eyes. "Anyway, one-night stand or not, I know what Morgan and I have is going to last." God, I hope it lasts.

"Of course it will." Lauren forces her brows together as if she's trying to convince herself. She plucks a stargazer the size of her palm from the bucket, and holds it up as if she were making a toast. "To Morgan and Ally."

Kendall is quick to do the same and hands me one as well.

"To my big brother and Ally," she sings.

Lauren presses her lips together and holds back tears as if she were really happy for me. "Though they be few, may you enjoy every moment you have together."

And there's that.

She knows our days are numbered, and in my heart, so do I.

My phone vibrates in my jeans and I take a few steps away to see who it is. It's probably Morgan, and he's going to make me feel tons better by saying the right thing because that seems to be his gift.

It's a text from a blocked number.

You better watch your back bitch.

What the hell? I stare at it in disbelief for a minute.

I slip the phone back in my purse and don't say a word to Lauren or Kendall.

Morgan

The sun rides high and strong overhead like a bucking bronco at the rodeo, drilling its rays in my eyes until they sting. The scent of a freshly mowed lawn swims through the air like the finest perfume, and my hands instinctually want to strangle a bat for the hell of it.

"You got this, man." Cruise pats me on the back as we watch Garrison's baseball team, the Gladiators, connect ball to bat just before my walk-on tryout. I fessed up to Cruise like some whipped pussy regarding how I feel about Ally, and what I was going to do to up my odds of staying. I guess I kind of wanted the moral support. The only other alternative was Mom, and, with it being just days away from her wedding, I didn't want to bother her.

The guys are hitting the shit out of the ball and the pitcher is blowing some serious smoke. These dudes are beyond good.

"Yeah," I say doubtfully. "I should have probably warmed up. But I got this."

I watch as guy after guy launches the ball across the field in long, easy strides, as if the bat had somehow morphed into a missile launcher.

On second thought, I'm not so sure *I got this*. In fact, those balls may as well be flying to Oregon, the way they're knocking them out of the park. Maybe I'm not that great. Maybe the team back home was mediocre at best, and I've been happily clueless all along.

Fuck. Looks like I'm about to be laughed off the field. There goes the chance of having some weepy-eyed happily ever after with Ally.

My phone buzzes.

It's Paige.

My entire body freezes, and I stare at the phone for an inordinate amount of time.

"I'd better take this." I pick up and walk toward the chain-link fence. "Hello?"

"Morgan?" Paige's voice chirps from the other end of the line.

"Yeah, what's going on?" A million scenarios run through my mind. Maybe she changed her mind and had the test anyway?

"I had the baby."

My heart sinks like a cinder block.

"You what?" My throat constricts at the idea, cutting off my vocal cords right along with my balls. "Are you okay? Is the baby okay?"

"Everything's fine. I thought I felt a cramp, and it turned out it was baby time."

My blood runs cold. She knew I wanted to be there for the birth, at least in the next room.

"He's six weeks early. They had to put him in the incubator, but they say he'll be fine. I guess stuff like this happens all the time."

"I'll get on the next flight out," I offer.

The coach blows his whistle in my direction and waves me over.

Shit.

"No," she protests. "You don't have to do that. I've already had both him and Clint tested. We should know on Saturday," she says that last part quietly. I'm pretty sure it's not me she's rooting for.

"Saturday." I nod stupidly into the phone.

"Jordan!" The coach roars my name out like a warning. "You want this or not?"

"The baby," I whisper. "So it's a boy, huh?"

"A beautiful boy. He's got a gorgeous head of dark hair. It's hard to believe he's mine." Paige is a redhead whose entire body glows like a warning light. Clint's got dark brown hair so it could go either way. "Take care, okay?" she whispers, as if she's trying to soften the blow. "I'll call you as soon as I know the results."

"Got it. Take care of yourself and the baby." A boy. That could be my boy, my *son*.

I hand the phone to Cruise and jog over to home plate, my head spinning with the paternal possibilities.

The baby is here.

I pick up a bat and give a few solid swings to warm up. The pitcher launches one in my direction, and I jump out of the way.

Shit. It was good. I just overreacted.

If I have a baby in Oregon it's going to make it near impossible for me to relocate to Massachusetts. And I wouldn't dream of asking Ally to move to Oregon. She has Ruby. She needs to be near her sweet little girl.

I miss the next ball, nothing but air. Almost threw my back out trying to connect with that one.

Fuck.

The pitcher eyes the coach as if to ask if this is for real.

"It's for real, asshole," I whisper.

The ball comes at me like a comet and I swing—then like a dream I hear that lovely sound every baseball player wants to hear as the ball and bat connect. I watch as the ball flies twice as far as I've seen it go all afternoon. It sails into the reaches of the blue expanse until it's nothing but a speck on the horizon.

"Good show!" Cruise calls out while a few of the guys offer a spontaneous round of applause.

It would have been a home run—just like Ally and me.

———

The Elton House Bed and Breakfast is playing host to Mom's nuptial rehearsal. The lawn is rolling and lush, decorated with flower petals the girls picked up this afternoon. It looks like someone dumped a box of Trix cereal all the way down to the altar if you ask me, but pretty nonetheless. My stomach's been going off for the last two hours and I've been seeing food in everything because I haven't eaten jack shit since I got that phone call.

I hook my arm through Mom's and walk her down the aisle, as I've been prone to do with the exception of the time or two she eloped, but my eyes migrate over to Ally. She's sitting off to the side, her long creamy legs crossed over one another. She's so damn beautiful. I could never expect her to sit around and wait for me while I finish up school.

Kendall and Cruise stand under the lattice arch where the wedding coordinator belts out demands like some sexed-up dominatrix.

I walk Mom over to Andrew, who looks more than enamored by my mother in her svelte black dress. She looks more "merry widow" and less "blushing bride" but who knows? This could be a twofer—the guy looks far more aged than any of her other suitors.

"Okay!" The wedding coordinator claps. "It's a wrap."

I head over to Ally and we take a walk in the direction of a weeping willow.

"That was the second time I received applause today." I dot her lips with a kiss. Ally smells like a rose, like an entire floral boutique, and I always want to remember her like this. "How come you don't clap for me in bed?" I go for humor but miss by a mile and end up sounding like some depressed teenage girl who wonders why no one likes her.

"Did someone clap for you in bed today?" She pulls me in by the back of the neck and licks the periphery of my lips as a token of her lewd affection. "You said that was the second time."

Crap.

"Did I say that?" Perfect. First I have a son in another state and now I almost blow the surprise I was hoping to knock her socks off with—my baseball tryout. Not that I know I'm the father—not that I know if I have anything to knock her socks off with. The coach said he'd review some online footage I sent over and get back to me. Looks like I'm all about the questions today.

"*Hey.*" She hooks me tenderly by the chin and turns me toward her. "Everything okay? You seem kind of lost."

"You're with me. How can I not be okay?" I glance over her shoulder at the brimming buffet. It's finally starting to smell like food out here and rumor has it there's a steak with my name on it. "I got the call today." My eyes fill with tears as soon as I say it, and I blink them back. Shit. The last thing I want to do is cry like a schoolgirl.

"The call?" She looks perplexed for a moment. Her pale eyes squint at me just before her perfect bowtie mouth opens as the realization sets in. "Oh, God. What did she say?" Ally pulls me deeper into the property, away from prying ears.

"She said she'll know on Saturday." There. It felt good to lance the wound and get it out. I would have gone insane trying to keep this from Ally. "She had the baby early. She said he's doing fine."

"A boy." She mouths the words as she twirls her fingers through my hair. There's so much sorrow on her face, clouded with a touch of joy. That, in a nutshell, is exactly how I feel. "Guess what, Jordan?"

"What?" I'm almost afraid to ask.

"I'm not leaving your side once on Saturday. When that phone rings, I'll be right there with you."

I pull her in and wrap my arms around her so tightly it feels as if I'm about to push through.

I want to tell her I never want her to leave my side, but I don't. The truth is the entire girth of the country could clog the distance between us soon. And I'm not quite sure I can stop it from happening.

Can I?

———

After the festivities, I head over to the club to set up the bar and mark the cards to ensure I win every fucking hand tonight. I think I've seasoned the bad boys of Massachusetts enough into believing I'm a mediocre player at best. It's time to make a few corrections.

I asked Ally to catch a ride over with Cruise and Kendall so we could drive home together but really that flat tire and that dead rodent on her car have me more than a little on edge, and I don't want her alone. It's just too many mishaps in too short a span. Either God hates that Honda or there's a jealous rage brewing in the background that's about to turn explosive.

The lights are on down the hall in the blue room—the Poker Room. I had the bulbs in each room replaced to match its mood—red for sex on heels, and blue for don't look so down when I steal all of your fucking money.

Great. I must have forgotten to flip the switch off last night. I'm pretty sure that qualifies Cal to yank some more cash out of my ass.

The faint scent of perfume startles my senses. Nice. I'd think maybe it was left over from last night, but I'm starting to get hopeful that I'll find Ally ready and willing to give me a lucky hand.

I widen the door and a blonde in a trench coat spins on her bright-red heels—Blair.

She drops her coat. Her pale, bony body is naked as the day she was born.

"You're welcome," she says before lunging at me and diving her tongue straight down my throat.

11

LOVERS AND FIGHTERS

Ally

The lavender sky sparkles with a million shining stars. It looks fake, like a piece of felt laid out with too much glitter poured over it. By the time we arrive at Rock Bottom, a crowd has already congested the entrance. Business is booming, but it won't be for long—not with fall semester hanging over our heads like some scholastic guillotine. If we're lucky maybe we'll have this kind of business on the weekends, but then again the sororities and fraternities like to hold their own parties.

"Are you still upset?" Kendall slings her arm over my shoulder as we fight to make our way inside.

"What's she upset about?" Cruise asks, genuinely interested.

I'm thankful Kendall hasn't clued him in yet. That's the thing with having girlfriends who are practically already married to their other half. It makes you wonder if any of your secrets are ever really safe.

"School's coming up so fast." I nod toward the club. "Morgan can't stay." I shake my head. "We haven't really talked about it." Who needs loose-lipped girlfriends when my own tongue betrays me? What's next? Confessing to Cruise the fact I had debilitating cramps last week?

His lips twitch to the side. "I wouldn't worry too much about it. When two people care about each other as much as you and Morgan, things have a way of working themselves out."

I expel a lungful of air. It was as if I were holding my breath and Cruise said the exact words I needed to hear to breathe again.

"You're right." I say it a little louder than necessary. "Things do have a way of working themselves out." They had better, for my sanity's sake.

We hit the entrance and Cal taps me on the arm. "Where's that knuckleheaded boyfriend of yours?"

"Here, somewhere. And, by the way, the only knucklehead around here is you for not hatching this brilliant plan yourself." I give an impish grin as I make my way past him. The place is pumping tonight with wall-to-wall bodies. I swear we're break-ing twelve different fire codes. Although, if we go down for something of the illegal variety, safety issues will be the least of our worries, what with the gambling ring, the quasi house of prostitution, the underage drinking as evidenced with Molly— tragically the list goes on and on. But still, something feels dif-ferent about tonight. You can feel a whole new energy. It's as if the tail end of summer has encouraged everyone in this room to let loose.

"Great news!" A female voice rides high behind me, and I turn to find Lauren with two drinks in hand.

"What's that?" I gawk at the chocolate-looking vial with whipped cream ready to float off the top.

Kendall comes up behind her and holds up yet another whipped concoction.

"Blow jobs all around!" She raises a glass to me.

"What's the occasion?" I ask, accepting the potion with its obscene moniker.

"Do we need an occasion to get down and dirty?" Kendall hoots. "Tonight everybody parties!"

"That's right, ladies." Lauren wrinkles her nose. "And this will be the only time I swallow." She hikes her drink into the air. "Actually"—she gives me a look that spells trouble—"I have a surprise for you."

"For me?" Since when does Lauren dole out surprises?

"That's right. I felt really bad about stranding you this summer and essentially leaving you without a place of your own." She makes a face. "So . . . I went out and got you an off-campus apartment just east of sorority row. No worries about driving to all the hot parties, all you'll have to do is carry those pretty little high heels." She gives a quick wink.

"Lauren!" I squeal and give her a hug as best as I can without spilling the emissions of my glass. "You didn't have to do this. You're way too nice to me."

"I had to." She gives a long blink. "It came up so fast, I knew it'd be gone by afternoon so I snagged it. All I did was pay the first and last. And if you ever have a tough time with rent we can work something out. Besides, how often in life do you get to choose your neighbors?"

"Neighbors?" I try to contain the urge to jump but can't seem to do it.

"Okay," Lauren shouts over the music, trying to calm me. "Now we have a serious decision to make." She holds the indelicately named drink out in front of her. "Do we use our hands? Or mouths?"

Kendall and I laugh and knock into one another in the process.

The cool liquid splashes over the front of my dress in one quick spurt.

"Oh shit."

Lauren hacks out a laugh. "Looks like you're the victim of a little premature ejaculation!"

Lauren and Kendall crack up like they've never laughed before. I guess there's nothing a little crude humor and an apartment to call my own can't fix because for the first time in weeks I'm in a celebratory mood. In fact, I wouldn't mind a little climax myself. Speaking of which. Where is my own personal ejaculation station? Surely he's ready and willing to please. Plus, I can't wait to share the news that we finally got our own place!

Then it hits me, fast and furious: there is no we.

Morgan Jordan will be gone in a week.

———

The women's restroom leaves a lot to be desired, three stalls that by the end of the night are the most sought-after seats in the house. But it's still early and there's nary a line so I walk in and inspect the white frothy stain on the front of my dress.

"Disgusting," I say, plucking at the mess just above my stomach. I snatch a paper towel and embed the cream into the fabric. "Gross." I let out a hard sigh.

"You are, aren't you?" Blair pops up in the mirror like a ghost and begins adjusting the collar on her preppy dress. She's wearing a single strand of pearls around her neck and a plaid headband in her neatly flat-ironed hair. Her fiscally sound fashion sense makes me want to stick my finger down my throat.

I wish I could say I'm not jealous of Blair—that her daddy's money doesn't make me wish I had a familial monetary IV injected into my bank account. In truth, a part of me is very much envious.

My new plan of action—the *only* plan of action—is to ignore her. After all, I did get to strip off her clothes and send her in a virtual mosh pit filled with horny frat boys. Rumor has it she made a lot more than sixteen dollars that night.

Her bitchy BFF, Erica, pops out of the stall and appraises me as if I were a parasite.

Lovely. Maybe walking around all night with a giant stain on the front of my dress isn't that bad. In fact, accessorizing with real semen would be more pleasurable than occupying air space with Blair and her ditzy sidekick.

"So, I just had this wild sexual fantasy play out," Blair coos to her partner in fictitious sexual crime while trying to entice me into listening in on their tawdry conversation. "I mean, there wasn't much to it—just a trench coat and heels—but he didn't mind. He says he likes it simple because the girl he's with always tries too hard. She feels the need to overcompensate by wearing things she can't afford. Pity because she cheapens everything she touches."

My cheeks burn with heat.

"All right, Blair." I pivot on my heels. "Obviously you weren't with Morgan. You're just trying to make me think you were so you can cause another misunderstanding like you did with Kendall and Cruise. Morgan wouldn't cheat on me. Not tonight, and for damn sure, not with you."

Her mouth opens as she feigns surprise. I can feel her hatred pulsating off my body as she rides her gaze over me.

"Oh, Ally, you flatter yourself." She gives a snippy tight-lipped smile that makes me want to wring her neck. "I'm not trying to break anybody up. You see, Morgan and I have had this thing going ever since he came into town. Only we don't kiss and tell. You want to know what he calls it?"

My brain wants to fire off some smartass comeback, but I'm too pissed to think straight.

"Oh, I'd love to know." I toss my hair back as obnoxious as possible. "Then I can compare it to what he calls you in private." Not that he's ever referenced her as anything other than what her mother felt moved to call her. Morgan is too much of a gentleman. Ironically, I distinctly remember Rutger referring to her as Horse Face. I guess money doesn't buy you manners.

She leans in, her eyes on fire with a vicious level of joy.

"He calls me his *dirty little secret*." Blair bites down on a blooming grin.

My body freezes, my adrenaline spikes—the next thing I know my hand connects with her cheek in a violent slap.

"You bitch!" Blair nurses her wound for a moment with her hair swept across her face.

Her hands spring to my shoulders. Blair pushes me into the sink and slams my head against the mirror.

"Shit," I yell as a sharp pain travels through my spine.

Blair snatches me by the scalp. She yanks me down only to introduce my face to her knee.

I let out a guttural moan as she shoves me against the wall.

"Ask him," she shouts. "Ask your precious little boyfriend whose body he was pressed against, *loving* with that animal tongue of his, just before the club opened?"

"What?" I glance up at her before gaining my footing.

"That's right, Ally. It was just me and him, right there over the poker table, and it felt real good." She holds herself as if reliving a memory. "But I don't have to tell you. You already know how good he can make a girl feel. Or didn't you get over your little problem? He told me all about your inability to—"

I don't wait for her to finish. I charge her like a bull ready and willing to inflict some serious bodily injury. I don't know how she did it, but she hit every sexual detail right on the head. As much as I'd like to cry bullshit, I can't.

Maybe in the end the joke is on me. Maybe in the end, Morgan Jordan is nothing but a player, someone who barreled through Carrington one summer looking for a good time wherever he could get it.

I latch onto Blair and her brassy tresses with the skunk roots coming in, and knock her against the wall. A group of girls wander into the bathroom and scream as they witness the bruising.

"Say you didn't sleep with him." I grind the words through my teeth.

She tries to dislodge my grip, but I won't relent.

"Erica!" she howls.

"Say it!" I shake her so hard I swear her hair is going to fall out in my hands like a bad Halloween wig.

"I wouldn't lie to you, Ally. I was *with* him!" she shrills.

I jostle her body as we tug and wrestle until we slam into an open stall.

"That's it," I mutter, maneuvering her head toward the water-filled basin.

Blair shoots off a few wild kicks my way like a mule in heat. Her fists pummel against my chest, but I'll gladly accept the bruising in exchange for what's coming next. I slam her head into the toilet seat and secure my knee between her shoulder blades.

"Take it all back, and I'll let go." My heart thrashes against my chest. Blair Lancaster has gotten under my skin for the very last fucking time.

She looks up with a wicked sense of determination. "We did it just before the club opened." Her lips curve with a devious smile. "The last thing he said was, thank God you're not boring like Ally."

"Crap." It takes all of my strength to submerge her successfully. I hold her under, a good few seconds, before flushing the toilet with my elbow.

Blair rises with a bionic strength and bolts over to the sink. She sticks her head under the running water, screaming at the top of her lungs for antibiotics.

Pfft. Like that's going to cure her of the bitch virus that's been plaguing her since childhood.

"Go ahead and scald your face, Blair. You might melt that ugly scowl off and actually score some friends who would help you out in a bind," I say, shooting Erica a look before I head back into the club.

Now—to find my cheating boyfriend.

Morgan

I'm one hand away from taking good old Rutger and his high-brow pals to the cleaners when Ally stomps in with her hair a little wilder than I'm used to.

I blink a quick smile up at her and get back to my cards.

Damn, the girl is hot.

"I'm out." Pennington tosses in his hand and shakes his head.

Nice. The fact I just financially spanked Cruise's little brother is just an added bonus to the mayhem that's about to ensue.

Ally gives a pressured tap on my shoulder. "I need to speak with you."

"Just one second, babe." I nod without taking my eyes off Rutger. His cable-knit sweater is knotted around his neck despite the fact we're in the middle of a tropical heat wave. Everything about him spells douche.

"I'm sorry, but this can't wait." Her voice trembles, catching me off guard.

I glance up. Her eyes are filling with tears faster than I can swipe the change from the preppies' pockets.

Crap.

"What happened?" I try to sound discreet, holding my hand close to my chest.

"You tell *me* what happened." Her voice is so loud it cauterizes my eardrums.

"You mind?" Rutger barks up at her. "Step the fuck out, Ally. Save the girl drama for later."

"Hey, *dude*, don't talk to her like that." I say it low, trying not to set him off since we're moments from a monetary exchange that can have the same life-altering effects as a lotto win.

"You don't talk to *me* like that." He says it cool, plucking through his deck without bothering to look up. "I'll talk to my girl any way I please." He shifts the toothpick in his mouth from one end to the other.

"My girl, huh?" I huff because I know it's not true. "Not in my club you won't." My blood starts to boil. As soon as I clear the table of all the green I'm going to strangle the shit out of good ol' Rutger here and make it look like an accident.

He huffs a quiet laugh as if he heard and accepted the challenge.

"You don't own this place, Jordan—my friends and I do." His eyes rest heavy over mine. There's a haughty air about him that affirms the fact this guy is a terminal asshole. "I can have you shut down in ten minutes. You've got no liquor license. You're violating some serious gambling codes. And I'm pretty sure prostitution is still illegal in Carrington County." He smears a shit-eating grin across his face. "You're trash, Jordan, just like your girlfriend." He glances up at Ally and winks.

I flip the table over, landing the four of them flat on their designer asses.

Ally screams as if the building were about to blow up.

Pen and his buddies instigate a money grab, but I skip the currency and go for the gold instead. I pick Rutger up by his pretty pink collar and drag him across the room in one quick pull.

"The only piece of trash I see is you." I grind it through my teeth.

"Morgan, *no!*" Ally screams as if I'm about to commit a felony, and I just might.

With everything in me I want to smash his ugly mug in, kick him in the nuts for even *thinking* about Ally that way.

I thrash his ass against the wall and get into his slobbering face.

"Ally is a *person*," I hiss, nose to nose. "She's got feelings just like everybody else. She's never hurt anybody or bullied them, and that's exactly what you and your *friends* seem to get off on. Just because you have a couple of dollars to rub together doesn't mean you get to treat people like shit. None of your friends are real and the only chicks you'll ever score will be there for the bonus. Nobody will ever want you for who you are because nobody likes a lying sack of shit." I push him out the door and watch as he stumbles into a wall.

The room drains, leaving Ally with a semi-pissed look on her face.

I shut the door and barricade it with a chair.

"You wanted to talk?" I pick up the table and spot a stack of cards pinned beneath it. I let out a little laugh. "Well, looky here." I hold it up for her to see. "They were taking me for a ride all along. The rich-boys club wasn't giving away a dime of their daddies' money tonight."

Ally doesn't lose her hard edge, that unwavering cold look.

"Were you with Blair Lancaster tonight?" She cuts me the death stare and lets me know my balls are up for the skewer.

Shit. I think I know where this is headed so I opt for the truth.

"Yes."

Her face smooths out; her features bleach, pale as plaster.

"Yes?" Her mouth contorts, disbelieving.

"Let me guess." I step forward and wrap my arms around her waist, but she's quick to push me away. I pull back and hold out my hands like a common street criminal. "Okay, it looks like I'm right. Whatever the hell she said to you I swear it was a lie. In fact, why don't I give you my version first, and you can compare and contrast. I've got no problem with that since I have nothing to hide."

"Let's hear it, Jordan." Ally takes a seat on the edge of the table and folds her arms tight across her chest. Her body language alone lets me know I can go screw myself. And if I want to get laid, I might just have to.

"Okay. I got here early, and noticed a light on, right here in this room."

She makes a face like she might be sick.

"I assumed I left it on, but I came over to check it out just in case there was some idiot milling around." I pause, trying to remember in detail what happened next. "I opened the door and Blair was standing here in her coat. She dropped trou and was naked as a jaybird. Believe me, Ally, I've seen skeletons at Halloween that were more attractive than what she was trying to offer." She gives a little laugh. "Then," I continue, "she said, 'You're welcome,' and slammed into me. I immediately jumped back and told her to get the fuck out."

"Then what?" Ally's eyes brim with tears, but she's determined not to let them fall.

"Then . . ." Shit, then what? "Oh, that's right, she said, it could be our 'dirty little secret.'" Why does it feel like I just stuck my head in a noose? "Look, Ally, I don't how the hell she knew to say those buzzwords and to be honest, at that point I was making my way back to the truck to get the liquor. I wasn't sticking around to have a conversation with her."

"So that's it?" Her brows notch together at the tips and she looks vulnerable as a schoolgirl.

"That's it. I swear. Why—what else did she have to add?"

Ally's mouth opens like she's about to say something but she pauses. "She just said some stupid stuff. We got into it and that was about it." She presses her lips together like a good cry is still an option. "She knew some stuff, Morgan." She shrugs. "You wouldn't tell her anything personal about me, would you?"

"What?" I take a step in and wrap my arms around her waist. "God, no. What did she say? Did she say something about Ruby?" I can't imagine anything more personal than that.

"No." She shakes her head. "It was nothing about Ruby." Ally swallows hard. "She probably dug around and filled her head with a bunch of crap to use against me. Looks like tonight was her night to unload the ammo." She glances at her shoes and gives a hard sniff.

"Ally," I whisper just over her ear. "I swear I would never hurt you like that." My heart breaks at how devastated she is. I have no idea what Blair told her, but the look on Ally's face is enough to let me know it was pretty shitty. "I love you." I kiss her cheek. "I only want to be with you, ever, Ally—and there is no greater truth."

"Really?" It comes from her as a barely there whisper, as if she finds it hard to believe that anybody would ever want to be with her.

"Really." I dot my lips over hers.

I suppose this isn't the right time to fill her in on the facts that the dancers never showed tonight, that Steven wasn't here to man the liquor, and I had to hire some frat boy to tend bar for the evening. Everything went to shit after Blair hexed the place with her ghost of a body, but I'll be damned if Ally and I fall apart because of it.

My cell buzzes in my pocket, and I pluck it out. It's a text from a blocked number.

You just fucked with the wrong person. See you in hell.

I slip it back in my pocket. It's probably Rutger and his band of brokers, emphasis on the "broke"—then I remember they mopped up the money before they left the room and I'm the one who's broke.

I push a tiny smile out at Ally. She's all I need.

"I'm sorry." She gives a slow breath. "I guess I just let her get to me."

"Hey, it's okay." I trace her lips with my finger.

"Thank you for defending me just now with Rutger. You didn't have to do that." Ally leans in and I take in the scent from her sweet perfume. "He's a total ass. I never did pay attention to half the crap that defecated from his mouth."

My chest rumbles with a tiny laugh.

"I'm glad." I touch my finger to her chin and gently lift it until she looks right at me. "You're a smart, beautiful woman, Ally. And if someone tries to tell you otherwise, don't believe them. You're important and you have a good heart." I lean in and land a tender kiss over her pillow-soft lips. Something pinches deep inside me. Ally has my stomach melting like that of a sixteen-year-old. "I don't ever remember anyone making me feel this way," I whisper. "I think for the first time in my life I truly know what love is. Thank you for giving me that."

Her eyes widen, her lips press in. She runs her hip over my crotch, and I tick to life like an obedient puppy. I give a wicked half smile, hoping she'll catch on to the implications.

"*Oh*"—she gives a little laugh while rubbing her thigh over me, and I happily bloom to life—"it looks like someone's glad to see me." She runs her hand inside my shirt, smoothing over my chest in one heated rush.

"I'm always glad to see you." I sink a heated kiss over her neck, and she lets out a groan. I toss the cards down over the table and growl, holding back a smile.

"It looks like you're still in the mood to play games."

"Are you in the mood to play games?" My lips curve in a crooked grin as I run my tongue over her lips. I can hear the club pulsating in the background like a bongo drum, and I wish to God we were anywhere but here.

"Sometimes I think life is one long game." She glances down a moment. Ally is just one step away from tears. Blair really got in her head. And God knows I'd love to help her forget Blair and all her bullshit. She looks up at me with those lime-green eyes and holds my gaze. "You ever wonder if you'll win, Morgan?" It comes out far too serious. Ally is on the verge of an all-out sob, and I'd do anything to comfort her. Damn Blair and her stupid antics. She and Rutger should hook up and leave decent people like Ally the hell alone.

"I always win." My hands race over her back. "I have you, don't I?" Shit. That didn't sound quite the way I meant it. "I mean." I shake my head. "I probably shouldn't say anything else.

You turn my brain to Jell-O. You're just too damn hot to focus on anything else." I ride my eyes over her chest without meaning to—but with her dress cut down to her belly, who could blame me?

Her hands melt down the front of my chest. Her fingers fumble with the button on my jeans.

"Maybe neither one of us should talk." She dips her cool fingers into the back of my boxers, and I let out a choking breath. "Maybe we should—"

I crush my lips over hers before she can finish the sentence. My body aches and my bones feel like they'll shatter if I don't have her right fucking now. Ally unzips my jeans and pulls my hard-on free from my boxers.

"You sure know how to get to the point." I say it quietly as I bite over her earlobe. I dip into my pocket and pull out a condom.

"Armored response. I'm impressed." A tiny dimple depresses into the side of her cheek. "I bet you're just waiting to bend me over this table." She pulls back and takes me in with her sleepy eyes. "Well, Jordan? Looks like you've got a boner to contend with. I think you'd better do something." She morphs back into the Ally I know and love, incredibly sexy and bossy as hell. "You just going to stand there with that golf club hanging out of your Levi's or are you going to try and swing it?"

"Oh, sweetie"—I gurgle a soft laugh—"you have the wrong sport. This is a bat, and I'm about to score the home run of a lifetime." I pull her in by the back of the neck and sear my tongue over hers like I'm putting out a fire. "Turn around," I whisper hot into her ear.

Ally spins and pulls her hair to one side as I nuzzle into her neck.

"Bend over." I say it with a little more feeling and her mouth opens as she looks up at me. Ally complies and lies belly down over the green felt. I glide my hands over her panties and tug them down, torturously slow, inch by inch until they fall to her ankles. I kick out her legs and a laugh bubbles from her.

"Pull up your dress for me." I step back, not wanting to miss a moment of the show. Ally reaches down and carefully inches up her dress. A black curtain of lace rises over the mound of her perfect ass and a groan churns from my gut.

Her dress puddles around her waist, and I'm mesmerized by her pale perfection. Ally's got a banging body, a face that could make an entire army of angels jealous, and a heart of solid gold.

"Shit," I moan, taking her in. Ally Monroe is every wet dream I've ever had rolled into one. "I'm going to open the door and let everyone see how fucking beautiful you are." I sway toward the exit, and her hips jump in my hands. "I'm teasing. I'm greedy. I want this all to myself. I want to keep you like this forever. You can be my lucky charm the next time the boys and I get together to play. Of course, you'll have to assume the position."

"You're not funny," she purrs with that sexier than hell drawl. "And by the way I'm getting cold."

"Mmm," I moan, running my hands over her bare bottom. "Sounds like I'd better heat things up." I run my hand down over her wet slick and plunge a finger deep inside her. Ally gasps, clawing at the table as if that was what she was waiting for this whole time. She so fucking wet, she's practically crying onto my hand. "You're almost there, aren't you, Ally?"

She pants into the table. Her pale hair spills out over the expanse of it.

"I bet you'd like it if I made you come right now, wouldn't you?"

"Morgan." She grinds her hips into me, begging for that very thing.

"I want you to wait for me, can you wait for me?" My breathing grows erratic. I'm about to fucking lose it. Hell—I don't think *I* can wait for me. I roll the rubber on fast and furious and let out a heartfelt groan as I rub my cock along her heated slick.

Ally moves her hips like an invitation so I accept and push myself deep inside of her, one strong thrust after another. I stare down at Ally with her hair splayed over the table in loose ringlets, her long, pale fingers begging for something to hold onto. I want Ally to hold on to me, forever.

I pull out and spin her around, landing her legs over my hips. Ally leans up and locks her lips over mine as we ride into that beautiful oblivion together. I reach down until my thumb finds a home between her heated thighs and she begins to lose control.

"Right now." I give it in a ragged breath over her mouth and we detonate together, shaking and trembling with a groan locked in our throats.

"I would die before I hurt you, Ally," I whisper, still out of breath.

"I know." She buries her lips in my neck.

But I'm not so sure she knows.

⌒

Saturday, on the evening of my mother's next and hopefully final jaunt down the aisle, Kendall insists we gather in Mom's bedroom and offer our moral support. I watch bored from the mattress as

Cruise's mother, Sam, puts the finishing touches on Mom's hair, trying my hardest not to let my mind wander to what might be taking place in this room in just a few short hours.

"Looking good." I say it like I mean it. Although I'm not too sure my mother needed a cheering section while having her hair set in rollers.

"We're getting there," she sings. She's got a smile on her lips that looks almost foreign. I'm glad she found someone who makes her smile. I don't remember her smiling so much with the other clowns she leashed herself to.

"Now, Morgan"—she starts slow—"we just need to find you someone special and our family will be complete." She gives a quick wink.

I glance over at Kendall and wait for it.

"Morgan does have someone special." Kendall gives an impish grin, sounding all of thirteen in the process. She looks nice in her lavender gown, her dark hair swept up with loose curls dusting the sides, but I won't tell her that. I'll leave the compliments to Cruise and save mine for Ally.

Mom and Sam *ooh* and *ah* over the morsel Kendall tossed in the air.

"So who's this girl that's swept my little prince off his feet?" Mom's eyes pop like dinner plates. The bright-blue shadow she's wearing does her no favors, but I don't say a word.

"Ally." Kendall is quick to dispense the latest Carrington gossip.

"Ally?" Sam nods in approval. "She's a sweetheart, that one. Works at Starbucks, right?"

"*Did,*" Kendall corrects. "She got canned. Anyway, she's had it pretty tough in general so that explains her attraction to Morgan." She cuts me a brief wink.

"I know Ally." Mom comes to as if she's just catching on. "She's the one who's been staying at the house with you. Looks like a little summer romance was brewing all along."

"Just summer?" Kendall twists in my direction. Her eyes drill into me with the subtlety of a jackhammer, and for a stunned moment I wonder if Ally has the same question.

"Looks that way." I still haven't heard back from the coach. Maybe I'll head back to Oregon and finish out fall semester, then move back permanently in time for Christmas. I'll be back for Kendall's wedding. That might be a nice way to surprise Ally.

Who the hell am I kidding? It's killing me not to see Ally right this fucking minute, and she's in the backyard. I'll never make it to the gas station, let alone the next state.

"Well"—Mom turns toward the mirror as Sam pokes her fingers into Mom's hair—"you just never know what the future holds. I thought I left Carrington for good, but a part of me was rooting for the love I left behind. Who knows? Maybe Ally will be sitting right in this chair twenty-five years down the road and you'll be the groom waiting downstairs."

"Twenty-five years?" Kendall scoffs.

That's a whole lifetime.

"People move on." Mom reapplies her lipstick. "Marriages—*kids* happen, and before you know it you're both leading different lives."

An image of Ally and Rutger driving around in that kit car of his runs through my mind, and a wave of jealousy rips through me, wide as the sea.

Twenty-five years. I couldn't make it twenty-five minutes.

Nope—I'm definitely going to need to figure something out.

The Elton House Bed and Breakfast has been transformed both inside and out to reflect the blessed event with an explosion of flowers in every shade of pink. The willows blow in the thick, humid breeze, and the perfume from the roses fills the air.

I spot Ally standing near the altar and my stomach bottoms out. Her hair glows platinum as the sun illuminates it from behind. She outshines the roses—all of nature can't compete with her beauty.

The wedding hymn vibrates through the air, and I take Mom's arm.

"It's time," I say. "You ready to do this?" A part of me felt like asking if she wants to run like hell.

Mom's eyes glitter with tears. I've never witnessed her so moved to marry anyone. I'm hoping that's a sign of a marriage that spans the length of years, or at least that Mr. Right Now hangs around long enough for me to remember his name.

"Oh, hon," she whispers, "I've been ready for decades."

Decades. I swallow hard as I glance over at Ally. I don't plan on letting decades slide by.

We walk down the aisle, slow and measured, my eyes never wavering from Ally's. She's flirting, licking her lips, her neck arching back just enough; it's not until I get close enough that I notice she's holding back tears. A part of me would like to think she's imagining what it would be like walking down this aisle with me standing at the other end. I try to picture her derelict brother giving her away—me waiting with an ear-to-ear grin.

I'll be damned if this is the last weekend we spend together. I just need to figure out what the hell to do. But, I can't just walk away from baseball—can I?

My heart skips a few beats as I glide past her. I hope this isn't some big euphemism for what the future holds—me moving on without her. It's times like this life squeezes my balls just enough to make me want to puke my guts up.

The ceremony goes on with the usual pomp and ultra-boring circumstance until Mom and her new hubby exchange a peck on the cheek.

The crowd breaks out in applause, and Mom and Andrew trot back down the aisle. I head over to Ally and press a kiss just shy of her lips. I'm pretty sure if it were our wedding day we wouldn't be pecking at one another. A lewd grin begs to erupt as I consider the possibilities.

The three-piece strings section continues to play long into the outdoor reception that comes complete with a catered buffet from a local five-star restaurant. Andrew may have let Mom have her way by choosing a humble venue, but he's gone balls out when it comes to the finishing touches.

"You were great up there." Ally blushes as she says it.

"And you're beyond gorgeous," I hum over her lips before pressing in a kiss.

She glances over my shoulder. "Lauren's calling me." She makes a face. "I'll be right back. Hold that thought." She bounces her lips off mine before trotting off.

Molly pops up like a diligent little stalker. Her nipples play peekaboo over the low rim of her red dress, which shows off her most prized assets. She leans into me with her cleavage in my face like she's trying to put my dick on notice. Swear to God, if that doesn't spell out tramp on a stick I don't know what does.

"Looks like we're getting closer every day." She breathes it over my face, and a blast of whiskey rakes over me.

"Yup, we're practically brother and sister," I say, looking past her at Ally, who's already making her way back.

"Oh"—Molly runs her finger down my chest—"I wouldn't say that, but if you want me to call you *daddy* that could be arranged." I catch her by the wrist before she hits pay dirt, and Ally slips an arm around my waist just in time.

"How's it going, Mol?" Ally bites down over her lower lip as if it's taking everything in her not to pull out the claws. I think I like this side of Ally, protective with a touch of insane jealousy on the side.

"Always sticking yourself where you're not wanted." Molly sways on her heels. "You're just a thorn in everybody's side. Especially mine." She shoots Ally a look that spells out an ass-kicking with more intensity than some of the physical ones I've distributed.

I pull Ally in and kiss her cheek. "You're definitely not a thorn in my side."

"Oh, is that so?" Molly takes a step forward, her tits thrust in my face like a threat. "You just think you can dump me and move on?" Her eyes reduce to slits, sharp enough to castrate any male in the vicinity. "I suggest you rethink this, *Morgan*." She says my name as if this bullshit just got real. "Choosing someone like Ally over me can and will prove to be a fatal move. Being with some-one like her"—she shakes her head, her face rife with vengeance—"that's just a slow suicide." She stalks off in the direction of the B and B, and I'm not too sorry to see her go.

"Someone's PMSing." Ally bubbles with a laugh as she pulls me to the side just under the weeping willow.

"Did you send me a rose today?" Ally circles her arm around my waist as the smile melts from her face.

"Uh . . ." Did someone send her a rose today?

"That's okay." She shakes her head. "I didn't think it was you. It was silly."

"Since when are roses silly?" I'm not opposed to pretending I sent it. "And why wouldn't I send you one?" I'll send her a dozen to make up for it.

"Because it was black." Her eyes sharpen on mine.

"Black?" What the fuck?

My phone rings, and I pluck it from my pocket. It's Paige.

I glance up at Ally as the color drains from my face.

"Is it her?" Her brows knit together with worry.

I nod and pick up.

"Morgan?" Paige sounds a hell of a lot happier than she did a few days ago. I'm not too sure what to read into her all-too-chipper mood, but I'll bite.

"It's me. How's it going? Everything okay with the baby?" My heart thumps wildly. My ears pick up on the sonic boom going off in my chest.

The world spins unnaturally. The ground gyrates beneath my feet as Ally puts her head on my shoulder.

"Camden is doing great. He's doing *real* great. He doesn't need a respirator or anything. They want to keep him at the hospital a couple more days to keep an eye on him, that's all." The line goes quiet, and I forget to breathe, let alone ask the pertinent questions. "I got your results."

"Great. I'm ready." Am I? Am I ever going to be ready to be someone's father? His *dad*? God knows mine wasn't. I hope it's not a hereditary trait.

"It's Clint's baby. I'm not sure whether to say I'm sorry or not, but Camden's not your son."

A wave of relief pushes through me so fast and hard, for a second I start to black out. Then, more pronounced than ever,

I realize that I do want to be a father, I want to be a dad to a perfect tiny being that happens to be the product of me and the woman I love. I glance down at Ally, who's getting ready to bite right through her lip, and I shake my head.

"Congratulate Clint for me, will you? I'm sure he's beautiful."

We hang up and I swing Ally around in a circle. The whole world comes to life; the air is sweeter, lighter, and every possibility is open once again for Ally and me. I plant a heated kiss over her lips that helps melt me back into my own skin. Morgan Jordan is free to move to the Eastern Seaboard any fucking time he likes. Now if only I can get the baseball world to comply.

Ally pulls back and I set her feet on God's green earth. I'm just happy to be here, be anywhere with Ally.

"One day it'll happen for you"—she runs her finger over my eyebrow—"and it'll be the right time with the right girl." She glances down a moment. A look of sorrow sweeps across her face as if she's jealous of this other girl.

"Would you want to be that girl?" My cheeks fire up with heat, testifying to the fact I'm one hundred percent whipped.

Ally opens her mouth to respond just as Kendall, Lauren, and their respective not so better halves crop up to join us.

"Why so secret?" Kendall arches a brow like we might have big news to dispense. Leave it to Kendall to make something out of nothing and leave me looking like a douche.

"No secrets." Ally shrugs as I pull her in and drop a kiss on her head. It's great like this with her friends—having Kendall as a part of my life again. Even Cruise is starting to grow on me. Deep down, he's a pretty cool guy. Kendall's lucky to have him.

"Oh, come on." Lauren pushes her shoulder into Ally. "We saw all that, hugging—the celebratory spin."

"Morgan's leaving next week." Ally sounds a bit too animated, like she's glad to be rid of me even though I know she's covering for the phone call. I hope. "In fact"—she takes a step back and faces me—"I want to apologize to you, right here in front of everyone." She takes up my hand and looks me in the eye.

I'm not so sure I want to hear the big apology. I'm positive she's got nothing to be sorry for, and, if she does, it's certainly not to me.

"When I first laid eyes on you"—she shakes her head a little, her eyes already pooling with tears—"I judged you. I saw how vexingly gorgeous you were, and thought this is a guy who can and *does* take home anybody he wants. Then I saw all those tattoos and I decided you were wild—untamed. I judged who you were based on what you looked like and how much money you had in your wallet." She sniffs hard, cutting a quick glance to the ground. "Morgan, you're the kindest soul on the planet, and I think you know how much I care about you, so it's really important for me to say I'm sorry. I hope you don't mind, I wanted to say it out loud, in front of my closest friends—I wanted to share how much I love you—how much you mean to me." She looks up at me from under her lashes, her face pink from her admission.

I pull her in and rip a wet kiss right off her lips. "I think you're pretty amazing too."

Lauren and Kendall break out in a choir of *aww*.

Ally tightens her grip around my waist and we indulge in a deeper, more meaningful kiss. A part of me wishes this were our wedding.

Then I would never have to worry about leaving.

Ally would be mine forever.

I hope she will be one day.

12

RUBY SKY

Ally

In the morning, long before the first rays of sunlight spray over the northern hemisphere, Morgan buries a heated kiss in my neck and rouses with a groan.

"Are you looking for a repeat?" I murmur. Last night's sex was spectacular. Correction, it wasn't sex. Last night was all about celebrating our love.

He grazes over my thigh with his long, hard answer, and I twist in his arms and meet him with a kiss.

"A repeat would be impossible." He plants a scalding kiss directly into my ear, and my body tingles as I let out a breath.

I'm savoring, *memorizing* all this for the fallout of his departure. I hate that he's leaving, and I hate that neither of us has brought it up. Maybe it's not that big a deal to him? Maybe I've read way too much into what's happened between us this summer.

"Why, pray tell, is a repeat impossible?" I was sort of hoping for a rather spectacular minute-by-minute replay, especially the part where he launched me into the outer realm of pleasure with an orgasm that had a life of its own—a shooting star that went on like a blaze of glory. Morgan is a god, creating a whole new universe, with me as his clay. This was divine, glorious, and right. It can't end. Not like this, not now, not ever.

"Because"—he draws me close until our stomachs sear one another—"every time we're together it's something new, something better." He presses a quick kiss over my lips before reaching to the nightstand for a condom. "And, right now, I want to make everything new." He touches his mouth to mine with a sweet roaming kiss. "Everything better."

Morgan lands over me and hikes my hands up over my head just as the first ray of dawn pierces through the slit in the blinds.

"This is turning out to be a good morning." He whispers it low, seductively.

"I think this is a great way to start every morning." There. I broached the topic, popped the balloon of our discontent, and now the ball is in his court.

"Me too," he whispers with a measure of grief in his voice as he lowers a kiss to my lips. Morgan cups my breasts fully in his hands and covers me with his mouth until I'm aching for him in every way.

Morgan holds up the condom, a loose grin playing on his lips. I take it from him and open it, pull it over him, never losing our gaze.

I wrap my legs around his back and guide him in until he gives. Morgan thrusts in all the way until it feels as if he could burst from my throat. I hold him there like that by the small of his back. This was it, the big countdown. Every moment had reduced itself to a limited-time offer. Morgan dips into me, crashing his lips over mine.

It's sweet like this, filled with angst, the pleasure and pain both physical and emotional. Tears pool in my eyes, and I don't fight them. There's a hole forming in my heart because I know it's going to hurt like hell not to reach over and feel him right there next to me.

Morgan glides his hands down my body, slow and heated as if he were tracing out my curves for a final time, rubbing his thumb over me until I'm choking for air.

"Let's do this together," he whispers.

"Let's." I want to do everything with Morgan, but I'm too afraid to say it—too afraid I'm the only one who wants anything other than *this* together.

Morgan thrusts into me, unrestrained, uninhibited by the loud crack of the headboard knocking into the wall like a shotgun blast. He moves me with him every step of the way until I feel like I'm going to burst. I bury a kiss in his left dimple as he pants in my ear, alive with his lust for me.

"Shit, Ally." He glides his lips over my mouth, my cheek, right up over my ear. "I'm gonna come." He chokes out the words and quivers over me just as I explode into a million blissful pieces. I let out a cry that shrills through the virginal morning like the serrated edge of a knife.

A hard thump lands against the wall, and I clap my hand over my mouth in mortification.

"I think that was *Cruise*," I whisper. "I bet he's congratulating you," I pant just shy of a laugh.

"I think he was congratulating *you*." Morgan collapses over me before rolling off to the side. He hikes up on his elbow and gives a sad, slow smile. "Ally"—he says my name in a heated whisper—"why couldn't this summer last forever?" It comes out barely audible, almost as a private thought that has somehow escaped his vocal cords.

"I don't know." I lay my head over his chest and listen to the wild drumming of his heart. My own heart cries out *Don't go* with every morbid thump. But I'm not sure he hears it.

And if he did, would he listen?

———

"Ruby Christie is four years old today." I say it out loud as Morgan drives us down miles of country back roads that lead to the Christies' spacious home. As soon as Tess heard Morgan was joining me, she opted to drive out on her own and give us some alone time on the way over. I'm glad she did.

The bright-red bicycle in the back of the truck is already assembled thanks to Morgan and his toolbox know-how. That boy knows his way around all of the pertinent equipment, that much I know is true.

"Did it go by fast? Ruby turning four?" Morgan's dimples dig in, content, and it melts me just to look at him.

"Lightning quick. It really does feel like it was just yester-day I was lying in that hospital bed—that tiny baby wrapped in my arms." I leave out the part that it was the most painful day of my life—that Tess held me while I sobbed for weeks, *months*, to get over the initial trauma of losing my precious baby. It was like losing my mother all over again. "I don't know what I would do if I didn't like the Christies." I say it so low, I'm not sure he heard me. The thought of someone not being kind to her, or denying me the right to be a part of her life, would have been too much to bear.

"I can't imagine how tough that was." He shakes his head, still staring out at the road. "But I'm glad you like them and that they're so generous with Ruby. You think she'll be okay with me showing up?"

"Are you kidding?" I bubble with laughter at the thought of Ruby meeting Morgan. "She'll probably want to marry you." True story, but no sooner do the words stream from my lips than my face turns beet red from saying something so stupid to begin with.

"Sounds like she's a girl who knows what she wants—just like her mom." He gives a quick wink.

I'm just about to turn up the volume on my sarcastic superpowers when my phone buzzes in my hand.

It's a text.

See you in hell.

I stare at it an inordinate amount of time. The number is blocked just like the last time.

"You okay?" He dips his gaze over me a moment before returning his focus to the road.

"Just Tess." The truth is I don't want to lose any part of this precious day by entertaining the lunacy that is Molly or Blair or whoever feels the need to try and scare the hell out of me. Rory and the insanity that existed between us those final few days comes back to life. He swore he'd never forgive me if I told the police. My heart gives a few tempered thumps. So many damned possibilities to entertain.

Even that black rose lying over the seat of my car had me rattled. The doors were all locked, the windows rolled up. How the hell did it get inside?

I power down my phone and bury it at the bottom of my purse. No use in giving the lunatic in question any more airplay in my mind. Instead, I sink into my seat and gaze out the window at the evergreens and the kaleidoscope of sugar maples that speed by in a dizzying blur.

This is Ruby's birthday—Morgan's last Sunday on the East Coast for quite some time. I'll deal with Molly or Blair, or whoever the hell it is, once he leaves. I won't let anyone get away with this bullshit.

I glance over at the handsome prince by my side, his dark hair, the face of a fallen angel. The only person I'm letting get away, apparently, is Morgan.

After another half hour, we come up on the house, and we struggle to find a parking spot on the street.

The Christies' home is decorated both inside and out with a kitten theme, giant, small, fluffy, hairless—pictures of cats in every incarnation are plastered to the walls.

A small crowd of children and parents stream throughout the property.

"This is amazing!" I beam over at Janice as soon as we walk through the door.

"Well, thank you!" Her eyes enlarge as she glances back at Morgan. "I've been up since midnight stuffing goody bags, and I dreamt of cats trying to claw my eyes out all week long." Janice perks up as she steps toward Morgan. Her eyes elongate over him like a pair of oval mirrors as she nods with approval.

"Janice, this is Morgan. Morgan, Janice." I don't take my eyes off her. Janice has many talents but concealing how she feels isn't one of them.

They exchange hellos and he shakes her hand like the gentleman he is. She engages him in polite small talk, and I swim just taking it in. I can't imagine what it would have been like if I ever brought Rutger here. Rutger would have commented on the lack of a waitstaff, balked at the ceiling fan instead of a chandelier.

But Morgan is sweet, *humble*, and well-versed in all the areas in which Rutger is severely lacking. It's apparent I dodged a bullet with that one. Thank God for Kendall and her mother's wedding or I might have missed out on the best summer of my life.

Janice claps her hands together and straightens her back.

"Well, it looks like you've got your head screwed on straight. I'm really impressed, especially about your upcoming baseball career. I'll have to tell my husband to keep an eye out for you. Baseball is his passion."

Something warms in me as she gushes over Morgan. She gives a quick wink in my direction before disappearing back into the kitchen.

"Mama!" A tiny voice squeals as Ruby runs over. Her hair is up in two perfectly curled pigtails. She has on raspberry-colored lip gloss, and her cheeks sparkle with glitter.

"Well, look who it is! It's the birthday princess!" I press my lips to her cheek and spin her around in a circle. Ruby is light as a feather and smells of clean linen and fresh summer rain. "Ruby, I'd like you to meet someone." I hike her up over my hip. "This is my friend Morgan. I thought I'd bring him to help celebrate your big day."

"You have a boyfriend?" Her face twists up like she's trying to hold back a laugh.

God. Who knew Ruby would put two and two together?

"I eat cookies with boys at school," she says to him in lieu of hello.

He nods. "I'll eat a cookie with you anytime." His eyes pierce through a brilliant glacier blue, and my stomach pinches at the sight.

"Cookies!" She springs out of my arms and races toward the yard, where there's a sprawling display of confections to choose from.

"Told you she'd fall in love with you."

"Like mother, like daughter." Morgan's killer dimples implode as he offers a sweet smile.

I bite down over my lower lip. I swear I might bawl like a baby any minute.

"Like mother, like daughter." I say it quiet, unsure if either Ruby or me falling for Morgan is a good idea.

Morgan pulls me close and wraps his arms around my waist.

"Hey, you two!" Tess bobs by and places a giant red gift bag on the table. "Cool it, will you? This is a family show."

Tess looks immaculate in street clothes. I can't remember the last time I saw her in jeans and a simple white T-shirt.

I give a brief hug and we follow her outside to the heart of the party.

"So," she starts, "I have an announcement."

"You have a job lined up for me in the fall?" I'm only half teasing.

"Nope." She pinches her eyes closed a moment. "Morgan, don't let her dance. I can't stand the thought of not being there to protect her."

"What do you mean, protect me?" For a moment I think Tess knows something about my not-so-nice rose-gifting stalker. "And where are you going?"

"I'm leaving." She shrugs with a playful grin on her face. "I got a job at that gown club in New York, so I took it." She turns to Morgan. "Technically that's high-end dancing, but in reality it translates to less dancing, more dollars, and lots of fancy dresses."

"Is Dell okay with this? What the hell am I saying! Who cares what Dell has to say? Congratulations!" I offer Tess a huge strong hug. I can't help but think she's escaped some involuntary incarceration. "But I'm shocked you'd leave Pretty Girls, not to mention your boyfriend."

Morgan glances up at me when I say it.

"Ex-boyfriend," she corrects. "Besides, you were right, Al. I need to explore, see what's out there, not chain myself to Dell and his sheltered club forever." She rolls her eyes. "Dell says I'll come back."

"You will," I say. "Only it'll be to visit *me*." I pull Tess in and take in the vanilla scent of her hair. Tess has worn the same fragrance since our childhood. The same perfume my mother wore.

"You're thinking about her, aren't you?" She says it sweetly, combing her fingers through my hair the same way my mother did.

I don't say a word, just press my lips together and nod.

Tess always knows when I go there.

"How I wish she could be here to see Ruby," I whisper.

"She'd be proud of you, Al. You know that, right?"

Tears spring to my eyes as Tess tightens her grip around my shoulders. *"Hey."* Tess bounces back and claps her hands. "You gotta come visit me in New York!"

"If you insist," I tease, averting my eyes as if this would be more than difficult.

"I'll go with you." Morgan dips his gaze toward me with his tragically sexy smile. "We should see a Broadway show when we go." Morgan pulls me in by the waist, and I melt into him.

My entire person springs to life with hope. Maybe Morgan Jordan does want something more than a summer fling. Or maybe I've just become his go-to vacation girl.

Janice wrangles the crowd together for gifts. Ruby looks like she might blow if this doesn't happen soon, while her sisters dance around her in a circle. They look like sugared fairies, and I try to etch the beauty of the moment into my mind. Ruby tears through gift after gift, amassing far too many toys and clothes to comprehend, and Janice is kind enough to save my gift for last. She motions me over to present it.

I pull Morgan aside and run my hand over his chest. "Would you mind rolling it out to her?" I ask. "I really want to see the look on her face." I've waited all summer for this moment.

"You bet." He dots my lips with a kiss.

Ruby jumps in my arms, and I hold her tight.

"What is it, Mama?" Her eyes grow large as tennis balls as Morgan wheels over her bicycle, complete with a wicker basket and a shiny, silver bell.

"A big-girl bike!" She jumps out of my arms and bolts to her new wheels, nearly taking Morgan out in the process. Ruby hops on, fearless, as her feet twirl over the pedals. Morgan holds on to the back and guides her down the concrete expanse until she flies like a speed demon down the makeshift basketball court.

"She's doing it!" Janice hops by my side. "She's going all by herself!"

Morgan watches as Ruby rides around in circles. He's there waiting, ready to catch her if she falls, just like he did me.

"He's a real good guy, Ally," Janice whispers. "I'd say he's a keeper."

"Yeah, I know."

I just can't figure out how to keep him.

Morgan

The week glides by like a sailboat cutting through the sea, the wind of time propelling it along at unnatural speeds. It's time to pack up my suitcase and not one ounce of me is willing to do it.

Wednesday, Cruise offers to ride shotgun while I drive down to Garrison to speak with the coach. It's the last party trick I can think of to let me blow off Oregon once and for all. I'm set to leave tomorrow, so I'm not above falling to my knees and begging for a batboy position.

School starts next week both here and back home. It's like someone hit the fast-forward button on August and forgot to let go. Summer in Carrington filled me with a world I didn't know was possible, one in which something as intangible as love could actually be felt, touched, held—and in my case, love came in the form of a sweet girl named Ally. Just the thought of heading back to Oregon fills me with dread. My life back there had become nothing more than an empty shell. Having a prime baseball scholarship once meant I had the world by the tail, and now a light's been cast over it, exposing it for what it's been all along—nothing without someone to share it with. Not even something as rewarding as baseball could hold up to what I had going with Ally—still have, and hopefully always will.

"What happens if you don't get it?" Cruise asks as we cross the lawn toward the athletics department.

"*Gee*—glad I brought you along, sunshine." I shoot him a look. "I don't know what the fuck happens if I don't get it." It comes out far more maudlin and less pissed than I was hoping for. "I haven't gotten that far yet. What about you? Kendall mentioned something about a failed attempt at getting your doctorate. What's plan B?"

"I'm living plan B. And the B stands for bed-and-break-fast." He lets out a curt breath. "Besides, I got kicked out of the program. I didn't fail." He does a double take at someone at the top of the stairs. "That happened."

I glance over and lo and fucking behold if it isn't Satan in female form: Blair.

Cruise lets out a hard sigh. "She reported some question-able behavior and happened to document it in the process. Case closed."

"Got it." I can tell by the look in his eye there's more to the story. "Did that questionable behavior happen to involve my sister?" Not that I need the dirty details, and I do believe they're dirty. The words *questionable behavior* are rife with sexual implications.

"I'll take the fifth."

There you go.

Blair scuttles over as fast as her high heels will allow, cut-ting us off just as we're about to head into the athletics building.

"Hello, Morgan." She gives a wide sniveling grin. "Rumor has it you'll be staying around." She disregards Cruise entirely and runs her hand over my chest uninvited.

"Maybe, maybe not. Either way, it's none of your business." I take the next step toward the building and pause. "And by the way, I didn't appreciate you lying to Ally and making it sound like we knocked boots over the poker table."

Cruise's eyes expand like Ping-Pong balls.

"And," I continue, "I don't know what sources you used to dig crap up on Ally but the only one that came out smelling like a sack of lying shit was you."

Her chest expands, her tight lips press in until they disappear, and for a second I'm positive she's going to break down and cry.

Crap. I've done a lot of shitty things but telling off a girl, well, this is a first.

My shoulders sag because I know what's coming. "Look," I whisper, "I'm sorry things aren't working out the way you want, but you can't keep running around trying to take people down because they don't want to have a relationship with you. I'm sure there are plenty of guys out there who would, but you just keep going after the ones that are taken."

"For the record"—she takes a bold step forward, seething in my direction—"you didn't seem to mind me too much when you came into town."

"That's because I didn't know any better." I say it dry, not meaning to slit her throat with my harsh words, but according to the look on her face I did just that. "Everybody makes mistakes, Blair. Why don't you accept the fact that you have too? Move on. Head for greener pastures, where you're wanted, and stop trying to crucify people who've found happiness elsewhere."

Blair remains stoic, stiff as a statue as Cruise and I brush past her.

"Well done," Cruise says as we head up the stairs. "It's too bad it fell on deaf ears. Blair could have really learned something today if she was a decent person. That girl is hell on wheels. You just lit a very short fuse, my friend. If I were you, I'd look out for the boom."

We enter the cool of the building and meander all the way down to Coach Wexler's office only to find it dark with no sign of life, for sure no sign of my scholarship.

"And there's my luck for you." I blow out a breath of frustration. "I guess I'm out of here tomorrow as planned."

"Is that what you want?"

"No, but I'm not sure if I have the balls to give up my baseball scholarship."

"Maybe it's time to think about growing a bigger pair." He lets out a sigh as if I hit a wall.

Why does it feel like there's no hope of staying? I'm pretty sure Ally wouldn't want me hanging around while both undereducated and underemployed. Baseball's always been the out—the safeguard for my future, and now everything seems up in the air.

"Dude, you can visit." He slaps me on the back as we head back outside. "That's what long weekends and even longer plane rides are for. Plus, there's always next summer."

"Next summer." I shake my head at the idea. It feels like another lifetime away. "What would you do if you were me?" I'm not too sure Cruise gets the fact I've got a whole lifetime of baseball riding on the tail of this decision.

"I'd probably drop everything and move, but I'm stupid that way. Besides, Ally knows how much baseball means to you. She wouldn't want you to do that."

I give a bleak smile as we head back out into the haze of late afternoon.

Cruise would drop everything and move.

I nod at the idea. I just might be stupid like that too.

My phone vibrates, and I yank it out of my jeans. It's a text from a blocked number.

RIP Rock Bottom.

A dry laugh rumbles from my chest. It's probably Cal pushing me to clear my shit out of his place. He has the gift of subtlety.

"Would you mind dropping me off at the gym?"

"Sure, I was just heading there myself. Did Kendall ever ask you to be a part of the wedding?"

"Nope." Great. I have a feeling we're about to elevate our bromance to a whole new level.

"Well, *I'm* asking. We're keeping it simple, just a best man and best woman. I was thinking about Cal but I'd rather have family. What do you say? You think you'd want to stand up for me on my wedding day?"

"Yeah, man." I give him a gentle sock to the arm. "I got your back. But if you hurt my sister I might have to break it."

"Deal." He socks me back with a little more meaning behind it. "You'll be paired with Molly."

"Perfect." It comes out far more sarcastic than intended.

"Thanks for letting her down easy. I know she's been after you all summer. Once she gets her teeth sunk in something, she doesn't know how to let go. She can be a little demon."

That not-so-veiled threat she delivered at the wedding runs through my mind.

"Yeah, a real demon. You've got more than a few of those running around Carrington." Molly, Blair, Dell—just to name a few. How in the hell am I supposed to pack it up and go back west, knowing Ally is out here with a target on her back?

The Carrington Fitness Center is brimming with bodies I've seen night after night at the club. If anything, Cal owes me for augmenting his business both day and night.

Tonight is my last night at Rock Bottom.

I hightail it down to the basement and take in the expansive area. The hint of alcohol and cigarettes lingers in the air. The wind picks up and howls through the cavernous space like a damn ghost. And, come this time tomorrow that's exactly what I'll be leaving in my wake, my ghost.

Back door is open. We've never used that door. Cal probably forgot to shut it this morning.

I head in that direction and the memory of every good time I've had in this place comes back to me—girls laughing, dancing, the bastards running a game in the back under my nose—making love to Ally here as if we had the rest of our lives to do it. And now, I've got less than twenty-four hours to touch her, feel her, listen to her breathe. Speaking of which, it's time to head home for a little while and do just that.

Home. A huff of laughter escapes me. Home is where Ally is, and that feels right in every way.

A low, guttural roar emits from behind like something heavy being dragged across the concrete.

I turn just as my feet are kicked out from beneath me, and I land hard on my side.

"Shit." The air depresses from my lungs.

I glance up in time to see a lead pipe aiming straight for my head.

13

BURN FOR YOU

Ally

The sky above Carrington spins like a kaleidoscope in blues and swirls of early evening pink, as Kendall and I drive to Starbucks to meet with Lauren.

"It feels like enemy territory," I whisper. I glance behind the counter. There's no sign of my former supervisor, Gretchen, which I'm totally glad about. Today was pure torture, and I have no plans to add to it. Kendall and I melted away precious hours buying things for Morgan's going-away party. One thing is for sure, Morgan's going-away party is going to suck. Not having him around is going to suck even more.

"I can tell he's on your mind." Kendall pushes her cheek in and looks decidedly like him in the process. It's not only going to be a living hell without him, it's going to be impossible to be around Kendall. She's basically him in female skin.

"He's always on my mind," I lament.

Penelope greets us with an uneasy smile.

"The usual?" She bites down on her lip as if a narcotics exchange were taking place.

"Yes, and one more for Lauren." I shake my head. "You know, I can still come here. I'm not breaking the law."

"I know." She frowns as she scrawls our names on our respective cups. "Did you know Gretchen is gone? You should totally try and get your job back."

"No way! What happened?"

"She went ballistic and one of the employees, who shall remain anonymous"—she blinks a smile—"filed a complaint. Melinda's in charge now."

"Really?" Melinda loves me. "I'll totally talk to her."

"She just got in. I'll get her." She speeds off as if that was the plan all along.

Lauren walks in just as our drinks are ready.

"Go ahead and take a seat," I tell them. "I'll be over in a minute."

Melinda comes around the counter and offers a robust hug as if we hadn't seen each other in decades. Melinda is older, and wiser, and has always reminded me a lot of Janice in her own maternal way. The blonde pixie cut sort of helps cement the connection.

"Al, this place isn't the same without you." She pulls back and examines me for a moment. "What's going on? You look like your dog just died. You don't have a dog, do you?"

"No, worse. I have a boyfriend and he's leaving me."

Her tiny mouth elongates in an *O*. "Guys are such jerks. Come back and work for me, and we'll dish about this while slogging down lattes."

"Work for you?" I wrap my arms around her neck. How I miss those apron-wearing, paycheck-riddled Starbucks days. "I accept, but do you think there's any way you can up my hours?"

"Done." She gives my hand a quick shake.

And with that, my dancer days are firmly behind me, even though they sort of were to begin with.

She hands me a smock and adds my name to the schedule as I make my way back to Kendall and Lauren.

"I start next week!"

"Cheers!" Lauren holds up her cup. "Everything's falling back into place."

I shrug.

Everything but Morgan.

"Ally"— Kendall clears her throat, her affect falling flat a moment—"I hate to even bring it up, but after the wedding, when you apologized to my brother, I have to say I'm happy that you did it but I was also kind of hurt."

"You were?" My heart sinks like a boulder. For some reason I thought she was going to say it was sweet or just, well, anything but hurt.

"I was." She looks indignant that we're not on the same page. "Morgan is kind, caring, and gorgeous. The thought of you thinking less of him because he doesn't come from money, actually . . ." Her voice grows small before disintegrating to nothing. "It made me really sad."

"I get it." I swallow hard and nod.

"Ally had it rough growing up." Lauren is swift to come to my defense.

"So did I," Kendall counters. "Welcome to the club. But I would never judge anyone because of how much money he can pamper me with."

"I'm so sorry, and I *beg* your forgiveness." I blow a breath from my cheeks. "Okay, here it goes. When I was fifteen my mother died. We were always broke, *always*. Tess sort of took over and made me promise I would aim financially higher than our mother did when looking for a mate." I pause. "My dad took off before I was nine." I can feel a knot building in my throat

ADDISON MOORE

but I press through it. "Anyway, Tess said it was just as easy to marry a rich man as it was a poor one, so of course, being young and rebellious, I refused to listen."

Kendall blinks back in surprise.

"I fell in love with an idiot. And, honest to God, I fell harder because he gave new meaning to the word *broke*. He was everything Mama Tess warned me about and then some. Anyway, flash forward a year later, I was knocked up, and he was staring down the barrel of an attempted murder charge."

She gasps.

"It gets worse," I assure you. "The day he went out on the hit, I was supposed to go with him, but I ended up sitting on the bathroom floor puking my guts up for hours with morning sickness. It turns out Ruby was already saving me." I pan the two of them with their matching wide-eyed stares, their mouths rooted to the floor as I pour my life story over the table easy as spilling coffee. "Rory, her biological father, and the people who had the misfortune to be in his presence—they all went to prison." I pause to keep from crying. "They tried to cover for him and ended up doing time. That would have been me. I know for a fact I was dumb enough to tell a lie or two to try and help a friend out. Not that he was much of a friend. He was a constant nightmare in my life. Turns out he was cheating on me the entire time. Anyway, I did an about-face on my poverty dating stance ever since and didn't give a slow blink to anyone Tess wouldn't approve of. That's actually why I ended up at Garrison. Tess swore I'd meet someone special there as opposed to the other schools I was looking into—*and* she was right. Because of you, Kendall, I did."

"*Aww*," Lauren and Kendall sing in unison.

"I'm really sorry I acted like an imbecile. Do the two of you accept my apology?" I shrink a little when I ask.

"Of course!" Kendall lunges at me with a hug that feels like a balm over my judgmental soul. Kendall is Morgan's flesh and blood, and she already feels every bit like family to me. At least with Kendall around I'll always have a little piece of Morgan here.

My phone buzzes in my pocket and I fish it out. It's a text from Morgan.

I've got a big surprise for you sweetheart. Meet me at the club.

"You mind catching a ride home with Lauren?" I ask Kendall and flash the text at the two of them.

"Not at all." She presses out a sweet dimpled grin.

"Just so you know"—I secure my purse over my shoulder— "Morgan is more than enough for me. I could live happily on canned soup for the rest of my life just knowing I have his killer smile to come home to night after night." I lower my lashes because that's the very thing I don't have.

"Go on, get out of here." Lauren averts her gaze. "You're going to make me all weepy-eyed and ruin my mascara."

"I'm out of here."

And unfortunately, tomorrow, so is Morgan.

———

Rock Bottom is dark and empty. The faint odor of something caustic overcomes my senses as soon as I step inside, and I can't quite put my finger on what that stench is. Smells like industrial cleanser, or turpentine. Maybe that's the surprise? Maybe Morgan painted a giant mural over the wall asking me to marry him. Now that would be the best surprise ever. Not that we're even close to the matrimonial phase of our relationship. We're more at the *I hope to see you at Christmas* phase, which is alarmingly close to the *thanks for the hookup, see you around* phase. Face it, we're all but over. Summer and Morgan both came and went in a blur, and all I have to show for it are bad tan lines and heart-stopping memories.

"Morgan?" The sound of my voice echoes through the basement. It's too dark to properly see anything down the hall. I bet he's in that Poker Room with his clothes off just waiting to give me a special good-bye. Perv.

As I head in that direction, a smile twitches on my lips because I totally approve of the perv in him. I hope he's buck naked just waiting for some much-needed oral attention. God knows I'm ready to give it. In fact, I say we cancel the going-away party, which was looking to be a downer anyway, and I hold him hostage with my body until he complies with my demands and stays in Carrington forever.

"Ally?" A man calls from behind me.

"Morgan?" I whisper. Funny, it didn't sound like Morgan. In fact, it didn't sound *familiar.* I spin on my heels and freeze.

A tall man with scraggly hair and a lewd smile stares back at me—Dell.

"Hey there, sweetie. Bet you're real glad to see me." The light catches his greasy locks, with their brown and blonde skunk highlights. His clothes are filthy with splotches of mud caked over his jeans. His face is slicked with sweat.

"Been working out?" I say, sidestepping my way toward the exit. I've never seen Dell at the club before. I doubt he's got a membership to Cal's health club. The only thing Dell does for his health is cardio by way of the smallest organ of his body, and according to Tess, *small* is the operative word.

"Do you like what you see?" He taps his stomach. The light shines down over him, revealing cherry-stained eyes. He's stoned out of his mind, and this panics me. "I can give you a piece of this if you like." He comes in close and touches his hand to my cheek.

"I have to go. Someone's waiting for me." I try to jet past him, and he catches me by the elbow.

"What's your hurry?" A greasy smile slides up his cheek, and my heart starts in on a death rattle.

"Morgan?" I cry out, trying to break free from Dell's hold. "What the hell are you doing here?" I pant. "Let go right fucking now. The club is opening in just a few minutes."

"No, hon, it's not." He tightens his grip on the soft underbelly of my arm before relenting. "You see, I've been observing your little joint venture with that sleazebag boy toy of yours. Opens at ten, closes at three." He glides into a malicious grin before his features harden without notice. "I should have never let you into my club. I should have thrown you and that trash sister of yours out a hell of a long time ago."

I shoot an open-palmed slap across his face without thinking.

"The only piece of crap here is you." I spit it out with venom. That's one judgment I won't be taking back anytime soon.

Dell brightens a unique shade of crimson. He seizes onto my arm with a vice grip.

"A fucking slap?" He spits in my face as he says it. "I guess that's what I get for doing gutter trash like you a favor." He jostles me to the center of the room and slams me against a supporting column that's thick as a telephone pole.

I push past him harder than before and make it five feet out before he drags me back by the hair.

A harrowing scream rips from me—so loud and shrill, it catches even me by surprise.

"Shut up." He knocks me into the pole head first, hard enough to send a vibration reeling through the metal.

Dell snatches up my wrists and shackles them around the beam as he secures me from behind.

"Shit!" I try to free myself but my hands are completely locked in this position.

"You took everything from me." He produces a pack of cigarettes from his back pocket and proceeds to pluck one out.

Shit.

I tip my head back and scream like a maniac.

"Tess is gone." He nods. "But you like that, don't you?" He narrows in on me. "You took off with about six of my best girls. Steven up and left." His eyes widen with surprise as if that one completely took him off guard. "You went and sucked my business dry until not even my regulars showed up anymore." He casts a quick glance at the ground and a part of me actually feels sorry for him.

"Oh, don't worry about the club," I blurt in a panic. "Tonight's the last night—in fact, we won't open at all. If I knew what it was doing to your business I would never have let Morgan open the doors." Great. Put this all off on your soon-to-be ex-boyfriend, who by the way . . . hey, where the hell is he? I parked right next to his truck in the lot.

"Oh, honey, I know you won't be opening tonight or any other night." He laughs nefariously, and a trail of shivers runs through me. "In fact, I've got this shithole covered with a touch of my affection to ensure it doesn't open ever again." He lights up his cigarette, and I watch mesmerized by the orange flicker emitting from the tip.

Oh God. My breathing grows erratic. A fevered sense of panic rips through me at whatever the hell he's about to do. He's probably going to burn his name into my forehead so I'll never forget him. My body pulsates with fear. I pant up a storm as if I just ran a marathon, rendering myself dizzy, ready to pass out from the effort.

Dell takes a step forward and offers me a hit, and I'm quick to refuse the offer.

He blows a stream of smoke into my face, forcing me to turn away and choke from the disgusting fumes.

"Enjoy the rest of your life, sweetheart"—he heads toward the exit—"what little you have left." He flicks his cigarette in the corner and a wall of flames erupts.

I let out a scream as a line of fire races around the room like inferno-inspired dominos. A soft explosion goes off as the fire expands to the carpeted portion of the basement in the distance. I watch in horror as the flames rush across the ceiling with their orange and blue tongues.

"No! *Dell!* Please . . ." My tears come fast and furious. "*Cal!*" I rub my arms up and down the pole until it feels as though my elbows are going to fall off and at this point I really wouldn't mind. "*Help!*" I wail with everything in me until my bones reverberate from the effort. I give one deep guttural cry after another, primal and hasty.

The room fills with smoke, dense and smothering.

"I can't breathe!" I choke on the words as they heave out of me. The thick plumes dance in my direction, taunting me with their necrotic fingers.

"Shit, shit, *shit!*" I engage in a series of guttural cries that no longer qualify as screams—then one final plea for mercy by way of the name of the one I love.

"Morgan!" I belt it out like a battle cry. His name quivers from my lips as the final memory I might ever have. The room sizzles. My flesh singes with heat. My lungs fill with smoke.

Can't see.

Can't breathe.

I slump forward as the world and everything in it burns to cinders.

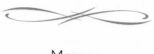

Morgan

The smell of old cigarette butts overcomes my senses until the urge to vomit takes over. My name comes to me from deep within a dream as I struggle to wake up. My head feels heavy and granular, like a sandbag.

"Fuck," I whisper. I give several long blinks. Something hard lies on the side of my face, and I reach up and grab it—my phone.

Dell's face is imprinted in my mind—that lead pipe looming above, then nothing.

I groan as I try to sit up. Feels like he force-fed me my balls. That's a hell of a parting gift from Carrington: impotence. Although I suppose it wasn't from Carrington, it was from Dell, the-hound-from-hell who thought it was best to personally deliver his parting shot. Rock Bottom is not happening. Got the fucking memo.

"Morgan."

There it is again, and for sure it wasn't in my dreams. This was real and panicked and holy shit if it didn't sound like Ally.

I try to get up and the room spins. The leg of the poker table sways before me, and I slap my hand to the top and use the surface to steady myself to my feet.

"Shit." I stagger toward the door, slamming into it as if I were drunk off my ass. I try the handle and my hand bounces off from the shock of heat.

Another scream erupts from outside, and I twist the knob with my T-shirt, but it doesn't budge. I give another hard yank, and the door swings wide as a vat of liquid spills into the room. Smells like paint thinner.

To the right a horrific glow catches my attention, and I bolt in that direction.

"Ally?" Smoke and fire—flames fanning out all over the place. It's hotter than hell, and that's exactly what this has become.

A weak cough emits from the middle of the room.

"Ally!" I shout, running blindly into the center. The smoke chokes me out and I fall to my knees, struggling to breathe; my head implodes on itself as the mother of all headaches hacks into my skull. "Al?" I cough as I lower myself further to the ground trying to gulp for air.

Fuck.

A pair of pink shoes catch my eye.

I rush over to the sandaled girl, not sure who I'll find. I pull in close and grab her by the waist. I know this body, those long, blonde waves of hair—"Ally."

"Morgan?" She rolls her head back over her shoulders, almost unresponsive, with her eyes glued shut. I try to pluck her loose but the bastard tied her to the post. I pull my keys from my pocket and start sawing the shit out of the zip ties holding her hostage.

Ally lets out a cry as she comes to.

"I'm sorry," I pant over her as the plastic gives.

Ally collapses as I hoist her over my shoulders. Adrenaline pumps through me with the force of a nuclear detonation as I bounce to my feet.

The smoke chokes me as I try to navigate us toward the exit. The fire breathes over us like a solar flare. I stagger like a blind man, wondering which way to go.

Can't fucking find the exit.

I pan the room, trying to get my bearings.

A plume of powder-like smoke shoots south of where I'm standing.

I'd swear on my life that's not the way out, but I follow the direction of the tornado of smoke until I trip and fumble toward a beautiful glimmer of night sky. I hold my breath until my lungs burn from the effort, until they threaten to burst the pressure as I struggle to carry Ally all the way up the stairs. A burst of fresh Massachusetts air penetrates our lungs as we choke our way over to the grass just shy of the building.

Molly barrels out from the parking lot with her face locked in horror, her finger pointing hard at my legs.

"Your pants are on fire!" Her voice drills through the air like an alarm. "I'm going to get Cal."

I land Ally on the grass and jump back to see my legs lit up in flames.

"*Shit.*" I wrestle off my jeans and stomp on them until there's nothing but embers left.

A fire truck screams in the distance as I make my way to Ally. I sit next to her and pull her over into my lap. Her face and hair are covered with soot as she sputters a tiny cough into my chest.

"Are you okay?" I fold my arms over her, burying a kiss in her neck.

"I am now." She cinches her grip around my waist. "I never want to let go of you."

"Then don't, because I'm sure as hell not letting go of you."

"Morgan." Ally looks up, her eyes crimson. "I'm so in love with you. I can't do this without you."

I plant a simple kiss over her lips. It's this moment that solidifies everything I'm about to do next. There's no way in hell I'm spending the next season of our lives clear on the opposite coast. I'll go home and clear my shit out and come right back.

My stomach pinches with a genuine ache for all those years I spent playing the game I love.

I swallow hard and glance down at her. I'm not sure why it feels like it has to be Ally or baseball. I'm not even sure if Ally *wants* a long-distance relationship. But at the rate I'm going I'll never find out. I'm not sure why I don't have the balls to ask. Maybe I can just walk her into it. Start calling, texting, visiting, and if she doesn't label me a stalker, we're good to go.

"We're going to figure this out." I kiss her just over the ear. "I love you, Ally." I trace out her features with my finger.

"I love you too, Morgan. Thank you for saving me." She closes her eyes and rests her cheek over my chest. "You keep saving me."

Nope. Can't leave Ally. It's becoming abundantly clear I love her more than baseball, more than my own life. I'll wait tables if I have to, just to be near her.

A team of paramedics races in our direction, and I hold her a little bit tighter.

"You're safe, babe. I'll always keep you safe."

Hours drag by as we give a lengthy police report and pay a visit to the hospital. Extensive X-rays prove I'm hardheaded, which for once is a good thing. I think. We're both sent home with nothing more than minimal smoke inhalation.

We head back to the house and explain the shit out of ourselves to Lauren, Cal, Cruise, and Kendall before staggering to the room and all but nailing the door shut.

"Did Dell make you text me?" Ally looks up at me from our bed, naked on the crisp sheets. Her bare ass rides perfectly high as her back dips in provocatively. Her feet are hooked in the air at the ankles.

"He did it himself." I run my hand over her shoulders and give a weak smile. My head still feels as if a tractor ran over it.

"I guess he was responsible for all that other bullshit as well. The black rose, the rat—the nasty text messages."

"You got the love letters too, huh?"

She gives a dull laugh as I land beside her. "I guess we could have used a little more communication."

I don't say anything. All I can think about is the fact I'm loading up the truck and heading out west tomorrow to pack up my life, and now would be the perfect time to address the Oregon-shaped elephant in the room.

"Did you think it was Dell?" I ask, running my hand up her thigh, nice and slow.

Ally swims up beside me and gives a series of gentle kisses.

"Not really." She bites over her strawberry-stained lip and lands a vine-ripened kiss just shy of my mouth. "I thought it might be Blair, or Molly, or—even Rory."

"Who's Rory?"

"It's a long story. He's the reason I judged you so hard. I guess you could say I judged him in reverse and dove into that relationship because I knew it would piss Tess off." She starts in slowly on how they met, how the asshole thought murder was a good way to spend his free time, and how now he's *doing* time.

"Shit." I pull her in close and blow a hot kiss over her temple. "I'm damn glad Ruby had you worshipping porcelain that night." I close my eyes a moment and try to imagine this summer without her, the rest of my life without her, but I keep coming up with nothing. And there it is. Life without Ally would be an impossibility. I already know this.

"He can't hurt you, Ally. I won't let anybody ever hurt you."

Ally pulls back and stares intently into my eyes. The moonlight illuminates the room in an entire nightscape of blues and purples. Ally is a goddess, a princess from some other world entirely. I don't know how in the hell I got lucky enough to get in her way, but I'm sure glad I did.

I dip a kiss into the hollow of her neck and she rises to meet me, her chest filling with approval at the tiny gesture of my affection. My hand rides up her hip before gliding into the warm slick between her thighs.

Ally lands her lips over mine and covers my body with the softness of hers. She moans into her kisses as she sprinkles them down over my chest, my hips, right over my stomach, and I let out a groan. I reach over and grab a condom off the nightstand and can't help but wonder if it's the last one we'll share, if there was a countdown on our lovemaking this entire time, and I was too stupid to realize it.

Ally takes the small foil square from me and tears it open. I can make out a sly smile buried in her cheek and she rolls it over me before straddling me with her knees and climbing onboard. Ally's eyes reduce to slits as she relaxes over me. A hard groan expels from her throat and she has me clenching the bedsheets. Ally rides me slow at first, steady, with her hair falling around her like a curtain, revealing and hiding her features at random. I don't take my eyes off her, just enjoy the hell out of listening to her breathing increase, her perfect body moving in rhythm to mine. I run my hand down her belly, touching the tangle of curls at the base before moving my thumb over her sweet spot until we're both right there.

Ally lies over me, pulling my face in with her hands, as we hit that magical zenith together with our bodies tightening and spasming in unison. We spend all night making love as if we were both on the way to the guillotine in the morning, and for all she knows, that's exactly where our relationship is headed.

Tomorrow is the day.

I push into Ally and she lets out a soft cry.

But the next several hours are all about us.

Ally presses her hand into the small of my back, and I collapse deeper inside of her. I never want this night to end.

I want to swim inside Ally Monroe forever.

14

THE LONG GOOD-BYE

Ally

Who the hell throws a good-bye party for someone you never want to see leave in the first place?

Early this morning the police called to let us know they caught Dell at the state line while trying to make a break for it in his rundown Chevy. I called Tess and she was horrified, but I told her to stay in New York, that we'd see each other soon enough. Now that Dell is out of our lives, we can all breathe a little easier. And, in light of that small legal victory, Kendall dubbed this a "double" celebration, but I was never planning to celebrate in the first place.

I toss the last of the paper plates and soda cans into the trash. To hell with recycling, I'm not in the mood to save the planet. I'm in the mood to save my relationship but can't figure out how.

The sun warms the backyard of the Elton House Bed and Breakfast as Lauren and I clear the picnic tables where we shared our last meal with the man I love. It all sounds so dramatic. It feels so freaking tragic. I'm afraid I'm not going to be able to hold back the dam anymore and I'll burst into tears like a three-year-old any second now.

"There's a big party tonight." Lauren sounds way too chipper, which just proves she's incapable of understanding how miserable I really am.

"Have fun." I cut a hard look to Morgan while he chats it up with Cruise and Cal across the lawn and the three of them spontaneously burst into laughter. Morgan glances my way, and his expression dims. I bet they were whooping it up over how easy I was for him. How good old Ally put him on the fast track for some serious summer loving.

I spear him with a look. How dare he make me fall in love with him and then drive out of town like it didn't even matter.

"*We* will have fun." Lauren harps on about Pen and his stupid party. God, I can't even stand the sight of half the people who will be there tonight, let alone the one who won't because he'll be logging miles across long, lonely US highways. Unless of course he stops at all the strip clubs along the way, a whorehouse or two, to keep him entertained. Something tells me Morgan Jordan won't be lonely for long.

"Earth to Ally." Lauren waves her hand in front of my face.

"I'm not going," I say without regard to whether or not we're still on topic. Frat boys and frat parties in general don't really seem to hold the same sway over me they once did. I have a feeling in just a few hours, nothing ever will.

"You have to. It's Sigma Phi's big end-of-summer fest. It's Pennington's deal, so that means champagne and caviar."

"It means beer and questionable sushi," I correct.

"Oh, come on. We'll get good and toasted and walk home to our new apartments. It'll be epic."

"No." I glare over at Kendall as she makes her way inside with Morgan, presumably to get his stuff together. I couldn't stand the sight of his suitcase this morning. It managed to piss me off and make me want to cry all at the same time.

"Oh, hon." Lauren reaches over and smooths her hand over my arm. "You don't have a choice."

I'm not sure if she means the party or the fact that Morgan's leaving. Maybe both.

Cruise and Cal head over, followed by Kendall, and my heart drops. It's like a funeral procession, only the dearly departed is taking off voluntarily to move on to greener scholastic pastures. At the end of the day, I was just another girl—a way to pass the summer, nothing but someone who helped him turn the pages of his carnal calendar. He's probably got some cute jersey chaser waiting for him back home who he swore he loved just before he got here. He probably broke her heart on the way over and now he's breaking mine on the way back.

Morgan comes out, leading with his silver carry-on—the silver bullet that's about to shoot right through my heart.

I'm sorry I ever let him into my life. I'm sorry I ever introduced him to Ruby or Janice or Tess. I've never let anyone in so completely before—never trusted a soul with my heart—and now I know why.

"This is it," Lauren whispers. "Be strong, girl." Her brows rise and she pouts a little when she says it. Lauren's been aware of my misery all along. The party was just a ruse to get my mind off things. "I got your back. 'Kay?" She ushers me over to his truck where everyone has gathered. Morgan slips his suitcase into the backseat with a depleted smile.

He glances up at me with his eyes heavy with sorrow, his dimples blinking on and off like some primitive warning signal.

SOMEONE LIKE YOU

Tears pool in my eyes and a knot the size of a fist swells in my throat, making it impossible to push out any words—not that I'd want to. I'm pretty sure *go fuck yourself* isn't on the short list of things he's expecting to hear.

"Call us when you get there." Kendall wraps her arms around his back and rocks him. "You know you'll have to come back for Christmas. You're in my wedding, remember?"

"Got it." He offers her a gentle pat. "*Cruise.*" He pulls him into a half hug. "Take care, man."

Cal slaps Morgan over the back, and suddenly I'd like to administer a beating myself.

"Drive safe, dude." Cal mock shoots him. "You'd better hope insurance springs for a renovation. And if it does, I expect you to be there for the grand opening."

"That's the plan." Morgan looks over and gives a killer grin that highlights his dimples in the most dramatic way possible.

I officially hate those dimples. I'd run and hide in one if I could. I'm so mad at myself for being such an idiot.

Lauren gives me a shove, and I lurch forward with a manufactured smile plastered to my face.

"Have a safe drive." It hacks out of me, breathy like an expiring balloon. Morgan pulls me in and holds me with his chest pressed against mine so tight I can feel his heart pounding like a lunatic in an asylum. Insanity would be the only way to explain his actions so it doesn't really surprise me that his organs are orchestrating a mutiny. The soft scent of his cologne warms me, and a fresh pang of grief rips through my body like the serrated edge of a blade.

"I will," he whispers softly in my ear and my stomach bottoms out like I just plunged down a mountain—a suicide drop straight to the sea. He pulls back with his brows narrowed, his lips just a breath away from mine. "Is it okay if I call you?"

An explosion of heat detonates inside me—a seed of hope born of nothing but sheer desperation.

"Call me anytime." I swallow hard as I align myself with Lauren.

What the hell was that? Where were the tear-filled *I love yous*? The *Can I speak to you alone a minute*? Who the hell is this imposter, and what did he do with the Morgan Jordan who ran his mouth over every inch of my body declaring his love for me until the sun came up?

Morgan keeps his eyes locked over mine. Those steel beams are relentless in pursuing me. They're trying to make me say something when we both know he's the one who should speak. His lips should form the words *I can't leave you. I'll never leave you, Ally, because I love you too damn much.*

But he doesn't say it.

Morgan climbs in his truck and fires up the engine.

He speeds off with a simple wave and takes off toward the highway.

He drags my heart right along with him.

Morgan

Fuck." I slap my hand down hard over the steering wheel as I head out of Carrington.

I should have told her I'll be back as soon as possible, that I've made up my mind to turn in my baseball bat and attend the local JC until I can get back on my scholastic feet. I'll always have law to fall back on—eventually. Ally would probably love to marry a lawyer one day, and, hopefully, the fact that that lawyer could be me will be an added bonus. But after that stunt I just pulled I'll be lucky if she looks in my direction ever again. It was pretty clear I was choking her heart, making her wish she never laid eyes on me in the first place.

I shake my head.

Married to a lawyer, I scoff at my stupidity. I'll be *needing* a lawyer once she gets ahold of a restraining order. That look on her face clued me in on the fact she was roasting my balls on a spit in private.

In an effort to turn this into some kind of romantic surprise, all I've managed to do is screw things up in a royal way.

Starbucks comes up on my left and I'm tempted to pull over, ask her to meet me here for one last kiss, but I suppose having someone meet you at the place where she got fired would be my second most unromantic feat of the day. It's like I'm going for the breakup gold.

Garrison edges over the side of the highway with its Gothic architecture.

I admire the expansive, rolling lawn. I can almost smell the freshly cut grass, feel the sun searing over my skin. A spike of adrenaline surges in me. I pull off and head toward campus.

Why the hell not? So I lose an hour off my trip. At least I'll have peace of mind knowing I did everything I could.

I park and trek over to the athletics department.

My heart discharges blow after blow like an assault rifle as I enter the cool of the building. The shadowed halls are empty, and the scent of the copy machine and warm paper thicken the air.

Coach Wexler's office is sealed like a tomb. I lay my hand over the door as if it were the casket that held both Ally and me hostage.

"Jordan?"

A male voice calls from behind me.

I turn to find the coach lifting his brows with surprise and nearly shit my pants.

"I was just coming to see you," I say, a little more enthusiastically than necessary.

"It's about time. We have a strict practice schedule. We're going to need to get your uniform ordered right away. I talked to your old coach and he seemed surprised by your decision. You haven't changed your mind, have you?"

I blink at him, stumped by what he's just said. It was as if I had willed those very words to stream from his mind, and I was waiting for him to realize his error.

"What's the matter?" He looks me over as if I might be wasted.

"Are you saying I'm on the team?" My body tightens in knots, my palms slick with sweat, and I'm pretty sure my deodorant just lost all its antiperspirant superpowers.

"Didn't your girlfriend tell you?" He pauses with his key partway inserted into the office door. "Cute blonde about yea-high?" He cuts his hand to his chest just the right size for a little maniacal blonde I know: Blair. Cruise was right, I should have run the other way.

"Nope, I guess she forgot to mention it."

"Then I suppose she forgot to mention the school is offering a full scholarship."

"A scholarship?" Every cell in my body vibrates like a live wire.

"It's all yours. You'll need to transfer your units and take care of the basics with the university, but you've got until late next week. Go ahead and get started on that and I'll meet up with you on the field Tuesday, four o'clock."

"Four o'clock, Tuesday. Nothing could keep me away."

I drift back out into the sunshine with my head still spinning from the news.

I've got a scholarship, a spot on the team, and best of all I've got Ally—I hope.

I reach for my phone to call her and pause.

No, for sure this is the kind of news that needs to be delivered in person.

But first, I have a little side project I need to take care of.

I pull out my phone and search through the archive of pictures.

They're all here, every last one.

15

THE GIFT

Ally

Alpha Sigma Phi is a hotbed of immorality and hedonism, as evidenced by the vast display of alcoholic beverages that would put the grocery liquor department to shame.

"I don't drink," I lament as Lauren tries to shove a peppermint schnapps in my face. "Things go very, very bad in my life when I drink." I shudder at the thought. "Coffee, I drink *coffee*."

"You can't get a buzz off coffee." She lowers her lids. Lauren is already more than fed up with me, and if she keeps trying to lighten my mood things are bound to get lethal.

"You can the way I make it," I mumble mostly to myself. Some old-school rock funk blares from the speakers and a group of girls from Alpha Chi scream as they throw their hands in the air. I spot Molly with a couple of girls from Delta house. She has connections through Pen's mom so they'll probably let her in by proxy, but this chapter of Delta is notorious for its particular taste in hazing. I'm sure she'll enjoy the hell out of it— she's twisted that way. I wonder if my path had never crossed Morgan's if she would have been his summer fling. I can't help but feel a little jealous over something that never materialized. I'm pretty sure I'll look at every pretty girl and wonder if Morgan would have hung around town for her, at least offered her a decent good-bye. In my heart I was hoping for a picnic on the beach, maybe a midnight swim, and a roll in the sand afterward, during which we declared our undying feelings under the lamp of a hot August moon. Instead I got the shaft, the *See you later, have a nice life,* and not even that.

Kendall and Lauren pop up, each brimming with smiles and giggles.

"This is going to be an amazing year." Lauren winks over at Kendall as if she knows something. "I mean, you got your job back." She nods over at me as if Starbucks is the cure-all for this indescribable ache Morgan left in me. "Plus, we're practically roommates again. I mean I'll hear everything you say, the walls are paper thin."

Perfect. Turns out, listening to Kendall and Cruise go at it was just the prelude. I'll have the non-pleasure of experiencing Lauren and Cal demonstrating what I'm assuming will be something akin to a tribal voodoo ritual. I'll need earplugs if I ever hope to get any sleep.

"That's fantastic," I say, lackluster.

Kendall wraps an arm around my shoulder. "And I could really use your shopping superpowers to help with all the little details my wedding is going to need. Lauren's got champagne taste, but I'd love to have someone on my team who knows the value of a dollar."

Kendall's right. Lauren's wedding budget alone could pull the space program out of fiscal purgatory.

"Okay, I'll help." A twinge of excitement pinches through me. The truth is, I love shopping on a budget. I think if I had dollars streaming from every orifice of my body, I'd still want to get the best deal on everything on the planet. It's in my genes, and after witnessing Lauren purchase a jacket for eleven hundred dollars last winter, I'd say my thriftiness is not such a bad thing.

Blair comes up to our circle with Rutger by her side. They have on matching white polos and navy sweaters thrown over their shoulders—the uniform of assholes.

"Quick, someone alert the country club," I quip. "We've got a couple of escapees slumming with the commoners. What's the matter, Blair? Run out of boyfriends to steal?" I glance over at Lauren. "You'd better check on Cal. If my calculations are correct, his is the next penis she'll try to deep fry with her designer vagina."

Rutger belts out a laugh, and Blair swats him in the stomach.

"You always were a classless bitch," she snipes at me. "At least I have someone in my life. Rumor has it you were ditched for those West Coast girls. I guess Morgan Jordan wasn't that into you after all."

Rutger belts out another laugh, and this time I swat him in the stomach.

There it is—the truth that Lauren and Kendall have spent all night skirting. There was a fire in my heart no one could put out, and now my enemies are hosing me down with lighter fluid, creating an inferno from an already out-of-control blaze.

"I wouldn't put too much weight on those rumors." A familiar male voice hums from behind.

I spin on my heels and my heart rockets right out of my chest.

"Morgan!" I wrap my arms around his gorgeous frame and lean my head against his chest. If this is a hallucination I want to enjoy it just a little bit longer.

He presses a kiss over my cheek and pulls me in tight.

"Hello, Blair," Morgan seethes. My body vibrates with the tenor of his voice as he growls over at her. "Coach Wexler let me know he shared some good news with my *girlfriend*."

I pull back and my mouth falls open at what this might mean.

His dimples dig in, but it's becoming evident he's more than a little pissed.

"Great news." He glances down at me. "I made Garrison's baseball team with a full scholarship."

"Morgy!" Kendall dives over to him with a hug.

"Almost lost it too." He glares over at the blonde she-devil in our presence. "That's the last time you get away with this shit. Cruise may have let you off easy, but I'm reporting you to every fucking authority outlet that will listen, starting with the school. The dean of admissions is very interested in speaking with you about tampering with another student's private affairs. He mentioned it was grounds for academic expulsion, which would be great since Ally and I will be spending the next several years here." He digs a smile in the side of his cheek. "So, Blair, you can take the next psychological vendetta you've got brewing and shove it up your ass because I'm not going to let you hurt another person. Except maybe him." He nods at Rutger. "I've never seen a better-matched couple." He picks up my hand and looks me in the eye. "We're the exception, of course."

Blair's eyes fill with fire. "I'm the only one in this circle who belongs at Garrison."

"You won't for long." Morgan wraps his arms around my waist and returns his eyes to mine.

Blair's mouth opens and nothing but choking sounds comes out. She glares at me with a not-so-veiled threat before spinning on her heels and taking off.

Morgan leans in and crashes his lips over mine, and the room, the people melt away. The music, the noise of the crowd dissipates until all I hear, *feel,* is the beating of our hearts pounding over one another's chests.

He pulls back and looks at me. Our circle of friends and enemies has long since disbanded.

"I've got a surprise for you."

"I love your surprise," I squeal, jumping up and wrapping my arms tight around his neck. "But you're all the surprise I need."

"This is a better surprise." Morgan gives a heartfelt smile and nods toward the door.

He leads us through the crowd, and we slip outside Sigma house under the feathered branches of a weeping willow.

"Wait just a second." Morgan dashes to his truck parked a few feet away and returns with a large square box.

"What's this?"

"It's for you." He hands over the flat package with a black-and-white checkered bow on top, and I'm quick to open it.

"Oh my God!" I gasp, removing the oversized scrapbook—then I see it—Ruby's beautiful face staring back at me from the cover. "Morgan!" Tears flood my vision as I open the book. It's page after page filled with pictures of Ruby growing up—including ones I've never even seen before. Pictures of those precious infant years—her first photo taken just hours after she was born. I flip the page, and my heart stops. The tears start flowing, and I can't control them. It's the picture Janice took when she came to the hospital to bring her baby home. She asked if she could take one of the two of us, and I didn't protest the idea. There I am, holding my precious angel, my teary-eyed face, nothing but a baby myself.

"This is the one," I whisper. "She went from my arms to Janice's right after this."

"I hope you don't mind I included it."

"No." I wipe the tears away with the back of my hand. "God, no. I can't believe she gave these to you."

"Actually, she let me take pictures at the party with my phone. I told her that I wanted to help replace your scrapbook, and she didn't mind opening up her photo albums."

"You did that for me?"

"I wanted to. I'd give you everything in the world if I could, Ally." His eyes widen and for the first time, Morgan looks boyish, vulnerable.

"In the world, huh?" I bite down over my lower lip. "Morgan, all I want is you in my life forever."

A smile of relief bounces to his lips. "Lucky for me, because that's exactly what I want too—you in my life forever." He pulls me in by the waist. His warm hands ride low over my back.

"I'm the lucky one around here." I slip my hands into his back pockets as his dimples press in deep as oil wells. "So I guess you'll be needing someplace to stay." I lick the rim of my lips with a promise.

"I've got sixteen bucks to my name, and I'm willing to make a trade-off." His hand curves over the seat of my pants.

"*Morgan!*" I laugh, jostling him in the process. My features soften as I take him in like this, so perfectly gorgeous and sweet I could cry. "I guess happily ever after does exist."

"I guess it does," he whispers. "I want you as a part of my life." He grows altogether serious. "Ally Monroe, will you be my forever?"

His words echo in the night long after they drift from his lips. They linger in the air like the crisp scent of jasmine, so sweet and delicious, you could never get enough.

"I want to be your forever." The words quiver from my lips. "I want to be your everything."

Morgan leans in and kisses me with a tenderness I've never experienced before. His lips press in soft; his tongue gives a careful swipe before dancing over mine.

Ruby's book is sandwiched between us, solidifying us as a family as we linger with hungry kisses that stream out into this new forever we're forging. The long braids of the willow brush gently over our shoulders. I can feel my mother watching us from the sky, smiling down over the two of us with her approval through the magical lavender night. She was right. I would find my forever when I least expected it, and here he is, warming my body with his love for me. I guess in the end my mother's wisdom prevailed—I got my happily ever after in the last place I'd think to look—and God, I'm glad I looked. Maybe Pretty Girls wasn't such a bad life move after all. Sometimes, a strange turn takes us exactly where we need to be. Sometimes when we fall, destiny makes sure the right person is there to catch us.

I'm glad I tore down the walls of judgment I erected during that crazy time in my life. It took a lot of growth and learning on my part, but with Morgan I was able to persevere.

With Morgan Jordan by my side the world has recaptured that rosy glow that died out so long ago with my mother.

He pulls my hand to his mouth before pressing in a kiss.

"I can't wait to build a future with you," he whispers.

"Perfect." I pluck a set of keys from my pocket. "Just got these today. Looks like we get to decorate our first apartment."

"Nice." He pulls back and his dimples go off like bombs. "I've got one word for you—taxidermy."

I belt out a laugh as we walk toward his truck.

"What's so funny?" He pulls me in close.

"Nothing. I'm all about compromise. If a stuffed deer makes you happy then I want that too."

"Really?" He blinks back with a grin. "Because I was thinking more like a bear." He holds his hand in the air like a claw. "I'm teasing. As soon as you walk into that apartment it's already going to have everything I'll ever need. It's going to have you." He presses a searing kiss over my lips. "I love you, Ally."

"I love you too, Morgan." I give him a quick peck on the lips. "Hey, what would you have done if you didn't get a spot on the team?"

"I was going to get the rest of my things and haul ass right back here. We'd figure the rest out later."

"*We*—I like the sound of that."

Morgan pauses. He touches his thumb to my cheek and admires me as if I were a treasure. "From now on it's you and me no matter what life throws our way. We'll get through it together. We're a team."

"We're a team."

Morgan presses in an explosive kiss under the dazzling starlit sky.

Summer was the prelude to the rest of our forever. It came and went like a shooting star, and, now, here we are, ready to turn the page and write the next line in our story. I'm pretty sure we're starting with the words *happily ever after.* You can't go wrong with an opening like that.

And with Morgan Jordan by my side, every day gets a happy ending.

Thank you for reading *Someone Like You*. Look for *Someone for Me,* the continuation of Kendall and Cruise's story, coming in 2014.

ACKNOWLEDGMENTS

To my wonderful readers, thank you for believing so strongly in *Someone to Love*. And because of you this book was born. I hope you enjoyed Ally and Morgan's story in *Someone Like You* just as much. Thank you from the bottom of my heart for all of your kindness and support. You really do rock!

Thank you to the wonderful folks over at Skyscape for helping my dreams come true. Thank you to Marilyn Brigham and the awesome Jenna Free for helping me through edits. And an extra thank-you to Jenna for putting up with me!

To my kids, thank you for doing the dishes. And to my husband, who kindly and wisely treated me to sushi each time I got frazzled, which was often. I may have manipulated that.

And finally, to Him who holds the world in the palm of His hands—I owe you everything.

ABOUT THE AUTHOR

Addison Moore is a *New York Times, USA TODAY,* and *Wall Street Journal* bestselling author who writes contemporary and paranormal romance. Her work has been featured in *Cosmopolitan* magazine. For nearly a decade, she worked as a therapist on a locked psychiatric unit. She resides on the West Coast—where she eats too much chocolate and stays up way too late—with her husband, four wonderful children, and two dogs. When she's not writing, she's reading.

Feel free to visit her blog at:
http://addisonmoorewrites.blogspot.com

Facebook: https://www.facebook.com/pages/Addison-Moore/140192649382294

Twitter: https://twitter.com/AddisonMoore